JILLIAN E. MARTYN

DIVINE ABOMINATION

iUniverse books may be ordered through booksellers or by contacting:

iUniverse
1663 Liberty Drive
Bloomington, IN 47403
www.iuniverse.com
1-800-Authors (1-800-288-4677)

ISBN: 978-1-5320-5411-2 (sc)
ISBN: 978-1-5320-5412-9 (hc)
ISBN: 978-1-5320-5410-5 (e)

Library of Congress Control Number: 2018909733

Print information available on the last page.

iUniverse rev. date: 08/21/2018

This book is dedicated to my best friend Carrie Anthony and my nephew Nick Martyn. Carrie, thanks for never letting me give up this dream and Nick, thanks for wanting it more action packed.

Introduction

Humanity has been on the downward spiral to destruction for centuries. From openly committing sin to global wars, they have led themselves astray. Carelessly, running from sin to sin, from vanity to gluttony, adultery to murder, the blemishes upon their souls kept piling up. Some assume they will merely ask for forgiveness upon their death beds. While others believe there is nothing beyond this present existence. Despite thoughts, beliefs and common opinions, not a single human was expecting what happened that day. Not a single soul was expecting Heaven and Hell to abandon us all…

One

Our Sentence

Before the fall of Humanity

Social media was in an uproar that day. Every form of connection and communication was wildly blazing. Televisions, radios and news reporters were eagerly awaiting updates on the current situation.

In many largely populated areas of the world, two beings had appeared. One was pale with a soft, gentle almost calming aura. Its white feathered wings demanded every viewer to gaze in awe. The other, snarled and growled, its aura was dark and cruel. Its huge tattered black bat like wings hung down its boney back. It was obvious to the average person that one was an angel and the other was a demon. Despite being natural enemies, neither appeared hostile toward the other. In fact, they appeared to be of the same mind. Both the Angel and Demon spoke in the common language of the area they were in.

The Angel was first to speak. "Humanity, our Lords have made a definite decision upon your fates. This decision will change the very existence of your world. You, who have abandoned us, shall be abandoned in return."

The Demon glared at the spectators in contempt as it hissed. "Rules, simple rules were put in place for a reason! Yet each and every day you flaw your perfect immortal souls."

The Angel closed its pale colored eyes and sighed before speaking. "Heaven and Hell will dissolve. Life shall continue on but not as before. Hear us Mortals! Hear us well. It is time for you to receive your long standing punishment."

The Demon looked like at any moment it would attack, yet it spoke in a calm tone. "Our Lords have waited too long to offer forgiveness. They have grown tired and annoyed. Some of you even have the audacity to question their existences. Our Lords will not wait any longer. They do not deserve such abuse and disrespect from your wretched kind."

The Angel glanced toward its growling partner. "Though we feel betrayed by those we protect and influence, those carriers of holy and unholy souls granted by our Lords. We do not begrudge you. Go forth and gather ten of your brightest scientists. In seven days we shall return. Upon our Lord's day of rest, we shall grant you an invaluable gift."

Without saying another word, the Angel zipped up into the sky. While the Demon seemed to just melt and vanish into the ground. They were gone.

Two

Action and Reaction

Panic and denial filled the first two days since the proclamation. Opinions on authenticity spread like wild fire. Those who took it seriously flooded the grocery stores collecting as much supplies as they could. Those who didn't laughed it off and continued on with their day to day lives. Conspirators were quick to blame the Government for such a nonsense hoax. They believed it was yet another Government attempt to increase their choke hold on the world. However, doubt and denial fell from every human being the moment the sky darkened.

The clouds in the sky rapidly dissolved and the wind came to a sudden halt. Animal sounds that were natural to the outside world fell silent. The moon rapidly eclipsed the sun and locked into place. Unlike regular eclipses that could cause people retina and ocular issues, this event could clearly be seen. It was obvious this wasn't a normal natural occurrence. The earth and all of its inhabitants were suddenly covered by a dim blue light. From morning to night it remained the same. The entire world itself appeared frozen in a deathly state of time. In response to the sudden drastic change, anarchy broke out. Anger and vicious attacks of violence quickly became the norm. Reacting to the mass hysteria and chaos, the Government decided they had no choice but to obey the request of the Angel and Demon.

A worldwide demand called for the most talented and intelligent scientists in their fields to Washington. Without hesitation, the request was responded to with optimism. Scientists quickly made their way to their destination as fast as they could. Upon their arrival, they were instantly sent for testing. Tests and questionnaires took up the majority of their time. Those who couldn't handle the stress or simply did poorly were sent home. Not being the appropriate time for pride or ego, they bowed out gracefully. By the end of the seven days, eight men and two women were victorious. Despite high intelligence, nervousness fell over them as the Angel and Demon once again appeared.

Three

Hope

The amount of spectators had massively increased since their first arrival. Anyone and everyone who could see or hear the message paid attention in a state of traumatized panic. Police dressed in riot gear, had a great deal of trouble keeping the screaming and scared crowds at bay. A wave of camera flashes hit both the Angel and Demon. Neither had a reaction until the Angel lifted its hand. As if a spell of silence stole all the words from the people's lips, the area instantly became quiet.

The Angel calmly approached the ten scientists. It was obvious that knots had formed in their throats. Sweaty palms and rapid swallowing confirmed it. The Angel reached its hands out toward them. Everyone gasped as two large vials appeared in front of each scientist. One was almost full and contained a blue liquid. The other was less than a quarter full and contained a white liquid with gold flecks. Without a word, the Angel stepped back and the Demon stepped forward. The Demon, just like the Angel reached its hands out and two more large vials appeared. One was almost full and contained a red liquid. The other was less than a quarter full and contained a black liquid with silver flecks. As the Demon stepped back, the scientists nervously took their gifts. All of their expressions seemed confused yet intrigued.

The Angel shifted its pale colored eyes toward the dim blue sky. "Mortals this ours and our Lord's last hope for you."

One of the scientists was quick to question. "W.. What is it?"

As if annoyed with such a question, the Demon hissed. "It is our blood and our Lord's blood!"

All of the scientist's eyes darted to the Demon in shock and disbelief. One of the scientists timidly questioned. "Why are you giving this to us?"

The Angel smiled a very gentle smile. "Our Lords though feeling betrayed are still very merciful. They cannot simply abandon this world leaving nothing behind. In your worthy hands are the means to create Heaven and Hell."

The Demon gave a slight nod. "The creators have given their creations the skill to create. The mortal hands that carelessly destroy, now can grant life."

The Angel moved its beautiful wings a little. Feathers fell then vanished before hitting the ground. "Our blood is complex, far too complex to comprehend in a single mortal lifetime. We shall grant the ten of you with an ageless longevity."

The Demon was quick to chime in. "Do not misunderstand Mortals. You are not immortal. Should your heart stop, should you fall victim to the sin of murder. You will be dead."

The Angel glanced toward the vials and sighed. "We cannot force you to take action. We cannot force you to create. Once our conversation has ended and we depart, all our influences over the world will depart with us. Mortals, do not wait to discover what that truly means."

The Demon's lips curled into an ugly sneer. "Rotting in one's own skin is a revulsion most mortals cannot stomach."

The Angel closed its eyes. "It is time. Farewell Mortals, I pray for your success."

The Demon didn't glance toward the Angel as it zipped up into the sky. "Know this Mortals, you cannot have Heaven without Hell. Good without evil, light without dark. We are of the same coin. You cannot create them without creating us."

Without another word the Demon melted into the ground and was gone.

Four

Man's Law

3 Months later.

Due to all the violence and decay of civilization, the military were now the upholders of the law. They kept their weapons drawn toward the increasing crowd outside the United Nations. Despite all the screaming and shoving, nobody was getting through the barriers. For today was the day the leaders of the world would gather together. Today was the day they would discover what the scientists had learned.

Only three out of the ten had arrived. One was a dark haired woman with thick glasses and carried herself very timidly. The next was a rather plain looking man with black hair. The last, was a man with sandy blonde hair and had a noticeable limp. He leaned on his metal walking stick as he moved toward the podium. Once there, his eyes darted toward the two armed soldiers standing beside each doorway. Before any of the scientists had a chance to compose themselves, one of the world leaders spoke up. "What have you discovered?"

The female scientist responded in a meek tone. "Their Helixes are very complex, much more so than our human ones."

"Nobody cares about that! Have you discovered the key to immortality?"

The female scientist looked toward her fellow intellects confused. “Uh… No. Were we supposed to be finding..?”

Before she finished her sentence, she was rudely cut off. “Of course you were! We have the perfect opportunity to put an end to any illness in the world. Be rid of world hunger and-”

The plain looking scientist cut the world leader off with a hiss. “Have you lost your minds?! Illness? World hunger? We have a much larger problem at hand. Our world is deteriorating all around us. It’s never day time or night time. It never changes!”

The female scientist barely nodded. “The toil upon the world has been massive. Women can’t even have a natural birth anymore. That is, of course if they can even get pregnant. C-sections have-”

“None of that’s important at this moment. With the right amount of money we can-”

The plain looking scientist shook his head in disbelief. “I can’t believe what I’m hearing! With the world in its current state, money should be the last thing on anyone’s mind. We should become a moneyless society.”

Those words were responded to with an immediate uproar of disapproval. “Money will solve everything!”

“The haves will steal from the have-nots!”

“Your job is to discover the key to immortality, not to decide how the world works!”

The female scientist suddenly snapped. She slammed her hands onto the podium. Any sign of meek and timid was replaced with anger and frustration. “Our job, as you call it, is to re-create Heaven and Hell. To create Angels and Demons! To create God for crying out loud! A task we were given by an Angel and Demon!”

One of the world leaders indifferently shrugged. “We don’t need Heaven and Hell anymore. Those divine laws have been replaced with our mortal laws. There’s nothing wrong with OUR legal system.”

The man leaning on the metal walking stick finally spoke. “That is your response then? We will merely stand by and watch as our world falls into ruin? Greed, wealth and mass chaos shall continue to reign? We, who have been given these superior gifts, shall continue to simply obey man’s law? We’ll simply ignore the endless days and nights? We’ll simply except that our elderly don’t die. They merely rot and breakdown in their own skin. We'll continue to think we as humans are the superior beings? I, unfortunately refuse to accept any of this." The man leaning on the walking stick lifted his hand as he continued. "And I refuse to accept the need for world leaders."

The moment he dropped his hand, the conversation ended in a hail of gunfire.

Five

Creation Lab

After the fall of Humanity

90 years later.

A brown haired woman dressed in a standard lab coat, groaned out of boredom. She repetitively tapped her forehead against an old school computer screen. She quickly lifted her head hearing a quiet snicker. A younger red haired man named Byron rolled his chair toward her. "Boring, isn't it?"

The woman shifted her blue eyes toward him. "My eyes are fried. Is all this past history really that important?"

Byron gave a short yet meaningful sigh. "Yeah, I mean those who transfer into Creation Lab need to know about the past."

The Creation Lab was where infants were artificially created. The process of creating a child was basically the same as nature's plan. One egg was needed from a female and one sperm was needed from a male. Unfortunately, since the fall of Heaven and Hell the human reproductive system produced more unusable material than anything else. That is of course, if it developed at all. Thanks to this misfortune, natural births had become very rare and quite difficult. Here in the Creation Lab, the female uterus had become replaced with machinery and computers.

Byron glanced at the woman's ID tag which hung from her lab coat pocket. It read 'Violet Harmond' "Where did you transfer in from?"

"Temperature Regulation."

Byron's eyes darted to Violet. "Temp. Reg? Are you serious? That's usually a job for an injured scientist. That or one that feels burnt out and needs a long break."

Violet spun her chair toward Byron as she spoke. "My daughter had trouble sleeping at night. Temp. Reg. is easy enough to handle. It gave me plenty of time to be with her."

"Sleeping issues? That's usually removed during conception." Byron suddenly snapped his fingers. "Harmond! Now I know who you are! You're Amos from Combat's wife, right?"

Violet smiled at his excitement. "Yes, I-"

Byron cut her off with a pained awkward expression. "You had a natural birth. Eek! You poor thing, I don't know why you and Amos didn't do it our way. You could have spared yourself some-"

A woman cut Byron off entering the Lab. "Byron, leave the newbie alone. Have you checked the chambers yet?"

Byron quickly wheeled his chair back over to his large terminal. "Yes Kelly. Uh... I mean I was just about to."

The woman named Kelly gently tapped the air. Many green screens appeared in front of her. As she ran her finger down one of the screens, she spoke. "Got any questions about our past newbie?"

Violet gave a slight shake of her head. "No. Well… Did the Director kill everyone?"

Kelly tapped another screen as she shrugged. "Don't know. Bryon, what are the results?"

Byron looked beyond the terminal, through the glass at fifteen egg shaped chambers. "Everything's normal. Seven is due in a couple days and four is still suffering."

Kelly gave an indifferent nod. "Just like it's supposed to. What about fourteen?"

Bryon sighed loudly shaking his head. "The pre-soul check says nothing's developed."

Kelly closed her eyes and muttered. "Damn." She looked toward Bryon as she continued. "Have the parents been notified?"

Bryon slowly nodded. "Yeah, and they said what they all say. It's soulless, send it to the experiments."

Violet instantly chimed in. "That's terrible!"

Kelly chuckled a little glancing toward her. "You'll have to develop a thicker skin to make it in Creation, newbie. If you've actually seen the soulless, you'd understand why parents just ditch them. Besides, it gives the Angels, Demons, God and Lucifer Labs more people to work on. I really don't think their work will take, but that's not Creations problem."

Before Violet had a chance to say anything else to Kelly, a woman with short black hair raced into the lab.

Six

Reject

Everyone's eyes darted to the woman in confusion. Kelly watched as she quickly began accessing files at Byron's terminal. "Emma? What's going on?"

The woman named Emma quickly tapped the air in front of herself. As the green screens appeared, she spoke. "I need back files on 2461."

Kelly walked toward Emma with a slight frown. The green screens she had been working on vanished. "So why come here? This isn't the Archive Lab."

Emma sighed trying to find what she was looking for. "We had a little trouble with the Helix booster shot. I need to check the Creation records."

Suddenly the many green screens Emma was working on overlapped each other. All except the second last one displayed a normal DNA Helix reading. The problem one, looked like the Helix had spiked wildly to one side. Emma hissed at the screens. "Son of a bitch!"

Bryon looked at the screens himself. "Whoa! What happened there?"

Emma began to work on Byron's terminal again. The green screens near her vanished. The clear glass leading to the chambers suddenly flicked on like a computer screen booting up. Suddenly an image was displayed upon the glass. A man was standing inside a cell. He was frantically scratching at his arms. Emma pointed her thumb at the man. "2461 is one of our new synthetic Helixes. He was the first who didn't react badly through the first stage. We've been closely monitoring his progress. The sudden spike is why he-"

Emma suddenly stopped short as the man released an ear piercing screech. His back began to swell as saliva gushed from his mouth. The bones in his hands rapidly grew larger and tore haphazardly through his skin. The man's rib bones slowly began to crack and find their way out of his flesh as well. Emma closed her eyes. "Ah hell, it's another nasty rejection."

Violet slowly stood from her chair. Her eyes were wide and locked on the suffering man as she approached the terminal. "W... What's happening to him?"

Emma glanced toward Violet. "You must be new here."

Byron smiled toward Violet. "This is Violet. You know, Amos from Combat's wife."

"Emma Witfield, Lead ADGL Tech. In answer to your question, his soul is being destroyed by the synthetic Demon Helix." Emma kicked her foot like she was having a temper tantrum. "Damn it! He had a pretty strong soul too. What a waste!"

The man's teeth quickly began form into sharpened points. He doubled over as blood poured from his mouth. His laboured breathing lifted and lowered his back erratically. Emma sighed pressing a button on the terminal. "Helix 3421, Murdoch?"

A man's voice responded. "Yeah?"

Emma glanced at the screen as black spikes slowly began to push out of the man's spine. "Are you anywhere near building 5?"

Murdoch was quick to respond. "I'm in 4. Why? What's up?"

Emma sigh a sigh filled with frustration. "Reject. Building 5, 4th floor, cell 8."

"Reject? So what? They're pretty subdued. Just give it a simple mercy kill."

Emma rubbed her temples like a nasty headache was forming. "It's not normal reject. It's a synthetic."

Murdoch's tone of voice instantly overflowed with annoyance. "Synthetic reject? God damn stupid scientists, screwing around with-"

Emma cut him off with a hiss. "Hey! This order was given down by Director Hart, himself!"

As if a fire had been extinguished, Murdoch's annoyance vanished. "Top order? Understood. Confirm location again."

Before Emma could respond, the cell door was kicked open. Her expression instantly shifted to confusion. "..Hang on Murdoch."

A medium built man dressed in army fatigues calmly entered the cell. He had blonde almost white hair. It was perfectly slicked back and not a single strand was out of place. The only part of his ghostly pale skin that was exposed was his neck and face. Pitch black sun glasses adorned his face hiding his eyes. His entire disposition just screamed strength and dominance.

Emma grumbled under her breath. "Oh, that's just great."

Murdoch who was growing impatient spoke over the terminal. "Location?"

Everyone in Creation Lab watched as the man approached the reject without a drop of fear. As if sensing him, the reject quickly lifted its head. It loudly snarled and growled slightly backing away. A slight smirk touched at the man's lips as he slammed his hand clean through the rejects skull. It looked effortless, like hot knife through butter.

Emma pressed the terminal button. "Forget it Murdoch, the Commander handled it." Not waiting for an acknowledgement, she switched intercoms over to the ADGL Labs. "Jeanne, We need maintenance for cell 8. Oh and if the Commander drops by, tell him the order came down from the Director."

Jeanne instantly gave a panicked whine. "The Commander's in the area?! Oh Hell!"

Emma disconnected from the intercom with a sigh. As she crossed her arms and turned away from the glass, her eyes darted to Violet. She only stared back at her traumatized.

Seven

The Commander

A slightly sympathetic smile took Emma's lips. "I guess you haven't seen the Commander in action before. Consider yourself lucky. The first time I saw it, it scared the hell out of me."

Violet swallowed heavily. "A… Are the rumors about him true?"

Emma shrugged indifferently. "Well, I guess it depends on the rumors. Is he our first successful double Helix? Yes. Is he the perfect experiment A? Yes on that on too."

Violet looked toward the floor nervously. It was obvious this whole conversation was making her uncomfortable. Yet, she didn't change the subject. "Uh... A- Actually, I meant about the L Helix."

Emma instantly began to fume. She didn't make a single attempt to hide her annoyance. "Yeah that's our perfect double Helix, the Lucifer Helix. An accidental success the ADGL lab can't even take credit for!"

Violet's eyes darted up to Emma. "Accidental?"

Emma kept her ticked off disposition as she spoke. "You know how women freeze their eggs-"

Byron cut Emma off quick. "She wouldn't. I mean Violet had a natural birth."

Emma's eyes darted from Byron back to Violet. It was obvious his words sparked her interest. "A natural birth? In this day and age? I didn't think that was even possible. Did it have a soul?"

Before Violet could respond, Emma tapped the air accessing the green screens. "Harmond. Harmond." Emma suddenly smiled finding the file she was looking for. "Ah! Here you are, Violet Harmond. Husband: Amos Harmond. Daughter-" Emma chuckled lowering her hands. The green screens vanished as she continued. "I should have recognized your name, your Kid's mother."

"Yes, she-"

Emma dismissively waved her hand cutting Violet off. "Anyway, most of us women give up our ovaries. As you already know healthy semen are in such low in amount. And because it doesn't regrow right, there are so many deformities. It's a mess. So to create life we use our higher chance for success method."

Kelly looked through the glass at the egg shaped chambers. "Without God, how can we expect the life cycle to continue on as nature intended."

Emma continued her story. "The Director was the first to donate his sample. I don't know who the woman's sample was. I was a newbie then and as far as I was aware of, nobody asked. We used every heathy sperm he had. It was failure after failure. The Director became so angry with the ADGL Labs. He kept blaming us for the failures. Try harder! Make it work! You get the idea. You can't force any of the ADGL samples to take. They either do or don't. The stronger the soul is, the higher the chances are. But that's all it is, a chance."

Emma forced an annoyed chuckle. "We were on our last chance when the Director arrived. Expecting failure, he threw one hell of a hissy fit and tossed the Lab. Smashing and destroying so many experiments. As he swept his cane along a table, he accidently knocked the Lucifer blood into the chamber. It took. It took completely. The Director accidently made Lucifer himself. Since then we haven't had even the slightest glimpse of another perfect experiment A. And creating another L Helix? It just simply passes through."

Violet shook her head in disbelief. "How can Lucifer exist without God?"

Emma confidently smiled. "Don't ask questions like that. We're getting closer each day. Our lab will create God soon enough." Emma continued as she walked toward the exit. "Well Creation Lab, I need to get back. If the Commander visited any of my Techs I'm sure they're more than upset. The Commander can make anyone cry."

Kelly glanced toward Violet. Before she could say anything, loud beeping flooded the room.

Eight

Hiding

Chamber four was flashing a blinding bright red light. Kelly didn't hesitate in running toward the electronically locked door.

Byron looked through the glass at the panicking chamber. "Is it dying?"

Kelly zipped her ID card through the lock and the door swished open. As she raced inside, she hissed. "Not if I can help it!"

Byron glanced back at Violet. His expression became confused seeing her working on the green screens. She was accessing personnel files. Once she found hers, she went under her daughter's name. A picture of a blue eyed girl with sandy blonde hair appeared. Under the picture was her identification. It read: Kid Harmond. Before Violet had a chance to do anything in the files, Byron questioned. "What are you doing?"

Violet instantly went flush as her eyes darted to him. "I… I was… uh..."

Byron wheeled his chair toward her. "I wouldn't suggest tampering with your daughter's ID file. It sends red flags up to the top."

Violet went red in embarrassment. "I… I wasn't..."

Byron began to tap the green screens she was working on. "When Emma asked about your daughter. I mean about having a soul. I knew what you were thinking. If her soul is strong, she could be a potential ADGL experiment. They never get the chance to work on anyone who was naturally born."

Violet's expression instantly weakened. She looked toward the floor as if she was ashamed. "I just want to protect my daughter."

Byron smiled slightly. "Yeah, that's what I figured. Kelly won't take long in there, so let's just shuffle Kid in the maintenance files. Moving a file doesn't send anything anywhere. I mean people change work locations all the…" Byron stopped short seeing Kid's Helix. Behind her Helix was a faint shadow. Byron's eyes darted to Violet. "She's a Helix?"

Violet's features weakened even more.

Byron smiled shaking his head. "Oh well, it doesn't matter."

Violet's eyes darted up to Byron in shock and disbelief.

Byron quickly moved Kid's file into the maintenance staff ID files. "There, now if anyone finds her ID here, just fall on the 'I'm new and must have put it in the wrong place' excuse. Anyone who checks things out will see that you are a new transfer. You'll get away with it, trust me."

"B… But why are you helping me?"

Byron smiled leaning back on his chair. The green screens vanished as he spoke. "I figured anyone whose willing work Temp. Reg. just to spend more time with their child is amazing. I mean, I've seen so many parents just indifferently abandon their not so perfect child all the time. It's obvious you love your daughter. And I'm guessing the reason you took this job was for this chance. Am I right?"

"Yes, Amos and I tried from the residential terminals but-"

"You're wasting your time there. Most files are far too protected to hack. So now that her ID's been moved to safety, are you going to transfer out?"

Violet shook her head with a smile. "No. I think I can really help out here. Thank you Byron."

Byron wheeled his chair back over to his terminal. He glanced through the glass at Kelly. She was frantically typing on the computer next to the distressed chamber. "No problem newbie. Now get back to work."

Nine

Everyday Quarter To Noon

Medical stations were located on each floor in every building. The largest was just off shot of the Combat area in building 4. Being at this particular location, it wasn't uncommon for many broken bones, deep gashes and other nasty injuries to be the everyday norm. Egos tended to fuel the desire to battle in Combat beyond a soldiers skill level.

Medical Technicians were always busy tending to the wounded which filled over half the beds. The women were dressed in white uniform dresses with a white hat. Upon their hats was a red cross. The men were dressed in uniform white pants and a short sleeve shirt. They had a red cross displayed on their breast pocket. This ancient style of clothing had been revived when it became too difficult to differentiate between nurses and doctors. A female Med Tech called out as she sprayed a medical chemical on a patient. "Hey! What time is it?!"

Mere seconds after her question was asked, a loud agony filled moan spilled into the room. Any Med Tech, who commonly worked at this Med. station, snickered. A very built man with brown hair and light blue eyes leaned weakly against the doorframe. It looked like he was in some grueling battle. He wore army pants, combat boots and a navy blue short sleeved top. Adding his own personal style to his military garb he wore black suspenders. He squinted his eyes shut gripping the doorframe for dear life. "Ugh! The pain! I'm dying!"

His pain was responded to by many snickers and head shakes. As if losing the will to live, he slid onto the floor. "It's all over! I… I see a white light!"

As he reached outward at nothing, a blonde Med Tech named Judith approached him. "Every day, Bridger, every single day…"

The man named Bridger groaned loudly. "Judith, is that you? Everything's going dark."

Judith shook her head crossing her arms. "Alright, where's the injury today?"

Bridger wasn't hesitant to thrust his finger toward her. There was the tiniest paper cut on his index. "See! See how horrible it is! Oh, the agony!"

Judith giggled not even glancing at it. "Is it even bleeding? I swear you're starved for attention."

Bridger couldn't hide his slight smirk. Being the Lead Med Tech for this station, Judith sprang into action. She quickly uncrossed her arms and snapped her fingers. "Bruno, we have an injured Helix! Helix 7923 Bridger. It's almost lunchtime and our hypochondriac is dying again."

Bridger forced an obvious fake frown. "Hypochondriac? How rude."

A dark skinned, dark hair and eyed man quickly raced toward them. "I got a Med kit Judith!"

Judith turned to the man with a nod. "Thank you Bruno."

The man named Bruno looked toward Bridger sympathetically. "Are you alright?"

Bridger watched Judith open the kit and take out a tiny pink bandage. She snickered patching him up. Bridger responded to Bruno so weakly, it sounded like his life was rapidly fading away. "I… I guess… I feel so frail but... but I guess I'll live."

Judith rolled her eyes carelessly tossing the kit back to Bruno. "Oh stop being so melodramatic. You could have just licked that wound and it would've healed."

Bridger suddenly leapt to his feet and firmly snatched his arms around Judith. "My savior!!"

Judith laughed patting his side. "Alright, Alright let me go!"

The minute he did, he glanced at the other female Med Techs. "So ladies, anyone want to join me for lunch?"

Being the everyday question, he was responded to with giggles.

Ten

Hanging Around

Bridger smiled leaning against one of the station walls. Despite being an everyday nuisance, he never once got in any Med Techs way. If a female Med Tech glanced in his direction, they were greeted with a friendly, flirtatious smile. In response to him, they would smile back or simply giggle. As Bridger comfortably crossed his arms behind his head, Bruno nervously approached him. "Bridger?"

Bridger didn't shift his attention toward him. "Yeah?"

"You're going on a Lab Mission tomorrow, right?"

Bridger uncrossed one of his arms. He snickered looking at the pink bandage. "Yup, I'm going to have to ditch this cute thing before-"

Bridger was cut off by a quiet beep in his ear. "…Helix 7923 Bridger?"

Bridger pressed the small button size silver tab in his ear. "…Yeah?"

The voice in his ear sounded like a very young man. "Are you at the Combat Med. station?"

Bridger smirked glancing around the Med. station. "Uh... No?"

The young man's voice wasn't hesitant to hiss. "Bridger, get back to work!"

Bridger couldn't help but to chuckle. "Dante, Is that you? It has to be. You're the only high strung person who contacts me."

"Of course it's Dante!! I'm the only one whoever contacts you!!"

Bridger glanced toward Bruno. He looked like he had something very important to say. "Other people contact me besides you Dante. You're not the only Helix I know."

Dante responded with a somewhat dismissive tone. "Yeah okay, I need you to pick up our Med. packs for tomorrow's mission. I'm a little behind in work. You know work, that thing you flake off on around lunch."

"But I'm nowhere near Combat's Med. station. You're really making me go out of my way to help you."

Dante snarled so loudly, Bruno could hear him. "Stupid! I can see you on surveillance!!"

Bridger looked directly at one of the less noticeable cameras. He smiled right before he stuck out his tongue. Before Dante had a chance to snap, Bridger spoke. "I'll grab them. Don't sweat it."

Dante's angered tone of voice only slightly calmed. "The Commander has called us for a debriefing on tomorrow's mission. Two hours after the dinner hour. Don't be late."

Bridger's amused disposition instantly shifted serious. "I got the memo. I'll be there."

Once Bridger released his ear piece, he turned his attention back to Bruno. "So... What?"

Being caught off guard, Bruno stumbled over his words. "O... Oh? Uh, yeah... uh..."

Bridger rubbed his flat muscular stomach. "I really need to get something to eat." As a Med Tech passed by him, he spoke. "Can I get Helix 2341 Dante's Med packs please?"

The Med Tech quickly nodded. Bridger glanced toward the stumbling Bruno. "Come on Bruno. I can't hang around here all day."

Bruno quickly got control of his nerves. "Do you think you can put in a good word for me with the Commander?"

Bridger's eyes darted to Bruno. "Good word? What are you talking about?"

"Well, I was thinking a fully trained Med Tech will be useful on missions. I mean I know Dante has a little training but-"

Bridger gave a quick 'Thanks' as the Med Tech handed him the mission's Medical packs. He then glanced back to Bruno. "It makes sense to me."

Bruno's eyes instantly lit up. "So you will?"

Bridger gave a slight nod as he walked toward the Med. station exit. "Sure. I have to go, see ya around."

Bruno was too ecstatic to give a response back. As Bridger left the station, he glanced toward the Combat area. Today's top ranking scores flipped on the screens near the entrance. The top rank belonged to Kid Harmond.

Eleven

Lunch

Standing patiently by building 4's cafeteria entrance was a young woman. She was dressed in simple sneakers, black pants and a baby blue sweatshirt. Her hip length sandy blonde hair was tied back in a high pony tail. The ID card clipped to her read Kid Harmond. Anyone who saw her gave a quick 'hi' or a smile. The young woman known as Kid didn't give any acknowledgement or even glance in their direction as they passed by.

A smiling blonde haired man with green eyes ran toward her. The ID badge clipped to his grey tack suit read Amos Harmond. Combat. He placed his hand on Kid's shoulder and spoke. "Well Kid, what are you waiting for? Go grab us a table. I'll get us something to eat."

Kid gave a slight nod walking into the large room filled with tables. It wasn't uncommon for groups of Techs working in different fields to have lunch together. For most busy Techs this was the only time they could be social. Most of the conversations were either simple gossip or complaining about their workloads. Kid sat down at an empty table away from the groups. She didn't once glance toward the chatting pools of people. Amos smiled toward her as he joined the lunch line.

A Tech standing ahead of him in the line glanced back. "Hey Amos, How's Kid doing?"

Amos smiled proudly. "She's killing all the top scores in Combat. Her reaction time is amazing. Not even a scratch on her. That's my girl!"

The Tech smiled at his beaming pride. "Is Violet okay with her training?"

Amos instantly went flush. "Uh… Well..."

"You haven't told her? Amos, you do realize if she finds out, she's going to kill you."

"Murder is a Sin. Even without God or..." Amos gave an awkward shrug. "Well, you heard the rumors. Murder is a sin."

The Tech chuckled as both of them began to put food on their trays. "I didn't mean she'd actually kill you. I just think she's going to be really angry."

"Well, don't go and rat me out, okay?"

The Tech laughed loudly. "I won't. But be careful, word gets around."

Before Amos could respond, a woman raced over to him. "There you are! I saw Kid so... Anyway, your wife is looking for you."

The Tech smirked watching Amos go flush. "I guess someone did rat you out."

Amos glanced toward the woman as he finished getting lunch. "Is she in our building?"

"Yeah, and she looks a little ticked to me. I wouldn't keep her waiting if I were you."

Amos gave a quick 'Thanks' as he approached the section for utensils. He began to mutter to himself as he collected the cutlery he needed. "Murder is a sin. Murder is a sin."

Anyone within earshot couldn't help but to chuckle hearing him. As Amos put the tray down in front of Kid, he spoke. "Here's lunch Kid. I need to go talk to your mother. I'll try and be fast. If you're done before I make it, just wait here okay?"

Kid gave a slight nod as she began to eat her lunch. Amos nodded in return before, he raced out of the cafeteria.

Twelve

Encounter

A very unpleasant figure stepped into building 4's cafeterias doorway. Anyone who caught sight of him instantly went flush. One of the many Techs got to their feet and yelled out. "Commander on the floor!"

Everyone instantly stopped what they were doing and got to their feet. Everyone that is, except Kid. She just continued to eat her lunch. The Commander glanced around the anxious room. Due to his pitch black sunglasses, nobody could tell who exactly he was looking at. Everyone just nervously stared straight ahead. There wasn't a single person who wanted to catch his attention. The Commander calmly walked into the cafeteria. Anytime the Commander paused in front of someone, they would instantly go flush.

The Commander suddenly glanced in Kid's direction hearing cutlery hitting a plate. His eyebrows lowered seeing her calmly eating her lunch. Kid didn't lift her attention as the Commander stepped in front her table. "It's customary to stand in the presence of a Commander."

A Tech from a neighbouring table spoke. "Commander, Kid doesn't talk. She's-"

The Commander suddenly turned his head toward the Tech. His eyes brows lowered as much as they could. The Tech instantly went flush and looked nervously toward the floor. The Commander shifted his attention back to Kid. "To your feet!"

Kid only continued to eat her meal. The Commander slammed his hands on the table. Not only was her drink spilled but the sound made everyone in the room flinch. Kid looked toward the mess then up at the Commander. He greeted her with a full frown. "I said, to your f-"

The Commander suddenly stopped short as his eyebrows furrowed in confusion. The image of Kid's body seemed to shift slightly. For a few seconds, she appeared blurry and grainy. It was as if a static zap had hit her. Then within a blink of the eye, she was back to normal.

The Commander quickly turned his attention toward his hand feeling Kid touch it. She gave a slight nod placing her pudding cup in his palm. His confused expression seemed to increase staring at it. Kid lifted her spoon then pointed toward the utensil section. The Commander didn't shift his confusion from the dessert. Kid leaned across the table to the Commander. She gently placed her fingers under his chiseled jaw and turned his head toward the section.

As she drew her hand back, she could see through the side of his pitch black sunglasses. Her expression shifted to confused catching glimpse of something silver. As she reached toward him, the Commander turned his head back to her. Kid stared up at him as he stepped back from her table slightly.

"I'm so sorry Commander!" Amos yelled running toward the table.

The Commander didn't shift his attention from Kid as Amos continued. "Kid hasn't been here long enough to understand things."

Violet quickly approached Kid. Without a word, she took her hand. Kid didn't give any resistance as Violet encouraged her to her feet. Amos awkwardly smiled as he continued talking. "She really didn't mean to be so disrespectful."

The Commander kept his attention locked on Kid as Violet led her out of the cafeteria.

Thirteen

Curiosity

The Commander opened the door to his office in the 6th building. In response to someone in the room, the lamp on his large desk automatically flicked on. Besides the simple lamp, the room had a dim blue glow. The dim blue light came from his ceiling to floor windows. The Commander approached his leather bound desk chair and sat down. Hooking his feet on the edge of his desk, he turned his attention to the eclipsed sun and moon in the sky. The 5th, 6th and 7th buildings were the only buildings tall enough to see the real sky. Every other building sat blissfully unaware under the facilities protective dome. The Commander glanced at the pudding cup Kid had given him. "Computer, access Helix files."

Many green screens appeared above his desk. The computer made a beep sound. "Limited access to Helix files. Passcodes are required-"

"Access granted Double Helix 6426 voice recognition."

After a few beeps, a few more green screens appeared. "Access granted. Welcome Commander."

"File on Kid Harmond Helix unknown."

After a few seconds of scanning, the computer beeped again. "No known file."

The Commander turned his head toward the green screens confused. "No known..? Check again!"

The Computer did as it was commanded to. After re-scanning the results were the same. "No known file."

"Check under Techs."

"No known file."

"Staff?"

"No known file."

The Commander hissed toward the green screens. "Search all files! Helix! Human! Military! Everyone!"

The computer began to do a thorough file scan. The Commander frowned as much as he could until the computer made a beep. "File located. Kid Harmond, Maintenance."

The Commander placed his feet back onto the floor. "…Maintenance? That's an odd place to put her personnel file. Computer location of Kid Harmond."

A 3D image of the large compound appeared on his desk. As the computer scanned each floor, it momentarily became highlighted. The Commander placed the pudding cup on his desk and stood up. As he walked toward the windows, the computer beeped. The Commander glanced over his shoulder at his desk. The roof of building 5 was flashing. The Commander turned completely then leaned against the ceiling to floor window. "Access the surveillance of building 5's rooftop."

Four of the green screens blended together making a larger screen. The screen flickered then the live feed from the surveillance camera was accessed. Kid was sitting on the edge of the building. She was calmly looking at the outside of the protective dome, carelessly swinging her legs upwards and downwards. It looked like any moment she could easily slip off the building.

The Commander removed his pitch black glasses. The irises of his eyes were a shining almost animalistic silver color. Circling his pitch black pupil was a very thin unnoticeable crimson red ring. "Fearless." He muttered locking his silver eyes on her. "Completely fearless."

Kid suddenly spun herself back toward the building and jumped onto the rooftop. Amos appeared on the screen offering his hand to her with a smile. Kid smiled herself as she ran toward him and took his hand. Once they walked off the camera, the Commander hooked his pitch black sunglasses back on. "They hid you in maintenance for a reason and I want to know why."

Fourteen

Two Hours after the Dinner Hour

A built, black haired dark eyed man stood confidently by the Commander's closed office door. He was dressed the same as Bridger except for the suspenders and navy blue top. His personal style was a three quarter sleeved black top. Kneeling beside him, working on his laptop was a young man with blue eyes and light brownish blonde hair. He wore a black baseball hat, windbreaker, pants, gloves and boots. His lips touched at a frown hearing a friendly voice.

"I'm not late." Bridger said leaving the elevator.

The young man frowned even more looking up at the smiling Bridger. "Yeah but you're not early either."

Bridger snickered giving an upward nod toward the man standing by the door. "Murdoch, are you as high strung as Dante here?"

The man named Murdoch ignored Bridger's question and asked his own. "Are we ready?"

Bridger glanced down at the young man named Dante. He quickly closed his laptop and stood up. He removed his baseball hat and began to fix his hair. Bridger waited until Dante was finished his grooming before he knocked on the door. A 'Come in' heard through the door. Bridger smiled opening the door widely. Murdoch wasn't hesitant to enter the Commander's office. As Dante went to follow, Bridger placed his hand on his head. Dante hissed as Bridger roughed up his once tamed hair. Bridger couldn't help but to snicker again being swatted with Dante's baseball hat. Once all three men stood in front of his desk, the Commander spoke. "What's the status on tomorrow's mission?"

Dante quickly answered his question. "The information you bought from your source checked out. Lab 6 is due to release a worldwide announcement on one of their creations. Rumor has it, they created 'God'."

Murdoch who was standing like a solider awaiting a command, scoffed. "I highly doubt it. What did it cost for that information?"

The Commander crossed his arms on his desk. "Two vials of synthetic D."

"That junk's dangerous, especially among the lost souls. Those people are nothing but a waste of space taking up air."

Bridger glanced toward Murdoch. "Yeah, but even rats have their uses."

The Commander turned his attention back to Dante. "Those who choose not to enter the safety of the many Labs aside. Do we have the blueprints on Lab 6 yet?"

Dante gripped his hat tightly. "Almost, there are a few gaps in the surveillance, but I'll get it done Commander. Even if I have to burn through the night, it will be done by morning."

Murdoch gave a brief shake of his head. "Don't exhaust yourself. The last thing we need is our communications not at their best."

"Don't worry, I'll be fine. …Uh Commander?"

The Commander didn't respond just kept his head pointed toward him.

Dante awkwardly swallowed. "I've made some improvements to your sunglasses. You'll be able to receive maps of the facilities and be sent codes, passwords and so on. They will be ready first thing."

The Commander turned his head to Bridger. "Explosives and Transportation?"

Bridger crossed his arms standing in a more relaxed stance. "Handled, I'll re-check them tonight, in the morning and right before we leave."

The Commander looked toward Murdoch. "Weapons?"

"I've made a few new adjustments to our battle suits. They're a lot lighter and easier to maneuver in. With Dante's help we've also improved the speed of our reloading systems in our Combat gloves."

Dante smiled proudly. "It wasn't that hard Commander."

The Commander leaned back on his leather bound desk chair. "We'll need five suits."

Murdoch glanced toward the other three men in the room. "Five, Commander?"

The Commander gave a slight nod. "There will be another joining our team tomorrow."

Fifteen

New Member

Murdoch was quick to question. "What? Who?"

Bridger chuckled shaking his head. "Well I'll be. I guess that idiot Bruno managed to win over the Commander."

"Bruno, the Med Tech? He had the nerve to ask me to put in a good word for him."

Dante quickly nodded. "Me too! He's always nagging me whenever he sees me. He even followed me into the bathroom once."

Bridger couldn't help but to chuckle. "You two should have done what I did. Say 'sure, no problem' then say squat. Everyone's happy."

Murdoch scoffed and turned his head in disgust. "I won't humor anyone."

Bridger smirked. "Well of course you won't. You have that mean Helix."

"It's pronounced Demon Helix and shut it."

Bridger chuckled as Murdoch turned his attention back to the Commander. "Dante's a good enough Medic Commander. All of our Helixes have the rapid healing skill. Besides, it's not like any of us get seriously injured anyway."

Dante's expression shifted to slightly awkward. "It's a good thing too. All I know is spray the med spray then slap on a bandage. Anything involving setting bones or something, I haven't got a clue about."

Bridger shrugged. “Like Murdoch said, we never get seriously injured. So, there’s no point in having a Med Tech on our team. I mean even Tech nerd here can shoot a gun.”

“Tech nerd?! I’m a Data, Information and Surveillance expert!”

Bridger ignored Dante’s annoyed demeanor and continued his thought. “But if you want a Med Tech to join our team Commander, I’m okay with it.”

The Commander shook his head pushing his chair back from the desk. “The Med Tech won’t be joining our team.”

Murdoch was quick to question. “Then who will be Commander?”

The Commander stood up and walked toward the ceiling to floor windows. “The Harmond girl.”

Everyone’s eyes darted to him. Murdoch wasn’t hesitant to react. “A civilian?!”

Dante’s expression shifted to confusion as he scratched his head. “Harmond? That name doesn’t sound familiar.”

Bridger snickered as he poked Dante in the arm. “That’s because you only did the basic Combat training. Kid Harmond is the daughter of Amos from Combat.”

“Kid Harmond? You mean the mute girl?!”

Murdoch was quick to protest. “Commander, I have to disagree with your decision. A civilian would just get in the way. Someone in the military would be better. Not by much but at least they wouldn’t just be hanging around.”

Dante was quick to jump on Murdoch’s ban wagon. “I think so too Commander. None of us want or even have the time to babysit a human.”

Murdoch stepped into the soldier’s ‘at ease’ stance. “An untrained human is-”

“None of us will be babysitting.” Bridger said cutting Murdoch off. “Kid Harmond is a Helix.”

Sixteen

Reasons

Murdoch scoffed shaking his head in disbelief. "You've been sniffing too much gun powder."

Bridger couldn't help but to laugh. "Gun powder is synthetically created. It doesn't have a smell."

"You know what I mean. There's no way that girl is a Helix. I haven't seen her in any of the booster shot lines. Only a perfect double Helix like the Commander doesn't need them."

Dante looked toward the Commander. His attention was directed toward the outside. "I heard a rumor amongst the Techs a long time back. A little girl wandered into one of the ADGL Labs and was accidently injected. The Tech just gave shots to everyone standing in line. Maybe that little girl was Kid."

Murdoch hissed almost instantly. "Based on what, rumors and gossip?"

"You need Helix booster shots to maintain a lot of things, especially sanity. Who's been giving them to her? Amos is in Combat so he doesn't have access to such things. What's her mother do? What Lab is she..?"

Murdoch snarled cutting Dante off. "None of that matters! She is not a Helix!!"

Bridger lifted his hands defensively as he spoke. "Calm down mean Helix. I know for a fact Kid Harmond is a Helix. And I have three really good reasons to prove it."

Murdoch's anger didn't increase but it didn't simmer down either. "And they would be?"

Bridger lifted his index finger. "One! I've been paying attention to the top Combat scores. I like keeping track of things like that. Last week Kid began to not just take them all, but dominate them. Now you know only you, me and the Commander-" Bridger patted Dante's head. "Sorry."

Dante swatted Bridger with his hat as he frowned.

Bridger snickered before he continued. "Us three and a few other Helixes are the only ones who can take on the hardest level. I mean without getting anything broken. And only the Commander can walk away without any scratches or bruises. Well, him and Kid."

"Wow! That's really amazing."

Bridger nodded in excitement toward Dante. "I know! And every day she beats her old top score!"

Murdoch gave an indifferent shrug. "None of that's important. You and I don't bother screwing around in those things anymore. I'm sure if we did, we'd do better and better each time too."

Bridger lifted a second finger. "Two! Have you actually ever looked at her, now I'm not talking a simple glance, I mean really looked at her?"

"Why the hell would I bother to stare at some kid?"

"If you did, you'd notice she phases."

Dante almost dropped his hat and his laptop. "Phases, you mean that freaky thing that makes a person look like they have lousy reception?"

"Yeah, but I don't think she can control it. When you stare at her long enough, it just happens. You swear you see her move when she hasn't at all. She just suddenly seems grainy and-"

The Commander cut off the conversation in the room. "She will be joining us on tomorrow's mission. This isn't negotiable. Murdoch, I want five battle suits prepared for tomorrow."

Murdoch instantly snapped back into a soldier waiting for a command stance. "Yes Commander."

The Commander shifted his attention to Dante. "Get back to work on those blueprints."

Dante was quick to nod. "Yes Commander."

As the three men turned to leave, the Commander spoke. "Bridger, stay."

Seventeen

After Conversation

Bridger and the Commander stood in silence as Murdoch followed Dante out of the room. The minute he closed the door behind them, the Commander spoke. “What is third reason?”

Bridger gave the Commander a look of confusion. “Commander?”

The Commander turned and faced the windows. “The first reason was her impressive scores in Combat. The second was her phasing skill. What is the third?”

Bridger awkwardly chuckled. “Well, it sounds really stupid but-” Bridger suddenly stopped short noticing the pudding cup on his desk. “Uh-”

“But?”

As if slapped back on track, Bridger continued. “It’s like a feeling.”

The Commander glanced back at Bridger. His eyebrows were furrowed. It was more than obvious he didn’t understand what Bridger meant.

Bridger placed his hand on his chest. “Something inside me just feels it. I know any Helix can sense another. But when I look at her, I feel- I don’t know, warm I guess.”

“Warm?” The Commander echoed back with a slight frown.

Bridger chuckled lifting his hands defensively. “I told you sounded really stupid.”

The Commander lowered his head toward the floor. “...Actually it doesn’t.”

Bridger's expression became questioning as he lowered his hands. "Commander?"

The Commander turned his head back to the windows. "Anything else?"

"No Commander. But I wonder if the reason I get that feeling from her is because she's another high A Helix. There isn't too many on my level."

"That would explain why Murdoch hasn't felt anything. Us, from Hell can sense one another. Those from Heaven are simply unimportant."

Bridger's lips only hinted at a frown as he thought. 'Gee, thanks Commander.'

The Commander tilled his head toward the eclipsed sun and moon. "Am I making a mistake having Kid Harmond join us?"

"We follow your lead Commander. If that's what you want, then that's how it is."

The Commander turned then approached his desk. "I need to deliver the mission criteria." As he scooped up a manila folder, he continued. "That will be all Bridger."

Bridger barely nodded being lead out of the office.

Eighteen

The Harmond Home

The temperature underneath the protective dome was comfortably cool. It was the appropriate temperature for a nice autumn night. Even though the sun and moon had eclipsed, within the dome of the facility day time and night time ran on a normal schedule. The Temp Regulators even made the seasons change. It went from winter to spring to fall back to winter. Summer was a hot, sweaty, uncomfortable, skin sizzling annoyance of the past.

In the center point of the facility was a large open grassy field. Not only was it a place for social gatherings, it was also the main passage to access all the buildings and Residential areas. The Commander didn't glance at the artificial night sky or stars above as he passed by many of the single floored homes. Having the exact same design and structure, only the last name of the resident and personal touches made them differ from one another.

The Commander opened the gate to the Harmond home. Once at the door, he carelessly pounded upon it. A frown took his lips not getting an instant response. As he lifted his fist to pound again, it opened. Kid had answered. She looked toward his raised fist then him. As the Commander lowered his hand, Violet called out. "Who is it Kid?!"

Kid didn't glance back or step away from the doorway. The Commander offered her the manila folder. "Take this. I'll pick you up in the m-"

Seeing who was standing on her doorstep, Violet cut him off. "Commander, uh... What..? T... to what do we owe this ple… ple…"

As Violet's sentence trailed off into nothing, the Commander spoke to Kid. "I don't wait on anyone. I will knock once then give you five minutes."

Violet's eyes darted from Kid back to the Commander. "Five minutes for what?"

"This will explain the basic outline for the mission. More will be explained tomorrow."

Violet instantly went flush. "M... Mission?!" The moment the words finished passing her lips, she ran toward the hallway leading to the bedrooms and yelled out. "Amos!!"

Amos stumbled exhausted out of one of the bedrooms. "What are you yelling about? It's been a hell of a day and-"

Violet snatched his arm and frantically rattled it. "The Commander, he..! he..!"

Amos' eyes darted to the open doorway. The Commander kept his attention locked on Kid. "Take the folder or go into the mission blind. Either way is fine by me and my team."

Amos forced a pleasant smile as he approached Kid. "Oh, good evening Commander. Would you like to come in for some coffee or anything?"

"No. I'm only here to deliver the itinerary for tomorrow's mission."

As Kid reached for the manila folder, Violet raced to her side and snatched it. Appearing almost in a state of frenzy, she quickly looked through it. Her expression went from worried to panic. "This is a Lab mission! They're the most dangerous! And..! And Kid isn't a soldier! Commander, she shouldn't be..!"

"Any Helix can be brought into a mission."

Violet slapped the folder shut and thrusted it toward the Commander. "She isn't a Helix! She isn't a soldier! She's my daughter! She..!"

Amos snatched his wife's shoulders, in an attempt to calm her down. "Thank you for stopping by Commander. What time does Kid need to be ready by?"

As if answering for him, Violet responded. "NO! She's not going anywhere!"

Violet aggressively shook the folder toward the Commander. All the papers inside came flying out. As Kid began to pick them up, the Commander spoke. “One hour after the breakfast hour.”

Amos pulled his bawling wife to his chest. “She’ll be ready.”

Once Kid picked up the last paper, she offered it back to the Commander. His expression shifted to confusion as he took them “You would rather enter into the mission blind?”

Kid responded with a slight nod. Before the Commander had a chance to say anything else, she closed the front door on him. The Commander gave a slight nod himself before he turned kneel and left.

Nineteen

Protective Parents

Violet broke from Amos' grip and snatched her arms protectively around Kid. "She's not going anywhere! She isn't a soldier!"

Amos sighed walking toward the open concept living room. As he sat on the back of the couch, he crossed his arms. "We can't refuse this Violet."

Violet squeezed Kid so tight her arms were pinned at the sides. "No! We finally managed to hide her and he comes along and-"

"We don't have any choice in the matter."

Violet screeched. "No!! I won't let her go!!"

Kid looked toward Amos. Her expression was a combination of sympathy and the need for help. Amos sighed again standing up straight. He spoke as he approached them and gently pulled Violet's arms away from Kid. "This isn't a request from a simple soldier. Or even a Helix soldier. This is a demand from the Commander. There's nothing we can do."

Once Violet's arms were finally pried away from her, Amos gave an upward nod toward the hallway. "Head off to bed Kid. Try to get a good night's sleep. I don't know what's in store for you tomorrow, but-"

"No! I won't let her go!!"

Kid looked at the tears coating Violet's cheeks sympathetically. She quickly hugged Violet trying to calm her down. Violet whimpered into her shoulder, hugging her back. "I can't put you in danger. I can't. Lab missions are-"

Kid softly stroked her back in a soothing manner. Amos nodded slightly. "Off you go, Kid."

Kid barely nodded letting Violet go.

Violet on the other hand only tightened her grip. "Amos, she's our daughter. I don't want her to go."

Amos placed his hand on her arm. "I don't want to let her go either but we don't have a choice. Kid will be okay. She's really good in the Combat simulators and-"

Violet instantly turned on Amos. "You let her try those barbaric things?! What were you thinking?!"

Amos instantly went flush. "Uh... Well, I was thinking that it's really boring just hanging around Combat all day. She wanted to try one, so I-"

Violet's anger shifted to Kid. "You wanted to try one?!"

Kid's expression instantly shifted to awkward.

Amos nodded. "I said it was okay. Now come on Violet, she needs her sleep."

Violet's anger was disarmed as her features broke. "I can't let him take her."

"It's past her bedtime."

Violet was hesitant to let her go but eventually did. In response to her freedom, Kid quickly hugged Amos then raced down the hallway. As Violet closed her eyes, more tears were forced out. "There's nothing we can do is there?"

Amos closed his eyes as well. "Come on, it's past our bedtime as well."

Twenty

Lost Little Girl

A small girl shuffled down a long dirt road. Blood was dripping from her side, mouth and many other injuries. Despite looking a stone's throw from death, she kept moving forward. She didn't glance behind herself hearing very loud engines gunning in her direction. An army hummer zipped by her. The gust of the wind it caused knocked the girl clean over. Three more hummers chased after the first. As the last zipped by, the driver noticed her and stomped on the breaks.

The girl didn't move an inch as the hummer came to a screeching stop. The driver was first to jump out. It was Violet, a much younger version of herself. She raced over to the small girl. She gasped seeing blood pouring from her injuries. She called out as she removed her lab coat. "Amos, get out here!"

The passenger door opened. Amos, a much younger version of himself, quickly climbed out of the hummer. He ran toward her as he spoke. "Oh no, did a Tech hit an animal?"

Violet gently placed her coat over the girl's shoulders. "I think they hit this girl."

Amos looked down at her sympathetically. "Is... Is the poor thing dead?"

"No, we have to help her."

Amos' eyes darted up to Violet. "Violet, you know we're not supposed to get involved with-"

"We need to help her Amos! She's just a little girl. I can't just leave her out here to die. I just can't!"

Amos looked toward his upset wife momentarily before he nodded. As he scooped up the injured child, he spoke. "Then we better get her in the hummer and get a move on. If we trail too far behind they're going to think there was a problem." Amos placed the small girl in the back of the vehicle. "How are we going to explain her, Violet?"

Violet smiled softly placing her hand lovingly on her husband's back. "We'll hide her. I'll give up working in the Labs and we'll raise her."

"She'll be our daughter?"

Violet gently brushed her fingers against the girl's forehead. "She needs us Amos. This little girl needs our protection. The facility can protect her. We can protect her."

Violet gasped awaking from the dream of the long ago past. Sitting up, she ran her hands against her sweaty face. "We were supposed to protect her." She muttered as her features weakened.

As she lowered her hands, she glanced toward Amos' side of the bed. His blankets were pulled back but he wasn't in the room. Violet pulled back her own covers and got to her feet. She quickly picked up her pale pink house coat from the edge of the bed. Putting it on as she left her bedroom, her eyes darted to Amos. He was standing in Kid's open bedroom doorway. Violet tip toed toward him. "…Amos?"

Amos glanced toward her as she stepped beside him. "I guess you couldn't sleep either. I know it's impossible but I wish we could hide her somewhere."

Violet looked toward Kid's bed. It looked like a large pile of blankets with only a lone foot sticking out. "Isn't there anything we can do?"

"Only the Director can overturn an order. But he doesn't directly involve himself in any of the missions. The Commander is the one that deals with them all. I hate to say it but he's completely right. He can choose anyone to join his team. Soldier or not, it's his choice. He can even choose one of us if he wanted."

Violet took Amos' hand and led him into the living room area. "What if we run? We can live in the world of the Lost Souls. I'm sure we can."

Amos gripped her hand tightly sitting down on the couch. "Security is a lot tighter than it used to be. That world is too dangerous for-"

"Lab missions are dangerous as well!"

Amos pulled Violet to sit down beside him. "Yes but she'll be working with soldiers. The Commander hasn't lost a single soldier on his team. I know she'll be more than fine but-"

"All I still see is that hurt little girl."

Amos rested the side of his head on her shoulder. "So do I sometimes, but then she kills the top score in Combat. Then I realize, we've raised a strong young woman. We have to except that and have confidence in her."

Violet sighed loudly just closing her eyes.

Twenty-One

Morning

The Commander dressed completely in black, pounded on the Harmond front door. Without having to attempt another so called knock, Amos opened the door. He had a tooth brush in his mouth and looked frantic.

"Morning Commander." He mumbled through a mouthful of toothpaste. "Kid's almost ready. Come on in."

The Commander just barely stepped inside.

Amos raced toward the kitchen area, it was directly across from the living room area. He quickly brushed his teeth then tossed his tooth brush onto the counter. "I'm so late!"

As he rinsed his mouth out with tap water, Violet entered the room. She instantly greeted the Commander with a full frown. "Why are you in my house?"

"I invited him in Violet."

Violet didn't shift her attention to Amos hearing him zip up the track suit jacket. "Kid isn't a soldier. She shouldn't be anywhere near these stupid missions."

The Commander mirrored her full frown. "These stupid missions as you call them, are what keeps our facility moving forward. Soldier or not, she will be joining my men."

Violet responded with an upset slight whine. "But why, there are so many other people just waiting for the opportunity to join you. Why take my daughter?"

"Why did you hide her in the Maintenance files?"

Violet instantly went flush. "I… I must have put it there accidentally."

"I highly doubt that. You were trying to hide a Helix. I suspect you or your husband has been stealing booster shots from the ADGL Labs to maintain her sanity."

Violet instantly began to fume. "How dare you?! We'd never-"

The Commander cut her off with an exasperated sigh. "Those five minutes are up."

As if knowing that herself Kid walked into the living area. She was dressed in a mint green sweater, black pants, sneakers and had her hair up in a high ponytail. Amos approached her with a smile and a hug. "Think of it like one of the Combat simulators and you'll do great. Good luck out there Kid."

Kid smiled, nodded and hugged him in return.

Violet's features weakened looking toward her. "Please Commander. I beg of you, don't take our daughter."

The Commander turned toward the open doorway. "Beg me all you want. I am taking a new soldier with me today. Kid Harmond will be joining my team and that's final."

Violet could feel herself on the verge of tears as the Commander left their house. Kid raced over to her mother and gave her a hug. Violet gripped her tightly as she spoke. "I'm going to be worrying endlessly about you Kid. Please come home to us safely."

Once Violet let Kid go, she smiled and nodded. After a quick wave, Kid raced out of the house. Violet closed her eyes feeling them over flow with tears. "We just handed our daughter over to the devil."

Amos' features weakened as he closed his eyes as well.

Twenty-Two

Choice

The minute Kid sat in the passenger seat of the army jeep, the Commander who was sitting behind the wheel with a rather plain expression, spoke. "Do you think I was a tad cruel to your parents?"

Kid's eyes darted to him. The Commander continued to look ahead at the white almost shinny roadway. "They're obviously very protective of you. Something I'm more than unfamiliar with. The Director merely sees me as a successful perfect double Helix. Always has always will. I guess it has made me cold toward those who care about their child."

Kid glanced toward her house. The Commander placed one of his always gloved hands on top of the steering wheel. On the knuckle of his glove was a small red rectangle microchip. "I'm not sure why they hid you. I can only assume it was because they didn't want you to be experimented on. That or the fact sometimes a Helix just snaps and needs to be put out of their misery. Either way doesn't matter to me. You are a Helix and it's in my every right as Commander to have you join my men. However-"

The Commander paused for a moment before he turned his head toward her. "Your parents care very deeply for you. They love you enough to even risk punishment for hiding you. So I'm giving you a choice. One I would never give any of my men."

Kid looked back toward the Commander. The Commander kept his attention locked on Kid as he continued. "Leave now and return to your family. Spend your time only battling in the Combat simulators. I won't bother commanding you to join my men. Nor will I mention your Helix file being hidden in Maintenance. If you are discovered it won't be because of me. Or-"

The Commander turned his head back toward the roadway. "Join my men. Give up the safety of the facility. See the world for what it really is. What it really has become. Risk your life alongside myself and my men. The choice is yours."

Without hesitation, Kid grabbed her seatbelt and drew it across her chest. Hearing the buckle lock into place, the Commander started up the jeeps engine. "You have made your choice."

Twenty-Three

New ID

The Commander drove down the white road to a dead-end. "First we need to get to the Launch Pad area. My team will be meeting us there."

Beside the driver's side window a green screen appeared. The Commander began to tap in a code before he spoke. "Voice recognition: The Commander, passenger, Kid-"

The Commander turned his head toward Kid as he stopped short. "Why would parents who so obviously care about you, give you such a simple name. It seems rather indifferent. I occasionally hear around the facility 'Kid this' or 'Kid that' or 'That Harmond Kid.' Don't you feel like you're lacking a name that makes you, you?"

Kid looked down at herself momentarily then shrugged. She then looked up at the Commander and shrugged again.

Before the Commander had a chance to say anything, a young man's voice spoke from the green screen. "This is Tech Lab. Is the lift unit non-responsive again?"

"It's fine."

The Tech instantly identified the Commander's voice and stumbled over his words. "Oh! U… Uh.. Commander. Uh... is there a pro-"

The Commander hissed back at the green screen. "I said its fine!!"

Not getting a response back, the Commander returned his attention to Kid. "Have you ever considered changing your name?"

Kid gave him a bewildered look, until the Commander suddenly shook his head a little. "No, forget what I said. Your name is yours and-"

Kid cut the Commander off by placing her fingertips over his mouth. As she lowered her hand, she looked down at herself and shrugged.

The Commander turned his head to the white wall ahead of them. "I suppose not being able to speak it would be rather difficult to give yourself a more personal name. If you want I can give you one."

Kid smiled slightly and nodded looking up at him. Seeing the movement of the corner of his eye, the Commander nodded himself. "I'm not quite sure what type of name you would like. I suppose off the top of my head, I would say 'Sinah.'"

Kid's eyes instantly lit up. She smiled full and quickly nodded. The Commander turned his head back toward her. Seeing her happy disposition, he barely nodded. "You like the name then?"

Kid now known as Sinah nodded again holding her full smile.

The Commander returned his attention to the green screens. "Passenger: Sinah Harmond. Location: bottom level."

The green screen flashed a couple of times then vanished. The ground below the jeep which was actually a lift began to lower. Once the vehicle was below ground level, the roadway above began to close. Every few seconds a red light flashed by them the further down they went. Once they reached the bottom level, the Commander drove off the lift. Sinah glanced back at it as it lifted back upward. She smiled slightly placing her hand on the Commander's arm.

The Commander glanced toward her as she pointed at him. He nodded slightly returning his attention to the underground passage. "Yes, I like your name as well."

Sinah shook her head then pointed at him again.

"I am known as the Commander."

Sinah's slight smile faded as she removed her hand from him and looked out the window.

The jeeps headlights and simple red emergency lights were the only illumination the underground passage had. As the Commander drove onto a second lift, he spoke. "Fallen. My name is Fallen Hart."

Sinah's slight smile instantly returned.

Twenty-Four

Toward The Launch Pad

As the platform ascended to the surface, the Commander now known as Fallen, spoke. "Do you like my name? I don't really bother with it. Normally, I'm called the Lucifer Helix or perfect experiment A. Under my creation file, my name is Fallen Hart. 'Hart' is my father's last name. I am Director Hart's creation. Once I became the Commander, that's all anyone knew me as."

Sinah smiled toward Fallen and motioned her hand at him.

Seeing her out of the corner of his eye, Fallen nodded. "I like your name as well. I think it suits you."

Sinah smiled as much as she could before she nodded in agreement.

As the ceiling for the lift began to open, Fallen glanced upward. "Murdoch is a master at hand to hand combat. He's my Offense and Defense equipment soldier. He's the only Demon Helix on my team."

Once the lift locked into place connecting them to another surface roadway, Fallen drove off of it. "Bridger has the same skills in hand to hand as Murdoch. He's my Explosives and Traps expert. The difference between Murdoch's high Demon Helix and Bridger's high Angel Helix is, Bridger will kill to prevent suffering. Murdoch will not only try to prolong it but will increase it."

Sinah looked around curiously. This was a road in the facility she had never been down before.

"Dante is a midrange Angel Helix. Physically, he's a low level soldier. Mentally, he's the best in his field. With time I'm confident his skills will only improve. He's my Data, Information and Surveillance soldier."

Despite feeling like they were outside, foggy glass walls were on either side and above them. Sinah narrowed her eyes trying her best to see through it. Fallen who noticed her attempts, spoke. "This is the only tunnel that leads to the Launch Pad area. There's access through building six but not by vehicle and security is a lot more annoying there."

Sinah's eyes darted to a large security booth at the end of the road. Two boom gates prevented them from simply driving through. As they approached, noticeable and hidden cameras turned toward the jeep. A man dressed in army fatigues, carrying a clip board calmly left the booth. Once Fallen stopped the car, the soldier approached the driver's side. Not glancing up from the papers attached to the clipboard, he dismissively spoke. "I'm sorry but you're going to have to turn this jeep around. We don't have any vehicles scheduled for-"

"Scheduled or not, we will be going through."

The solder frowned lifting his head. His agitated disposition instantly vanished seeing Fallen frowning back at him. He instantly stood up straight and saluted. "Sorry Commander, Sir!"

Fallen barely nodded, snatching the clipboard from his other hand. He quickly removed the pen from the clasp and signed the top paper. As he handed it back, the soldier glanced toward Sinah. "Uh.. C... Commander, protocol says we need both-"

Fallen turned his head toward the soldier cutting him off. "Two signatures aren't required. If you have a problem with that, take it up with the Director."

The soldier instantly went flush then waved them through. Once the boom gates lifted, Fallen wasn't hesitant to step on the gas.

The minute they passed the booth and gates, they were out of the facility. Sinah's eyes widened and darted around the open barren wastelands. The dim blue light seemed to highlight the nothingness. On this road in the distance was the brightly lit Launch Pad area. Fallen didn't glance toward her as he said. "Welcome to the world of the Lost Souls."

Twenty-Five

Chatter

Stadium lights illuminated every inch of the Launch Pad area. Despite actually being outside the facility, those working here always felt like they were inside. Dante and Murdoch were by two army hummers. Murdoch was making last minute inventory checks, while Dante was working on his laptop. He had it perched on one of the metal boxes that needed to be loaded into one of the hummers. A frown instantly took Dante's lips hearing a loud chuckle.

Bridger nonchalantly walked out from one of the hangers toward them. "I'm not late."

Dante didn't look up from working as he hissed. "Yeah but you're not early either."

Bridger glanced around at the many mechanics and working soldiers. "No sign of our newbie?"

Murdoch opened one of the metal cases. "The Commander went to go get her."

Bridger glanced at Murdoch's black shirt, pants, gloves and combat boots. He then glanced at Dante. Both were dressed exactly the same way Fallen was. "Are these the new suits?"

Murdoch handed him the same outfit. "Yeah, I got rid of that full body suit look. Taking a piss in one of those is a bitch."

Bridger chuckled. "Tell me about it. Zipping my front zip all the way down seems..." Bridger paused for a girlish giggle. "..Naughty."

Dante frowned tugging at his shirt. "I hate them either way. They're too damn tight and uncomfortable."

Bridger glanced toward Murdoch as he took a seat on top of one of the cases. "You're just upset because it shows off what little muscles you have."

Dante tossed Bridger a look that could kill. "Not all of us can be bulky and-"

"Careful now," Murdoch said with a slight frown. "I'm cut too."

Dante went a little flush before he forced angered tone. "You're sooo lucky Murdoch's here."

Both Murdoch and Bridger couldn't help but to laugh. Murdoch glanced toward his Combat gloves. Different from Fallen's red microchip, his as well as Dante's were white. "I made our newbie's top a little baggier. Not much, but being female, I figure she doesn't want to expose too much"

Dante glanced toward Bridger then the outfit in his hands. "Why are you just standing there! Get changed into your battle suit already!"

Bridger grinned pulling down his suspenders. "If you wanted to see me naked all you had to do was ask. You don't have to yell at me."

Dante frowned as his cheeks hinted at an embarrassed flush. He hissed turning his attention back to his laptop. "Shut up!"

Bridger chuckled removing his shirt. Shinning blue lines ran beautifully all over his back and chest. They didn't seem to run on any particular pattern. It just looked like his veins were glowing. "Come on cutie, sneak a peek."

Murdoch shook his head seeing Dante go even more red. "Why do you bug him?"

Bridger hooked his boot on the edge of one of the metal cases. "Well because you're too mean to bug."

Before Murdoch had a chance to respond, Fallen's jeep pulled up.

Twenty-Six

Sneak-A-Peek

The minute Fallen climbed out of the jeep, Murdoch leapt to his feet. He instantly stood like a soldier awaiting a command. Fallen approached his men as he gave the supplies a quick glance.

Sinah, who had climbed out of the passenger side glanced around curiously. Bridger smiled looking toward her. "She's cute."

Dante looked up from his laptop. Before he had a chance to comment, Fallen called out. "Sinah!"

Sinah quickly ran to his side. Fallen turned his head toward her then back to his men. "Sinah Harmond. This is our team." Fallen motioned his hand toward Murdoch. "This is Murdoch."

Murdoch gave a slight upward nod. Without having to be introduced Bridger chimed in. "I'm Bridger. Sinah huh? Nice name, much better than Kid."

Sinah nodded with a full smile pointing up at Fallen. Fallen motioned his hand toward a Launch Pad Tech. "And last is Dante. Murdoch, she's going to need a battle suit."

"Yes Commander."

The Launch Pad Tech handed Fallen a clip board filled with the Mission equipment forms. Once he removed the pen from the clasp, he quickly began to fill them out.

Murdoch removed the battle suit from one of the metal cases. Without even glancing up at Sinah, he spoke. "What size boot are you?"

Sinah looked down at her sneakers confused.

"Well?"

Bridger chuckled hooking on his second combat boot. "She doesn't talk mean Helix." Bridger smiled toward Sinah. "Could you show us one of your feet?"

As Sinah approached them, Murdoch glanced toward her sneakers. "9.5, maybe 10. You got big feet."

Sinah quickly looked down at her feet. Bridger, who was still smiling, chuckled a little. "Who cares? Welcome to our team Sinah."

Sinah smiled full looking up at Bridger. Murdoch indifferently offered Sinah her battle suit and boots. "Change into these."

Sinah quickly nodded taking them. As she walked back over to the passenger side of the jeep, Dante looked toward her. Not having a single drop of self-consciousness, Sinah didn't glance around as she began to change. Once she removed her sweater, Dante began to blush. Having never seen feminine nudity before, his eyes became transfixed on her. Sinah had very pale skin and wore a black bra. Bridger zipped up his black pants and began to put his arms in his shirt sleeves. As he hooked the shirt over his head, he noticed Dante's stare. "Hey!!"

Both Dante and Sinah's eyes darted toward him. Bridger frowned as much as he could at Dante. "Eyes on your work!"

Dante's blush instantly became a flush as he looked back at his laptop. As Bridger began to re-attach his suspenders, he glanced toward Fallen. He was looking in Sinah's direction as well. Bridger's expression shifted to slight disbelief. "..Really?"

Murdoch glanced back from loading one of the cases into the hummer. "Really, what?"

Bridger's eyes darted toward him. He forced a smile before he answered. "Hm? Oh, nothing."

Dante's blush returned as he turned his laptop toward the changing Sinah. Unbeknownst to her, he was recording. As she put on her battle top, Dante saw a flash of something. Before he had a chance to see what it was, his laptop suddenly flicked off. Dante frantically began to click on the keys. "No! No! Damn it!"

Bridger approached him with a look of concern. "What's wrong?"

Dante smashed his hands on the key pad. "My damn laptop got fried!"

"Can you fix it?"

"Not right now. It was my back-up so…" Dante glanced toward Sinah and thought. 'I swear I saw something.' Dante suddenly yelled toward the many Launch Pad workers. "Anyone want to run an errand?"

Twenty-Seven

Bridger's Red Scarf Discovery

A young mechanic raced over to Dante. In comparison to his fellow grungy mechanics, his coveralls were spotless. "I can help, what do you need, Sir?"

Dante sighed closing his laptop. "Do you know where the Tech Lab is?"

"I just transferred from there."

Dante's eyes darted up to him. "You're from Tech? What the hell are you doing here?"

The mechanic shrugged. "I got fried. I needed a break at least for a little while. So I figured use my hands not my mind. Do you want me to take that to Tech to get it fixed?"

"Do you do any side work?"

The mechanic was silent for a few seconds. When he did respond, he did in whisper. "Are we talking off the records kind of work?"

Dante shrugged looking toward Sinah. She was putting on her combat boots.

The mechanic gave a slight nod. "Sure, do you want me to fix it?"

"No, I need my hard drive saved. Especially the last few moments before it zapped out."

"No problem. I'll handle it"

Dante handed him the laptop. "Thanks. I'll be on a Lab mission for a while. When you get the hard drive, call my place. Leave a message with my mom. She'll make sure I get it." Dante suddenly laughed placing his hand on his chest. "Geez, I'm rude. I'm Dante."

The Mechanic laughed. "Everyone knows who you are Sir. You have the honor of being on the Commander's team. I'd be too nervous working with him personally. Anyway, I'm Alex." Alex lifted the laptop in his hand slightly. "I'll have this done in no time. I'll get your residential number from the personnel files."

Dante smiled. "Thanks Alex."

Alex gave a quick nod before he ran toward one of the hangers.

Dante sighed as he kneeled down to dig in his backpack. "Damn! A back-up would have been useful. Oh well I can always rely on my trusty…" Dante stopped short seeing a long red scarf inside. He instantly hissed ripping it out. "Damn it Mom!"

Bridger who was helping to load the metal boxes glanced toward him. "What's wrong?"

Dante aggressively shook the scarf in his hands. "How many of these stupid things do I have to ditch?"

Bridger smiled slightly glancing toward Fallen. "Are you getting rid of it then?"

Dante slammed it on one of the metal cases. "You want it, take it."

Without saying a word, Bridger snatched it, balled it up then whipped it at Fallen. It hit Fallen in the back of the head and over his one shoulder. Fallen frowned pulling it off himself. The minute he turned toward his men, Dante went flush. Bridger on the other hand forced an awkward smile. "Oops! Sorry about that Commander. I meant to toss it to Sinah."

Fallen gripped the scarf glancing toward her. The sweaters Sinah normally wore hid an hourglass figure. She was somewhat busty and had wide hips. She had a before the fall of Heaven and Hell, retro pin-up body shape. Back when women proudly had meat on their bones.

Bridger opened his hand out to Fallen. "I figured she'd like a little colour in her outfit. Women are like that. I'll just give it to-"

"I'll handle it."

Before Bridger could respond, Fallen approached Sinah and offered her the scarf. Sinah looked down at it then up at Fallen confused. Fallen tilled his head down to the scarf. "Just because you're surrounded by men doesn't mean you can't have anything feminine."

Sinah smiled taking the scarf and wrapping it around her neck. Being a rather long scarf, it draped very attractively down her back. Fallen lifted his head up to her. Sinah smiled even more as she nodded up at him.

Fallen gave a quick nod before he turned away from her. Bridger couldn't help but to smile seeing his slightly awkward expression. As he returned to filling out paperwork, Bridger spoke. "Well, well, well, I wasn't expecting that."

Dante glanced up from his old laptop. "Expecting what? Have you lost your mind? Why did you toss my scarf at the Commander?"

Bridger shrugged approaching one of the metal cases. "Nothing. No. I don't know."

Dante's expression instantly shifted to confusion. "What?"

Twenty-eight

Unregistered Helix

Murdoch handed Bridger a pair of Combat gloves. As he put them on, Murdoch spoke. "I guess I need to explain the gloves to the girl."

Bridger shook his head taking the second pair from Murdoch. "Her name's Sinah and I'll do it." Bridger picked up a small silver device from his case of explosives. "I need to explain the heart bomb anyway. Oh, you might want to chip her boots too."

Murdoch's expression shifted to questioning. "Her boots? Why?"

Before Bridger could answer, Dante responded. "She fights with her legs as well."

Both Bridger and Murdoch's eyes darted toward him. Bridger was quick to question. "How do you know that? I know because I've seen her fight. That and women are biologically stronger in their legs then men. So naturally you'd use your strongest points."

"I did a little surveillance research last night. I skimmed through a few of her record breaking Combat scores."

Bridger patted Murdoch's shoulder. "What do we expect from our Data, Surveillance and so on soldier."

Dante's lips touched at a frown. "So on?"

Murdoch gave an upward nod toward Sinah. She was curiously

watching all the busy soldiers, Techs and mechanics rushing about. "Give and explain the gloves. I'll get some extra chips."

Bridger nodded walking toward Sinah with a smile. "Your battle suit fit okay?"

Sinah's eyes darted to Bridger. She gave a slight shrug looking at the bunched sleeves at her wrists. It was obvious her arms weren't long enough for it to fit correctly. Bridger glanced toward Fallen. "It was really nice of the Commander to give you such a pretty thing."

Sinah smiled softly placing her fingertips on the scarf. Bridger glanced back at Sinah, seeing her soft smile he couldn't help but to smile even more. Bridger's tone and disposition suddenly shifted to serious. "Alright enough goofing around, put these on."

Sinah quickly nodded taking the Combat gloves. As she put them on, Bridger pointed at the white rectangular microchip on his own glove. "Now you see this?"

Sinah looked at his, then her own. Different from Bridger's, Dante's and Murdoch's chip, Sinah's was black. Bridger, who was about to continue his explanation, glanced toward her gloves. His expression instantly shifted to confusion seeing the black chip. "They didn't activate? That's not right."

Sinah looked up at Bridger confused, as he removed one of his gloves. "Give me one for a second."

Sinah quickly removed one and handed it to Bridger. The minute Bridger hooked hers on, the microchip instantly turned white. Bridger removed it then handed it back to Sinah. Once she put it back on it returned to black. Bridger's confused expression returned. "Still nothing? Okay, we know it's not the gloves. Is your ear piece on the fritz?"

Sinah stared back at him like she had no idea about what he was talking about. Bridger glanced at her one ear then the other. He barely nodded turning his attention to Fallen. "Commander, we have a minor problem."

Fallen handed the nervous Tech the clip board back. After a nervous 'Thanks' the Tech bolted toward the hangers. Fallen turned his attention to Bridger and Sinah. His tone of voice just screamed annoyance. "What?"

Bridger motioned his hand back at Sinah. "The Combat gloves won't work without an ear piece."

Dante's eyes darted up from his laptop toward them. "She doesn't have an earpiece?"

Murdoch glanced toward Dante. "She doesn't talk so technically she doesn't need one. The only thing is-"

Dante was quick to finish Murdoch's thought. "The earpiece is also a mental enhancer. It connects mind to equipment. Without them you're basically just wearing clothes."

Fallen frowned approaching Dante. "Being a hidden Helix, it would make sense that she wasn't registered."

Dante's eyes darted up to Fallen. "She wasn't-"

"Sinah's file is under the Maintenance files. Register her then put her under my personal files. That will hide her completely."

Dante quickly nodded tapping on his laptop. "Yes Commander."

Fallen turned his attention to Murdoch. "Check the med supplies for any extra ear connection."

Murdoch sprung to life and raced toward one of the already loaded hummers. "Yes Commander."

Bridger looked toward Sinah. "How did you avoid registration?"

Sinah only shrugged. Dante didn't glance up from working as he spoke. "If she became a Helix the way the rumor said, then she probably just slipped through the cracks."

Murdoch smiled finding a small white box amongst the medical supplies. "Okay, I found one. I'm surprised we even had such a thing."

Bridger chuckled. "I'm not. We can lose anything on a Lab mission."

Murdoch tossed the box to Bridger. "Clip her so I can chip her."

Bridger pulled a small button size silver tab out of the box. "This is going to be a little uncomfortable. Normally, a Helix gets registered really young so the pain's forgotten and…" Bridger suddenly stopped short for a chuckle. "What am I even thinking? You've got the top rank in Combat. This should be a snap for you."

Twenty-Nine

Heart Bomb

Having the earpiece pierced through her ear, Sinah made a loud sound of discomfort. Bridger couldn't help but to chuckle as she rubbed her sore ear. "And you got the top rank in Combat?"

Sinah instantly tossed him a frown. Bridger chuckled again lifting his hands. "Sorry. Sorry."

Murdoch glanced toward Fallen. His attention was locked on Sinah. Murdoch frowned slightly as he looked toward Bridger. "Do you think she's a high A Helix?"

"I know she is. Why?"

"Why can't she talk?"

"I'm not sure what you're getting at?"

Murdoch shifted his frown and eyes to Sinah. She was still rubbing her ear. "All of us have the rapid healing skill. If there was damage done to her voice box shouldn't it have healed by now? Obviously she can make sound, why not actual words?"

Before Bridger could give his answer, Fallen spoke. "That isn't important, Dante?"

Dante quickly nodded. "I got her Helix file Commander. Helix 7617 Sinah. She's now registered. Activating ear sensory device."

Sinah gasped feeling a sudden warmth flow from her ear then rush all over her body. Bridger's expression shifted to mild shock as the image of

Sinah became fuzzy for a few seconds. Once it returned to normal, Bridger spoke. "Your phasing skill will improve faster now."

Sinah looked up at Bridger confused. Seeing her confusion, Bridger smiled. "But then again, I don't think you even know you are doing it."

Suddenly the chips on Sinah's gloves flicked white. Bridger smiled even more looking at them. "Okay good. Now that we handled that, let's hook up your heart bomb."

Sinah's eyes quickly darted from her Combat gloves up to Bridger. Bridger smiled as much as he could. "It sounds just as horrible as it is."

Without saying a word, Murdoch approached then kneeled down in front of Sinah. Sinah's eyes darted down to him as he began to attach the microchips to the top of her boots.

Bridger ignored Murdoch and began his explanation of the heart bomb. "These are used for.. Well, let's just say it's for a 'nobody gets captured' kind of situation."

Sinah looked back up at Bridger as he awkwardly chuckled. "We're successful Helixes. Other Labs will probably want to-"

"Forget the reason! Just tell her what it does."

Bridger stuck his tongue out at the back of Murdoch's head. "Alright mean Helix. Can you give me a hand?"

Murdoch glanced back at him with a slight frown. "Why can't you handle it?"

As Bridger lifted his battle shirt, Sinah quickly averted her eyes from his naked flesh. Bridger pointed at his chest as he spoke. "I'm not wearing my heart bomb yet."

Murdoch released a loud frustrated sigh. Once he was finished attaching the microchips and both turned white, he stood up. Stepping back from Sinah slightly, he raised his shirt. Just like Bridger, he had beautiful shinning lines all over his chest. His glowing looking veins however were red. At the center point of his chest was a small silver device. It was the same device Bridger had in his hand. Bridger pointed at Murdoch's one. "Okay, Sinah have a look."

Sinah awkwardly glanced at Murdoch's chest then the device. Bridger snickered as Murdoch lowered his shirt with a slight frown. "It's like a panic button. You either die and it goes off automatically. Or you can set it off. Since we don't want our Helixes recreated or copied-"

"Recreated and copied are the same thing."

Bridger stuck his tongue out at Murdoch again before he continued. "First we get an electrical blast. Holy hell they hurt! It messes our Helix up something horrible. If you ever get zapped by an enemy all I can say is, try your best to shoot your gun in defense. Basically try to stay alive until your Helix recovers. It does pretty fast. Anyway, after the electric blast a few second later, you're blown to bits. Since the electrical blast messed up your Helix, any bit of you that they find is basically human bits. No Helix detected."

Sinah stared up at Bridger in complete and utter shock. Bridger smiled lifting the device. "I made yours special. Normally we sent ours off by verbal command. You know like Helix 3421 Murdoch heart de-"

Murdoch hissed almost instantly. "Don't set mine off, asshole!"

Bridger laughed lifting his free hand defensively. "My, my, so touchy, my goodness, you know I can't set yours off. It's voice recognition. Even at my crankiest, I can't sound like you."

Bridger turned his attention back to Sinah. "Yours is different, it has a manual response." Bridger glanced at Murdoch. "Of course, I'll explain that later. Now let's get down to combat."

Thirty

Unlimited Ammo

Before Bridger could get into the combat explanation, Murdoch spoke. "The instructions are simple enough, girl. All you-"

"Her name's Sinah. The ear piece works as-"

Murdoch frowned cutting Bridger off again. His tone of voice was short. "Picture a blade popping out of the tip of your boot. Don't picture it shooting out, just popping out."

Sinah gave both Murdoch and Bridger a confused look as they stepped to her side. She then shifted her confusion down to her boot.

After a few seconds of her just staring at it, Murdoch frowned. "Tap the back of your foot off the ground."

Sinah looked up at Murdoch looking even more lost. Murdoch growled throwing his arms up into the air. "I can't deal with this! I hate dealing with newbies"

Bridger tapped his kneel against the ground. "Like this. Now remember to picture a blade just popping out."

Sinah nervously nodded and did as she was told. She instantly jumped seeing a small blade pop out the tip of her boot. Bridger clapped his hands. "Alright! Great job! I knew you could do it!"

Murdoch scoffed crossing his arms. "Try doing that with a cluster of enemies attacking you."

Bridger waved his hand dismissively toward Murdoch. "We can handle things from here on mean Helix."

Murdoch shrugged indifferently as he walked away from them. "Yeah, fine."

Sinah smiled proudly at the blade in her boot. Bridger glanced toward Murdoch. The moment he sat down on one of the metal cases, Bridger stepped closer to Sinah. He wrapped his arm over her shoulders and turned her away from the other men. Sinah looked up at Bridger in a questioning manner until he began to whisper. "Once you place your bomb over your heart it will automatically attach. Don't worry it doesn't hurt. To work it.. Well to blow yourself up to bits."

Bridger showed Sinah the device and pointed at it. On the top was a small dial. "Turn the knob in either direction it doesn't matter, once it doesn't turn anymore. Cover it completely with your hand that will activate the electrical blast, then..." Bridger made an explosion gesture with his hand. "The end, got it?"

Before Sinah had a chance to give an acknowledgement, Fallen spoke. "Get Sinah a gun."

Bridger glanced over their shoulders at Fallen. He was standing a few feet away from them with a slight frown. He was locking and unlocking his chiseled jaw. Bridger quickly looked back toward Sinah. A slight smile took his lips as he removed his arm from her shoulders. After handing Sinah her heart bomb, Bridger turned to Fallen and nodded. "Yes Commander."

Fallen didn't shift his attention to the still smiling Bridger as he passed by him. He merely continued to watch Sinah. She was tapping the ground with her heels repetitively. The blade popped out of the tip of her boots then vanished. After a few seconds of watching her do this, Fallen approached. "Your ear piece is connected to each point of your offensive and defensive equipment."

Sinah turned quick to Fallen. She smiled proudly pointing toward her boots. Fallen didn't look downward, he just continued his thought. "Accessing weapons come natural to my men. They've been using them for a long time. Under panic, your mind may not focus on a single weapon. Lack of focus confuses the Combat gloves and nothing will happen. That's why.."

Fallen opened his hand but didn't glance behind himself. Bridger placed a handgun in Fallen's hand. Without hesitation, he turned the gun upward and began to shoot. The bang sound not only made Sinah jump but everyone working in the Launch Pad area. Fallen spoke over the gun shots. "That's why we carry a gun. When held in Combat gloves, you never need to reload. As long as you can pull the trigger you have a weapon."

Fallen stopped shooting. As he lowered the gun, he spoke. "Now access a weapon."

Sinah looked at her Combat glove with a slightly bewildered look. Bridger, who was still standing near Fallen, spoke. "They're like the Combat gloves in the Combat simulators. First you need to-"

"Get fully equipped then double check the hummers."

Bridger's eyes darted to Fallen. Fallen turned his head and looked at Bridger out of the corner of his silver eye. Bridger was quick to nod. "Yes Commander."

Once Bridger was out of ear shot, Fallen spoke. "Put on your heart bomb."

Fallen didn't turn his head back to Sinah as she reached down her top. Once the device attached itself over her heart, she approached him.

Hearing the movement, Fallen quickly shifted his attention back to her. Sinah looked up at him and gave a slight nod. After giving one in return, Fallen lifted his hand and tilted it backward. It looked like he was reaching for something. As he snapped his hand forward a throwing knife appeared in his grip.

Sinah's eyes lit up in amazement. She smiled excitedly placing her hands on his wrist. Fallen gave a slight nod before speaking. "When I toss this and repeat the motion, a throwing knife will keep appearing."

Sinah let his wrist go and tilted her hands back. Once she snapped her hands forward two blades appeared. After the initial shock of it working, Sinah jumped up and down happily. A slight smile touched at Fallen's lips watching her joy. Fallen opened his hand releasing the throwing knife. Before it hit the ground, it vanished. "Practice hitting the jeep we arrived in. I want to know if you can repetitively use your Combat gloves."

Sinah quickly nodded and turned to the jeep. Fallen watched Sinah excitedly whip knife after knife at it.

Murdoch frowned slightly glancing toward Sinah then Fallen. "Why is this girl joining us? This isn't some stupid little game."

Bridger smiled. "I think she's cute. And a little femininity will remind us how to be gentlemen."

Murdoch responded with a scoff.

Bridger couldn't help but to snicker. "At least you didn't belch."

Thirty-one

Final Touches

Once Fallen was convinced Sinah understood the function of the Combat gloves, he called out. "Let's pack it up and get out of here!"

Dante quickly closed his laptop and hooked it into his backpack. As he zipped it up, Murdoch spoke. "Don't forget to give the girl the basic supply pack."

Bridger grabbed a belt with a gun holster and three medium size pouches from one of the metal cases in the hummer. He carelessly tossed it toward Dante. "Catch."

Dante fumbled barely catching it before it hit the ground. Bridger tried his best to conceal his smirk. "You know, you may want to consider pumping some iron now and again."

Dante tossed Bridger a glare before he ran toward Fallen. "Commander, I'll give Sinah the basic supply pack rundown while you get ready."

Fallen barely nodded handing Sinah her gun. "Fine."

Sinah looked down at the gun in her hand then back up to Fallen. He was joining his other men. Dante looked up her releasing a defeated sigh. "…Damn."

Sinah looked toward him as he awkwardly chuckled. "When the Commander said, a girl was joining our team. I thought finally I won't be the shortest."

Sinah who was 5'7 looked at the 5'5 Dante sympathetically. Dante shrugged a little. "Well at least you're not 6 or over like the rest of them."

Sinah looked toward the 6'1 Fallen then the 6'3 Murdoch and Bridger. Even though Murdoch and Bridger were the same height, Bridger was a tad more built, which made him looked slightly shorter.

Sinah's eyes darted down to Dante as he hooked her belt around her hips. The moment he clipped it on, she stepped back from him with a slight frown. Dante's eyes darted up to her. Seeing her slight frown, he instantly went flush. "I.. I'm sorry! I.. I didn't think.. I Just wanted to make sure it fit okay. B.. But that's no excuse, I.."

Seeing his apologetic and uncomfortable features, Sinah smiled slightly. To stop his senseless rambling, she waved her hands defensively trying to calm him down. Once he did, he pointed at the gun holster. "Uh.. Your gun goes there obviously."

Sinah hooked her gun into it as Dante pointed at the pouch just beside it. "There's a small med kit in that one. It has a med spray, a few medium med pads and other medical junk like that. It's for emergencies or a quick patch up."

Sinah barely nodded as Dante pointed to the pouch near her back. "That pouch is your basic food supply. It's not that great. Nothing like the food here but it's fine for survival. Its job is to fill you up without weighing you down. When used correctly, you're supposed to be able to last a week on it, although I can eat them in a couple of hours."

Sinah barely nodded again as Dante pointed at the last pouch on her hip. "That's the important pouch. Inside are the Unbreakable Vials. UVs."

Sinah opened up the pouch and pulled out one of the clear vials. It was the size of a child's pinky finger. After taking it from her, Dante placed his index on the top and his thumb on the bottom. "During missions we come across all sorts of samples useful to at least one of the Labs. Be it enemy blood or flesh or plant life or food or whatever. This will make sure it arrives safely."

Dante squeezed the vial. It turned a blue color. "To activate it just squeeze it between your index and thumb like I just did. Then touch it against any sample of any size. The UV will liquefy around it then return to unbreakable glass. It will be completely safe and ready for travel. To deactivate it, just do the same thing as you did to activate it."

Dante squeezed the vial again returning it to clear. As he handed it back to Sinah, he spoke. “Now if you find any synthetic types. Especially ones already in syringes just touch it to the microchip on your glove. It will seal the tip and be ready to be brought back to our Lab as well. There’s no point wasting a UV on a synthetic. That’s pretty much it. Got it all?”

Sinah activated then deactivated the UV. She nodded putting it back into the pouch. Dante quickly ran over to his backpack as he scooped it up, he called out to Fallen. “We’re ready Commander.”

Fallen motioned his hand toward one of the hummers. “Murdoch, Bridger and Dante in that one. Sinah, you ride with me. Let’s move out.”

Without having to be told twice everyone raced to their vehicles.

Thirty-Two

And Away We Go

Murdoch followed closely behind the first hummer. A frown consumed his lips as he gripped the steering wheel. "Why'd he bring that girl onto our team?"

Bridger rested his elbow out the open passenger side window. "I think she's kind of cute."

Dante, who was in the backseat, checking map locations on his laptop, spoke. "You think everyone's cute."

"That's not true. I think you're adorable."

"I meant women!"

Bridger glanced back at him with a chuckle. "You're not a woman."

Dante instantly began to fume. "I know I'm not a-"

"Cut it both of you!"

Bridger looked back toward Murdoch. "That girl's name is Sinah. And I'd have her join our team too seeing how she dominates the Combat ranks."

Murdoch frowned as much as he could. "Doesn't the Commander think we're good enough to handle any situation he needs us to?!"

After a long silent pause, Bridger shrugged. "Are you jealous of our cute newbie?"

Murdoch began to wring the steering wheel with both of his hands.

"We are a fine team without her. Doesn't it bother you having some girl join us?"

Before Bridger could answer, Murdoch hissed. "What did we do wrong? Doesn't the Commander think our Helixes are skilled enough? Doesn't it just piss you off?!"

"No."

Murdoch scoffed. "Why the hell do I bother asking you. Dante?"

Dante looked up at Murdoch's reflection through the rear view mirror. "Yeah?"

"Doesn't it annoy you having this girl join us?"

"No."

Murdoch growled under his breath. "Damn A Helixes. The sons of bitches always stick together."

Bridger snickered leaning slightly further out the open window. "I trust the Commander's decisions. I wouldn't care if he wanted the whole facility to join us. It's his choice. He commands and we follow. Considering the type of Helix he is and the type you are, I wouldn't be questioning if I were you."

Murdoch instantly went flush. "A.. Are you saying I'm not loyal?!"

"I'm saying we do as the Commander commands. Nothing more, nothing less." Only getting a simple frown in response, Bridger snickered. "I wonder if petty jealousy is a trait all D Helixes have."

Dante quickly clicked on his laptop keys as he spoke. "Personally, I think Bridger's right. Sinah's scores in Combat are too impressive to simply ignore. The Commander wants the best team so that's exactly what he'll get. That's why our team is the only one called upon for Lab missions. Only the best can handle them. Besides if she sucks, she won't be on our team anymore. The Commander will just ditch her."

Murdoch muttered so quiet he was almost unheard. "..I guess."

Bridger couldn't help but to smile. Dante pressed his ear piece. "Commander, we'll arrive at our destination point in 53 minutes."

Fallen was quick to respond. "Fine."

Dante released his ear piece and went back to work on his laptop. "We'll be in map range in a few seconds."

Neither Murdoch nor Bridger acknowledged him.

Thirty-Three

The World of the Lost Souls

Fallen drove down a heavily damaged main street. This once booming city had become a desolate wasteland over run by trash, destruction and filth. The dim blue light which always covered the world, gave the city a gloomy uninhabited appearance. Anyone in the street Sinah did see looked dishevelled, scared and a little savage in the eyes. Fallen frowned narrowly avoiding some rubble on the road. "This place always annoys me."

Sinah quickly looked toward Fallen as he continued. "When all the Labs, Facilities, Safe havens or whatever you want to call them. When they were first built everyone in the world was given a choice. Come live in safety or remain out here. It didn't matter age, race, education, nothing mattered. The doors were open to anyone and everyone. Not only would you have the comforts of food and shelter, but you would have been trained in one of our many fields. And yet so many refused. So many people would rather just starve or fight other humans for survival. All of them choose to needlessly suffer. The problem with humanity is humanity."

Fallen's eyebrows lowered driving over a large pothole. After the hummer stopped rattling, he continued. "Even to this day our facility sends out trucks filled with food and supplies. We continue to try our best to save the Lost Souls. And what thanks do we get? Most of the time, our Techs get attacked. We've even lost a few. The fall of Heaven and Hell destroyed people's sense of morals."

As Sinah returned her attention to the destruction outside the window, Fallen's lips touched at a slight smile. "Of course, who am I to judge? We're about to attack a fellow Lab to get their Helix samples."

Sinah's eyes darted back to Fallen. Her expression just screamed shocked. Fallen glanced toward her for a split second then returned his attention back to the road. "You wanted to go into the mission blind."

Sinah barely nodded as her feature weakened a little. Fallen glanced toward her again, seeing her slightly upset disposition, he sighed. "You can wait by the hummers or stay with Dante. You don't have to involve yourself in this. I should have made sure you looked at the Mission details."

Sinah quickly shook her head but also had a questioning look on her face. Fallen who noticed her look, responded. "You want to know why we attack them for their Helix samples."

Sinah quickly nodded while Fallen gave a slight shrug. "I couldn't tell you even if I want to. The reason Director Hart wants them is something known probably before my time. As soldiers when we receive a command from the top we obey without question."

As Fallen opened his mouth to say something else, Sinah suddenly pointed through the windshield. Fallen's eyebrows furrowed in confusion as he looked in the direction she was pointing.

Thirty-Four

God's Party

In the distance was a large brightly lit mansion. Its colourful decorations and festive music stood out against the gloom of the world of the Lost Souls. Search lights dancing playfully against the sky, suggested this wasn't a celebration to miss. Even though this was Fallen and his team's destination, it didn't have the appearance of being a Lab. Elegantly dressed guests were welcomed in by security. With a smile they were waved through the open gates. If the fall of Heaven and Hell hadn't happened, this would be like an exclusive gala people would kill to get invited to. Fallen pressed his ear piece. "Dante what's going on?"

Dante looked up from his laptop toward the Manor. "I think they're having a celebration before the announcement."

Fallen glanced at the tall brick wall wrapped around the grounds. "Infiltration will have to be done with more caution."

Fallen took a sharp turn down a side street on the outskirts of the manor. Once he pulled around to the back, he pressed his ear piece. "Murdoch, we'll park here."

After a quick 'Yes Commander' Murdoch pulled up behind him. Both Fallen and Sinah climbed out of the hummer. As Fallen walked toward the second vehicle, he glanced at Sinah. She was looking up at the eclipsed sun and moon. Fallen, stopped beside by the driver's side window. "Dante?"

Dante shook his head checking all file results on Lab 6. "I can't find any records of a planned celebration Commander. Security also seems to be lacking as well."

Fallen's lips weren't shy at touching at a frown. "If they were successful in creating 'God' then their security has probably been moved. Protect what is precious."

"Do we abort the mission Commander?"

Fallen shook his head. "Bridger, mount a micro camera on the top of the wall. I want surveillance of the grounds."

Dante quickly removed a tiny camera from his backpack and handed it to Bridger. Once Bridger stepped in front of the protective wall, he effortlessly jumped up and hooked the camera just inside the perimeter. "Did I get it?"

Dante quickly clicked on his laptop. "Yup! Okay… uh..." Dante could see glass greenhouse buildings to the left of the manor and many parked vehicles to the right. Fallen put his hands on his hips and took a few steps away from the hummer. Dante gave a slight nod. "There isn't any sign of security Commander. All clear."

"Fine. Murdoch?"

Murdoch quickly got out of the hummer and stood like a soldier awaiting a command. "Yes Commander?"

"I want to hear the announcement first hand."

As Murdoch slightly nodded, Fallen continued. "Sinah and I will be attending the celebration."

Everyone's eyes, except Sinah's darted toward him. She was looking at a long faded graffiti design on the wall. Bridger was quick to protest. "But Commander we never openly-"

"I have right to know if my counterpart has been successfully created!"

Murdoch tossed Sinah a full frown. "Commander it's dangerous to bring a newbie directly into a potential battle field. I don't think she's-"

Fallen cut him off with a snip. "And it is my decision to make, not yours!"

Murdoch instantly lowered his head. "Yes Commander."

Fallen turned his attention to Dante. "Both Sinah and I will have an open line of communication. Dante pay close attention to everyone's movements and security's for both groups."

Dante quickly nodded keeping his attention locked on his laptop. "No problem Commander."

"Dante, you're sitting in an exposed area. Remember to keep that in mind."

Dante locked all the hummer doors. "I will Commander."

As Fallen walked toward the protective wall, he gave a slight nod. "Let's go."

Thirty-Five

Blending In

With an effortless tug on her hand, Bridger pulled Sinah onto the protective wall. Fallen watched Murdoch hang drop onto the manor grounds. Bridger patted the top of Sinah's head like a father comforting his child. "Sinah, protect our Commander. He gets a little reckless."

Fallen's lips touched at a frown as he turned his head toward Bridger. "What was that?"

Bridger instantly smiled lifting his hands defensively. "Nothing, I'm off."

Bridger jumped down beside Murdoch. Without saying another word, both raced cautiously toward the mansion. Fallen climbed down the wall then turned back to Sinah. She sat down on the edge then hooked herself forward. Fallen was quick to catch her before she hit the ground. The minute Sinah was placed on her feet, Fallen spoke. "Let's get a move on."

Sinah didn't get a chance to nod before Fallen ran toward the mansion as well. Sinah wasn't hesitant in giving chase. Dante clicked open a map on his laptop. "Commander, I've hacked into their outer cameras. There's a service entrance at the back of the mansion. Maintenance is currently using it. It should be easy to enter there unnoticed."

Fallen shifted the direction he was running to the back. Once there was a pause in maintenance personnel coming and going, Fallen and Sinah slipped inside. Fallen calmly yet cautiously passed through the packed storage room into a very busy kitchen.

Not a single person glanced twice at Fallen or Sinah as they passed by them. Chefs were either too busy preparing food or yelling out instructions. While servers were carrying trays of hors-d'oeuvres out of the kitchen as fast as their feet could carry them. Fallen led Sinah out of the kitchen and out of everyone's way. Before any of the security by the front door noticed them, Fallen pulled Sinah into the first room they passed.

After closing the door behind them, Fallen tapped the side of his sunglasses. A thin bright light shone from both joints of the frame. As he glanced around the room, it became clear they were inside a simple office. Bookcases filled with books were against every wall. While a large maple wood desk sat in front of a simple office chair. The overwhelming smell of dust and mold suggested this room hadn't been used for quite some time. Fallen tapped his sunglasses again. On the lens before his silver eyes displayed the map of the mansion. "Dante our location is right next to the ballroom, correct?"

Dante smiled hacking into the inside cameras. He accessed the office camera where Fallen and Sinah were. All he could see was Fallen's sunglasses light in the dark room. "That's right Commander."

Dante flicked over to the main entrance camera then the ballroom cameras. "Be careful Commander, there are two armed guards at each entrance point." Dante glanced at the front door camera feed. "A large crowd is approaching the main doors. If you want to blend in Commander, this will be a good time."

Fallen flicked off his lens map then turned his attention to Sinah. "I suppose we should play the part then."

Sinah looked up at Fallen confused. Her expression didn't change as he stepped closer to her. It did however, when he slipped his hand along the side of her cheek into her hair. "Do you mind if I remove your hair from its tie?"

Sinah instantly shook her head shifting her eyes nervously to the floor. Fallen gently pulled her hair forward and freed it from the ponytail. He then gently ran his fingers through it in a brushing manner. Once he stopped, he motioned his hand to her red scarf. "May I?"

Sinah's eyes darted up to his sunglasses. Seeing what his hand was directed toward, she shrugged. Fallen quickly removed her scarf then wrapped it around her hips hiding her basic supply belt. He then draped the remaining amount down the front and back of her. It looked like a skirt with two large slits on either side. Despite seeing that she was wearing tight pants, she looked like she was stylized rather fashionably.

Fallen removed his gun from its holster and handed it to her. Sinah watched as Fallen removed his basic supply belt and tossed it aside. As he took the gun back from her, he spoke. "Ready?"

Sinah gave a quick nod as Fallen hooked his gun into the back of his pants. After fixing the back of his shirt to hide the weapon, he approached the office door. Fallen tapped the side of his sunglasses shutting off the light. He whispered quietly opening the door and peeking around the doorframe at the two armed guards standing by the main entrance. "Give us the word Dante."

"Yes Commander. Security seems to be holding them up."

Fallen reached his hand back to Sinah. "We'll have to blend in quickly."

Sinah barely nodded taking his hand. Fallen didn't shift his attention from the guards as he spoke. "You look quite attractive Sinah."

Before Sinah could have any reaction, Dante spoke. "Now!"

The front doors opened widely, many loud party guests poured into the main lobby. As they made their way into the ballroom, Fallen and Sinah blended into the crowd.

Thirty-Six

Dancing with the Devil

Fallen hooked Sinah's arm around his elbow entering the ball room. He carried himself with such a calm dignified demeanor it seemed like he was an invited guest. Sinah on the other hand, glanced nervously at the dancing, drinking and socializing happy couples.

Fallen casually shifted his attention around the room. Instead of being tastefully designed, the large ballroom looked rather gaudy. It's off white and gold motif was assaulted by odd looking filigree. Even the golden decorations were more of an eye sore than anything else. Hanging very low from the ceiling were overly large obtrusive chandeliers. Beyond them, Fallen could see a second floor balcony. It wrapped completely around the ballroom. Only a few armed guards were wandering around up there. At the front of the ball room was a set of stairs leading to a small stage.

As Fallen shifted his attention to the armed guards standing by the entrances, he noticed them intently staring back. Fallen stepped closer to Sinah and whispered. "We're being watched."

Sinah, who had just finished a delicious stuffed mushroom she took from a server's tray, looked up at Fallen. As she began to look toward the guards, Fallen snatched her chin. Sinah's eyes darted up to him. Fallen gave a quick shake of his head. "It's best to act like we didn't notice. Shall we dance?"

Sinah's expression instantly shifted to awkward. It was obvious she didn't know anything about dancing. Noticing her discomfort, Fallen took then placed her hand on his shoulder. As he took her other hand, he placed his own hand on her lower back. "Just follow my lead."

Sinah barely nodded before Fallen led her into a waltz. Each time Sinah tried to look downward, Fallen spoke. "Just follow my lead."

Sinah barely nodded again trying her best not to step on him. Despite all the impressed comments from the guests, Fallen didn't once shift his attention from Sinah. Nor did he react hearing Murdoch's voice from his ear piece. "Found their version of an ADGL Lab. All locks are open."

Fallen's lips touched at a frown. "…Something isn't right."

Sinah gripped Fallen's shoulder with a slightly worried expression. Fallen kept his focus on her and their dance. "Remain calm Sinah. If there's any trouble Murdoch can handle it."

The moment Sinah's grip loosened, Fallen led her into a graceful spin. Once she was back in his grip, he gently dipped her backward. Sinah smiled looking up at the ceiling for that split second. Once standing comfortably back on her feet, the song ended. Anyone who had been watching happily began to clap at their performance. Sinah's smile shifted to slightly awkward and embarrassed.

As Fallen stepped back from her, a loud voice called out from the front of the ballroom. "Ladies and gentlemen, please direct your attention to the stage!"

Everyone, Fallen and Sinah included looked toward the small stage. Two armed guards stood by a beautiful young blonde woman. She smiled very sweetly toward her on lookers. One of the two guards a long side her, spoke. "Ladies and gentlemen, allow me to present, God."

Thirty-Seven

God

The beautiful woman being called God spoke in a soft, comforting tone. "Thank you so much for joining us this evening. I am well aware that our world is in a state of turmoil and dismay. I am also aware that my presence has been needed for quite some time." God bowed slightly as she continued. "Please allow me to express my upmost gratitude for your patience. My creation, though long needed was quite complicated."

Fallen's lips touched at a frown studying God. She wore an attractive white dress, complimented with delicate white beads and lace trim. Her pale skin made her pale blue eyes appear almost jewel like. Amongst the couples, she looked like the very image of purity. Running her fingers through her shoulder length hair, she spoke. "Let us end our world's suffering. Allow me to shine my mercy upon-"

"You're not God!"

Everyone's including Sinah's eyes darted toward Fallen. He hissed, pointing an accusatory finger at her. "This woman isn't God!"

God smiled softly as she nodded. "I understand that my creation is a hard thing to except. Humans have suffered by themselves for so long. Considering the fact a superior being hasn't been cre-"

"A superior hasn't been created? Is that what you were going to say?"

"Well yes, I-"

Fallen's expression suddenly turned cold. "You, girl, are talking to Lucifer himself."

All the guests either gasped or screamed. Without hesitation, they quickly moved away from Fallen and Sinah. Sinah glanced to her side hearing movement from the armed guards by the entrances. They were quickly and quietly encouraging everyone to escape the ball room unnoticed.

God still kept her soft comforting tone. "Lucifer, I am flattered you decided to join us for this celebration."

Fallen kept his full frown locked on her. "As my counterpart, you know I have no choice but to be here."

Dante's panicked voice suddenly spilled over both Fallen and Sinah's ear piece. "Armed guards are closing in fast!! It's an ambush!!"

Neither Sinah nor Fallen gave a noticeable reaction to his warning. God smiled softly. "Yes, we knew even a simple rumor of my creation would bring you to us."

Fallen quickly withdrew his gun and pointed it toward God. In response to his action, many click sounds from semi-automatic machines guns were heard around the ballroom. Having a gun pointed at her, made a few nervous sweat beads trickle down her forehead. A slight smirk took Fallen's lips. "Why, you almost seem afraid. As God, you should know full well that I can't harm my counterpart. Sinah."

Sinah's eyes darted to Fallen as his smirk shifted to an icy frown. "Remain calm and stay focused. Remember your weapon is only as strong as your will."

Sinah quickly nodded as Fallen's tone of voice became cold and heartless. "Kill them all."

Thirty-Eight

Questions without Answers

Before Sinah had a chance to obey Fallen's command, a loud masculine voice spoke from above them. "Now there's no need for that!"

Both Sinah and Fallen shifted their attention to the voice. A man dressed in a nice black suit and tie stood on the right side of the balcony. Two Lab Techs stood on either side of him. The rest of the balcony was full of armed guards. All of their weapons were aimed at Sinah and Fallen.

The man in the suit smiled confidently. "I knew a properly placed rumor would flush you out." The man chuckled placing his hand on his chest. "Where ever are my manners? Being in the presence of a superior being I should at least introduce myself. I'm Director Court-"

"I don't recall asking."

The man in the suit basically known as Director Court snickered at Fallen's response. "I was actually expecting a lot more rudeness from the Prince of Darkness. Tell me, why is Director Hart destroying his fellow Labs?"

Fallen didn't respond, he only kept his attention locked on the Director. Director Court frowned slightly at the forming silence. "We used to be friends. All of us scientists were. When he snapped, I thought 'Good, let us be the ones to create a better future.' But then he turned against us as well! Why? Why is he doing this to us?!"

Fallen noticed Sinah out of the corner of his eye. She was slowly removing her red scarf from her hips. Director Court hissed in frustration. "Answer me!"

Fallen who hadn't moved his gun from God, shifted his attention back to her. "You'll have to ask him yourself. That is of course, assuming we allow you to live."

Director Court closed his eyes shaking his head. After a defeated sigh, he spoke. "Though you are the one and only L Helix, you're not Lucifer. He is a superior being, not a lowly soldier merely obeying commands. It's tragic that you and I couldn't come to an understanding. Satan is all about bargains and-"

"I couldn't care less about who or what Lucifer was in ancient times."

Director Court's eyes snapped open and to Fallen. His expression and tone of voice screamed disbelief. "But your original Helix comes from him."

Fallen simply gave an indifferent shrug.

This action instantly made the Director fume. "A shrug?! That's your response, a simple shrug?!"

Fallen didn't shift his attention from God. Her dress and hair had become damp from nervous sweat. Director Court sighed loudly again. "As we speak, our soldiers have gone to kill your men."

Sinah wrapped her scarf back around her neck hearing Dante. "Murdoch, soldiers closing in fast! Bridger, more soldiers have been called in to your location!"

Murdoch gave a quick '10-4' and Bridger gave a quick 'Okay.'

Fallen who had heard the conversation, smirked. "And your soldiers won't know what hit them."

Director Court slowly shook his head in disappointment. "It's a pity we couldn't work this out." Looking toward Sinah, he questioned. "Girl, why are you following an obviously inferior reproduction of the original Lucifer? Why don't you join..?"

Fallen suddenly turned his gun. Without hesitation or even glancing in the Director's direction, he pulled the trigger.

Thirty-Nine

Ballroom Brawl

The bullet zipped clean through the Adams apple of one of the Lab Techs standing beside the Director. He made a god awful gurgling sound as blood gushed from his throat. Seeing such a terrible thing, God instantly began to scream. Director Court couldn't tear his shocked eyes from the Lab Tech. As he collapsed to the floor dead, Fallen spoke. "Enough of this pointless conversation, shall we Sinah?"

Without having to be told twice, Sinah kneeled slightly then did a very high backflip. In the air, she released a wave of throwing knives at the soldiers. Anyone hit was instantly killed. In response to the attack, the soldiers quickly began to open fire. Once Sinah landed, she turned to them. A slight smile took her lips as she whipped a throwing knife upward. The blade zipped through the wires holding up one of the large chandlers. Sinah didn't have a change in facial expression as it came crashing down right in front of her. Many soldiers quickly leapt out of the way. Those who weren't fast enough were crushed under the chandler's weight.

Fallen calmly walked through the fighting toward God. Anyone who tried to attack or was simply in his way, was greeted by an effortless kill shot to the skull. Once he reached God, she fell to her knees, whimpering. "Please... please don't kill me."

Fallen stepped beside her and turned back to the battle. His attention instantly locked on Sinah. Knowing that Fallen's gun was pointed down at her, God cowered in fear. "I was only doing what I was told. Please... Oh please don't kill me."

Fallen watched Sinah avoid each and every spray of bullets sent toward her. She reacted by sending blade after blade back at them. Each and every one of her shots was dead on target. "Who are you then?"

God covered her head with both of her arms. "M.. Morella, I'm Director Courtier's daughter. He said if we could just get you here then..."

"Then these will be the last moments of your deceitful life."

Morella instantly began to bawl. "Please! Please don't kill me!!"

Annoyed by her, Fallen hissed. "Shut up!"

Morella cringed and cowered even more. Fallen looked beyond Sinah as soldier reinforcements raced into the ballroom. They were armed with whips and what looked like police batons. One soldier snapped his whip around Sinah's arm. The soldier chuckled in amusement as the whip became electrical. His happy disposition quickly turned to confusion. Instead of messing up her Helix or even stunning her, Sinah's body instantly became grainy. Her phasing skill had automatically counteracted the effects of the electrical hit.

Fallen didn't make a single attempt to hide his smirk. "Let's see how you defeat her without the Helixes electrical weakness."

Sinah tapped her one heel then the other off the ground. As the blades popped out the tips of her boots, a soldier swung his baton toward her. Sinah was quick to grab it before it hit her. Again, her phasing skill protected her from any damage. The baton made a loud electrical humming sound in her hands. It was obviously set at a very high setting.

Sinah slammed her foot against the side of the soldier's ribs shattering his armor. She then released her boot blade into his unprotected side. As the soldier screeched and stumbled backward, she quickly slashed her second boot blade clean across his throat. Releasing the baton, he covered his wound with both of his hands feebly attempting to stop the blood gush.

Without hesitation, Sinah whipped the baton at another soldier holding the same weapon. It slammed aggressively against the baton in his hand. The over charge of the electrical current completely fried him and anyone in close proximity of him. The soldier who had his whip around Sinah's arm hissed. "Stupid bitch!! I'll kill you myself!!"

Sinah ignored being pulled toward him as she merely whipped blade after blade toward her targets.

Fallen shifted his attention upward toward the second floor balcony. Director Court or rather Director Courtier had long escaped. He had been replaced with many more soldiers. All of them were trying their best to shoot Sinah.

Fallen closed his eyes lifting his index finger. A small thin blade lifted from it. Fallen opened his eyes and pointed toward one of the soldiers. The thin blade zipped toward the balcony and slammed into the side of soldier's jugular. It looked like a fish bone was pierced through him. The small thin blade suddenly began to spin. The spinning became so fast it was as if the blade had become a drill. The soldier frantically clawed at his throat trying to remove it.

Once dead, Fallen pointed to the next soldier to repeat the process. The thin blade busted out its victim's destroyed jugular then moved onto the next. Slowly but surely, his small thin blade began to wipe out all the second floor balcony soldiers.

Once the soldier finally got Sinah in front of him, she turned her attention to him. Without hesitation, Sinah slashed the two blades from her hands across his throat. The force she used decapitated him. As his head fell from his shoulders, Dante spoke through the ear piece. "The soldiers have been commanded to fall back. I repeat the soldiers are backing off."

Sinah glanced around the ballroom at all the carnage. Injured and scared soldiers were retreating as fast as they could. Sinah smiled proudly removing the whip from her arm. She held her proud disposition walking toward Fallen and Morella.

Once the last soldier on the balcony was killed, Fallen lowered his hand. The small thin blade stopped spinning and vanished. Fallen shifted his attention to Sinah. "Get a sample from 'God' then, kill her."

Sinah's expression instantly turned sympathetic hearing Morella bawl.

Forty

Dimitri and Lyle

Morella sobbed uncontrollably. "I was only doing what my father told me to do! Oh please don't kill me!"

Sinah made a blade appear in her hand as she approached her. Morella cowered so much so she looked like a human ball. "Nooooo!" She whaled.

Sinah's look of sympathy was locked on her face. As she kneeled down to Morella, Fallen spoke. "It looks like it's time for the real battle."

Sinah stood up straight and looked in the direction Fallen was looking. Two men stood amongst the destroyed ball room. One was 6'2, very built and had black hair and eyes. The other was 5'9, had more of a wiry build and had blonde hair and dark eyes. Both were dressed like the many soldiers that Sinah and Fallen had defeated. The blonde carelessly kicked the leg of one of the dead soldiers. "Geez Dimitri, would you just look at this mess."

Dimitri glanced toward his partner. When he spoke, a heavy accent was heard. "Such slobs, how about we help them cleanup Lyle?"

Lyle shrugged indifferently. "Might as well."

Both Lyle and Dimitri lifted one hand high above their heads. The smashed chandler, the corpses of the soldiers and soldiers too wounded to move, suddenly caught a blaze. They didn't have the strength to even scream as they and everything else was burned to ash. Fallen didn't shift his attention from either men. "Deal with her. I will handle these two, myself."

Sinah barely nodded. As Fallen walked down the small set of stairs, Lyle noticed him. A frown instantly consumed his lips. As Dimitri dusted his hands together, he frowned toward Fallen as well. "Look Lyle, it's our so called Lord."

Lyle scoffed turning his head in disgust. "Lord? That's a laugh. Our Lord wouldn't have such a pathetic team following him. I mean what's that girl behind you?"

Fallen cracked his knuckles answering. "That's unimportant to a couple of low level D Helixes."

Dimitri released an animalistic snort befitting a demon. "We are Demons! This A-D-G-L junk your Lab deals with isn't us!"

Lyle was quick to agree. "That's right! And as Demons we will only follow someone worthy of our worship! And you, whatever you are. You are not worthy."

"Once we wipe you out, we'll be able to create a new and proper Lord. A superior Lord, our Lord Lucifer."

Fallen didn't make a single attempt to silence his chuckle. "That is assuming you two can wipe me out."

Lyle released a loud cackle. "My, my such arrogance."

"Enough of all this chatter, let's spill some blood."

Fallen's lips curled into a sneer. "Shall we then?"

Forty-One

Blood Splatter

Without hesitation, both Dimitri and Lyle raced toward Fallen. Fallen merely stood his ground holding his sneer. The second they were in reaching distance, Dimitri and Lyle went on the attack. Sinah watched as Fallen blocked each and every one of their strikes. Any time there was a pause or hesitation in their attacks, Fallen would strike. Fallen's hits were always open handed and across the face. After the third slap, Lyle hissed. "Stop bitch slapping me!"

Fallen shrugged and gave Lyle a forceful punch across the jaw. The force was strong enough to knock him clean off his feet. "Was that better?"

Lyle growled quickly standing up. "You'll pay for that!"

Fallen began to effortlessly block Lyle's attacks again. "You two claim I'm not worthy of your worship.." Fallen suddenly slammed his fists into their stomachs. Both Dimitri and Lyle doubled over. Fallen then gave both of them a shift uppercut. As they slammed onto their backs, he continued. "..I wouldn't want to be worshipped by such pathetic D Helixes."

Dimitri tried to sweep kick Fallen's legs out from under him as he screeched. "We are Demons!"

Fallen did a hands free backflip easily avoiding Dimitri's attack. Lyle snarled getting back on his feet and back on the attack.

Sinah looked toward Morella, she was still weeping uncontrollably on the floor. Sinah kneeled down and softly placed her hand on Morella's arm. Upon contact, Morella instantly flinched and sobbed even louder. "No! No! Please!"

Lyle's eyes darted in her direction, narrowly avoiding being punched by Fallen. "Hang on God, we're-"

Fallen snatched his hand around Lyle's throat and snarled. "She isn't God!!"

Before Lyle had a chance to react, Fallen tossed him into one of the ball room walls. The force caused a large chunk of the wall to crumble and crash down upon him. Dimitri leapt back from Fallen's attacks and called out. "Lyle, You okay!?"

Lyle groaned pushing the rubble off of him. "Ugh.. Yeah. Kill that son of a bitch already!"

Dimitri began to attack Fallen more aggressively. "You don't have to tell me twice."

Sinah grabbed Morella's arm. She instantly wailed and began to struggle. "No! No! I don't want to die! Noo!"

Sinah shook her head placing the blade beside them. Morella began to struggle as much as she could. Sinah gently began to tap the side of Morella's face trying her best to calm her down. After a few minutes of trying, she became fed up. She picked up the blade and gave Morella's fingertip a quick poke.

Morella's tears instantly stopped as did her resistance. Her traumatized eyes darted up to her. Sinah placed the blade beside them again and removed a UV from her basic supply pack. Morella only continued to stare at Sinah as she began to fill the vial. Her expression was a combination of scared and confused.

Once it was full and returned safely to its pouch, Sinah pulled Morella to her feet. As she leaned down to pick up her blade, she noticed at medium size vent at the back of the stage. Morella didn't resist as Sinah took her wrist and lead her toward it. Using the blade tip, Sinah began unscrew the screws holding the vent shut. Once the protective grate fell, she pointed inside. Morella's expression over flowed with apprehension. "Y.. You're letting me go?"

Sinah let her wrist go and pointed inside again. Morella stared back at Sinah as if she didn't understand what was happening. "You're not going to kill me?"

Sinah shook her head pointing toward the passage to freedom a third time. Morella's eyes filled with happy tears. She snatched Sinah into a relived hug. "Thank you! Thank you so much."

Sinah's expression shifted to slightly annoyed as she pointed to the vent again. This time her point had a more demanding disposition. Morella gave a few dozen more 'Thanks' before she crawled inside.

The minute she was out of sight, Lyle leapt in front of Sinah. "Thanks for letting her go. Now it's time to die."

Before Lyle could attack, Sinah slashed the blade in her hand across his throat. Lyle stumbled backward placing his hand on his gushing wound. He gurgled up blood as he spoke. "You'll pay for that, you little..!"

Before Lyle could finish his sentence, a fist slammed clean through his chest. The blood sprayed against the shocked Sinah's face.

Forty-two

Equality

Fallen who was standing behind Lyle, ripped his fist out of his chest. The second he flopped to the ground dead, Dimitri screeched. "Lyle!!"

Fallen opened his hand. Within his palm was Lyle's heart. Fallen indifferently dropped it then stepped on it. It made a loud squish sound under his combat boot. "I told you to kill her."

Sinah's expression shifted to slightly awkward glancing toward him. Her expression suddenly shifted to panic looking beyond him. Sinah quickly threw her weight against Fallen. As they fell, a slender metal arrow like thing slammed into her chest very close to her shoulder. If she hadn't knocked him over, the arrow would have hit the center of Fallen's spine.

Sinah made a sound of discomfort shifting off of Fallen and placing her hand near the throbbing wound. The arrow was sticking in her chest and out through her back. Fallen quickly sat up and grabbed it. Before Sinah had a chance to react, Fallen ripped it out of her and blindly whipped it behind himself. The arrow slammed into Dimitri's eye. Dimitri screeched in agony as he stumbled backward. Fallen glanced back at him as he got to his feet. "Are you alright Sinah?"

Sinah barely nodded covering the large open wound with both of her hands. Seeing the movement out of the corner of his eye, he nodded himself. As He walked down the small set of stairs, he spoke. "One low level D Helix down- One more to go."

Dimitri brought his shaking hands up to the arrow. He snarled tearing it out of his face. Blood gushed from his eye socket. "I'm a Demon!" It made a loud clang sound being tossed aside as he continued. "And I'm going to rip you and that bitch apart!!"

Before he could charge toward them, a pair of built arms wrapped around his chest. Dimitri's arms were pinned at his sides. Dimitri frowned glancing back at who was subduing him. "What the hell?!"

Bridger grinned looking at the side of his face. "More like, what in heaven?"

Fallen turned back to Sinah. As he helped her to her feet, he spoke. "Is everything in place Bridger?"

"Yes Commander. I didn't have any trouble. The soldiers here are mostly human."

Dimitri struggled aggressively in Bridger's arms. "I'm going to kill you too!!"

Bridger chuckled rattling him a little. "How are you going to do that? You can't even get out of my grip."

Dimitri grunted using all of the strength he had. Bridger smiled blocking his attempt with an equal of amount of his own. "Sorry D Helix but my A Helix can counteract anything you toss at me."

"I'm a Demon!!"

Bridger suddenly shifted his arm putting Dimitri in a head lock. "Either way, it all means mean to me."

Dimitri gripped Bridger's arm with both hands and snarled. "Face me head on you coward!"

Bridger reached his hand down his battle suit. "Naw, there's no point in doing that. We're evenly matched. I have to cheat to win." Bridger pulled off his heart bomb then attached it to Dimitri's chest. "Commander, get Sinah to a safe place!"

Fallen wasn't hesitant in pulling Sinah to a corner of the ballroom near the stage. As he pulled her protectively to his chest, he called out. "Do it Bridger!"

Dimitri struggled and snarled. "Let me go! Fight me head on!"

Bridger gripped him tightly as he called out. "Helix 7923 Bridger heart device-“ Bridger suddenly let Dimitri go and leapt to his left. Right before he landed he finished his command. “Activate!”

Before Dimitri had a chance to even touch the heart bomb, he was struck by the aggressive electrical blast. Being shocked by the zap, Dimitri only stood dazed for a few moments. Bridger quickly covered his head as the bomb was triggered and Dimitri was blown to bits.

Forty-Three

Boom!

As Bridger uncovered his head, one of Dimitri's arms flopped beside him. Bridger instantly jumped and clutched his chest. He couldn't help but to snicker at his surprise. "Well, it's a good thing I have a strong heart." As he stood up, he picked up the arm. "Think the ADGL Labs would think this is a good enough sample? Hm. Maybe not. We did electrically fry it so it is basically human now." Bridger shrugged hooking it over his shoulder. "Oh well. I'll give it to them anyway."

Fallen shifted his attention down to Sinah. "Are you alright?"

Sinah barely nodded looking up at him. She still had her hands over her shoulder wound. Turning toward Bridger, Fallen spoke. "Murdoch, do you have the samples?"

"Yes Commander. I'm on my way out."

Fallen glanced back at Sinah. The discomfort of her injury was clearly painted all over her face. "How much time?"

Bridger looked at his Combat glove then looked up at the ceiling. His expression suggested he was trying to figure something out. "Uh.." Bridger suddenly went flush as a panicked look fell over his features. "Let's get out of here!"

Fallen wasn't hesitant to snatch one of Sinah's bloody hands. Bridger waited until they raced passed him, before he gave chase. Once they cleared the front doors, they ran toward the protective wall. Murdoch ran toward then caught up with them. "Time?"

Bridger glanced at his Combat glove again before he yelled. "Take cover!!"

Without hesitation, all four slammed themselves to the ground. Fallen protectively covered Sinah's head with his arm. Not even a breath later, the mansion exploded. Fallen gripped Sinah tightly as flaming chunks of the manor fell all around them. Despite the sounds of destruction showering down upon them, Bridger's giggles could clearly be heard.

The moment the debris stopped falling, Bridger leapt to his feet. He cheered happily as he turned to the rubble and ash. Jumping up and down like an excited child, he yelled out. "Another successful explosion thanks to champion Bridger!!" Bridger lifted his and Dimitri's arm up in the air in triumph as he continued. "Helix 7923!! Champion!!"

Murdoch shook his head getting to his feet. "That was too close Bridger. It almost singed my butt hair off."

Bridger chuckled as he glanced back at Fallen. He was helping Sinah to her feet. "Yeah but wasn't it great!?"

Murdoch couldn't help but to chuckle himself. Fallen gave an upward nod toward the protective wall. "We're done here."

Both men quickly nodded.

Forty-four

Discipline

Dante let out a loud girl like screech as Dimitri's arm flopped on the hood of the hummer. Bridger laughed as loud as he could while peering through the windshield at him. "Hi Dante."

Dante went bright red in embarrassment. Trying to regain his composure, he rolled down the window and forced an angry tone. "Damn it Bridger!"

Bridger snickered putting his hands on his waist. "What's wrong? We needed a sample didn't we?"

Dante put his laptop on the driver's seat before he got out of the vehicle. "And why isn't it in a UV?"

"It was somewhat of a last minute kind of thing."

Dante glanced toward Fallen. He was helping Sinah down from the protective wall. "Well get it in one!"

Fallen approached Dante and Bridger. "Dante call in a clean-up crew."

Dante quickly nodded before he pressed his ear piece. "Helix 2341 Dante. Requesting a clean-up crew to-"

"You were given a direct command!"

Fallen and Bridger's eyes darted to the angry Murdoch. He hissed at Sinah as his eyes sharpened. "As a soldier, when the Commander commands, you obey! He told you to kill her. You should have killed her!"

Sinah's features weakened as she looked toward the ground. She didn't look up as he snatched her wrist and snarled. "You disobeyed the Commander!"

Fallen's attention shifted to Bridger. Though his eyes were locked on Murdoch, he was quietly removing Dante's gun from its holster. Murdoch raised his second hand. "You should have slaughtered that bitch!!" Murdoch swung his hand down to strike Sinah.

Before he got anywhere near making contact, Fallen caught his wrist. Murdoch's eyes instantly darted to him. Fallen's tone of voice though calm, was laced with noticeable hostility. "Let her go."

Murdoch instantly obeyed releasing Sinah. Fallen held his tone of voice. "Sinah get in the back seat of the hummer, Bridger in the driver's seat."

Bridger handed the confused Dante his gun back. He hadn't noticed that Bridger had disarmed him. Sinah quickly approached the first hummer. As she passed by Dante, he noticed her wound. "Oh! Uh.. Should I patch you up?"

Fallen wasn't hesitant in answering for her. "I'll handle it Dante. Once the sample of the D Helix is protected, load it and yourself in the second hummer."

"Yes Commander."

A few sweat beads trickled down Murdoch's forehead. "C… Commander, she.."

Fallen's grip on Murdoch's wrist tightened. "And since when are you the one to deal with disobedient soldiers?"

"I… I don't… I was just..."

Fallen closed her eyes and removed his sun glasses. "You've had an issue with Sinah from the first moment she joined our team. Did you think I wouldn't notice?"

Fallen's eyes snapped open and locked with Murdoch's eyes. "I suggest you learn how to get along with her and fast. Also-" Fallen's silver eyes sharpened, the unnoticeable crimson red ring around his pitch black pupil widened. "Remember your place D Helix. I give the orders and I deal with the discipline. Sinah won't be punished for a moment of mercy. Understand?" The widened crimson red ring began to bleed into the silver colour of his eyes. "Or are you willing to risk the hellfire that runs through my veins?"

Murdoch lost all colour in his face and couldn't swallow his worry fast enough. "N… No Commander."

Fallen hooked his sunglasses back on then let Murdoch's wrist go. "I won't have my soldiers fighting among themselves. Get along or get off my team!"

Murdoch was silent as Fallen walked away from him. "Get in the second hummer."

Murdoch wasn't hesitant in obeying his command. As Fallen got into the back seat with Sinah, he spoke. "Let's go Bridger."

Bridger quickly turned on the engine. "Yes Commander."

Forty-Five

Unpredictable

Fallen gently ripped the shoulder of Sinah's battle suit exposing her wound. "Sinah?"

Sinah looked up at him in acknowledgement. Fallen opened a few medium size med pads. "Are you angry with Murdoch?"

Bridger glanced up at Fallen and Sinah's reflection in the rear view mirror. Sinah shook her head a little. Fallen barely nodded, wiping the blood from the wound. The hole in her chest was almost completely closed. Sinah didn't have any reaction as he sprayed her injury with a med spray. "I'm glad you have the rapid healing skill as well. Is it sore?"

Sinah gave a quick shrug then nodded. Fallen began to bandage her up. "The pain will pass after a goodnights sleep. Tomorrow you'll be as good as new."

As she began to nod, Fallen spoke. His tone of voice was much more serious than before. "Sinah, you shouldn't have put yourself in harm's way for me."

Sinah's eyes darted up to him. Fallen's lips touched at a slight frown as he continued. "I've been through enough experimentation to know just how hard it is to kill me. Perhaps even impossible. This was a preventable injury. Carelessness like that will get you killed."

Bridger glanced up at Sinah's reflection sympathetically. She had a somewhat upset look on her face. Once Fallen finished bandaging her, he continued. "That being said, Thank you."

Sinah's expression instantly shifted to a shocked confusion. Bridger smiled slightly returning his attention to the road. Fallen shifted himself to sit properly in his seat. "I suggest you rest up a little. We'll be back at the facility in no time."

Sinah touched her bandaged wound smiling toward Fallen. Seeing her smile out of the corner of his eyes, Fallen nodded. "You're welcome. Now try to get some rest."

Sinah nodded getting comfortable in her seat. The minute she rested her head against her arm and pressed it against the window, she closed her eyes. After a few moments of silence, Fallen spoke. "Would you have shot him?"

Bridger's eyes darted up to Fallen. "Commander?"

"I noticed you grab Dante's gun. Would you have shot Murdoch?"

Bridger nodded in conviction looking back toward the road. "The minute his hand came in contact with her."

Fallen looked through the rear view mirror at Bridger's face. "Even with all the history our team has together?"

"It's not like that Commander." Bridger smiled slightly. "I would have done the same thing if he would have smacked Dante."

Dante awkwardly glanced toward Murdoch. Thanks to Sinah's and Fallen's open line of communication, both of them could hear the whole conversation. Murdoch only frowned gripping the steering wheel. Dante's eyes shifted down to the terrible looking red mark on Murdoch's wrist. It looked like Fallen had burned him.

"So then you felt like you had to protect a fellow A Helix?"

"Murdoch is different from Dante, Sinah and me. We're all loyal to you and will obey you and everything. But if and when 'God' is created-"

Fallen crossed his arms barely nodding. "Your Helixes will force you to only obey my counterpart."

Bridger gave an indifferent shrug. "I know squat about ancient times Heaven and Hell. All I know is Murdoch is the only D Helix on our team. And you personally picked him. That has to be important at least, that's what I think."

Murdoch's frown faded as Bridger continued. "I wouldn't say it to Murdoch he'll bite my head off. But I was protecting him as well."

Fallen's eyes darted to Sinah. "You think Sinah's dangerous?"

"I don't know. None of us do. We've haven't trained with her to know how strong she is. That makes her an unknown and unpredictable danger. Murdoch could have hit her and she could have snapped. Self-preservation can make any Helix vicious."

Fallen gently moved a few strands of hair from the sleeping Sinah's face. Bridger couldn't help but to smile watching him.

Forty-Six

Home again, Home again

Sinah's tired eyes slowly opened. Her expression shifted to confusion and slight panic seeing only empty seats. Sinah quickly sat up straight and climbed out of the hummer. Her demeanor was calmed once she saw Bridger. He was unloading the second vehicle. After placing one of the metal cases on the ground, he noticed her. "Well, hello there. Did you sleep alright?"

Sinah rubbed one of her eyes as she barely nodded. Bridger smiled slightly. "The Commander told me to let you sleep some more. I tried to unload the hummers as quietly as I could. I didn't wake you did I?"

Sinah shook her head before she glanced around with a searching look on her face. Bridger chuckled a little pointing beyond her. "He's over there."

Sinah quickly turned in the direction Bridger was pointing. Fallen was scraping the remaining chunks of Lyle's heart off his combat boot. Bridger couldn't help but to chuckle again as Sinah smiled and ran toward him.

Dante watched Fallen put the mud, guck and heart sludge into an unbreakable vial. "Uh.. I'm not really sure that sample will be-"

Fallen suddenly turned his head hearing Sinah running toward him. "It will have to do."

Dante glanced toward Sinah himself as she approached. He smiled slightly seeing the blood spray on her face. "How about I take a quick sample from Sinah's-"

"No, what's there is fine."

Dante barely nodded as Fallen handed him the safe UV. "Yes Commander."

Fallen watched Dante as he carried the sample over to the other collected samples. "Now that you've experienced one of our missions, will you be joining us permanently?"

Sinah smiled and happily nodded. Noticing the movement out of the corner of his eye, his lips touched at a smile also. "Good."

Sinah looked toward Murdoch. He was standing by the second hummer with a slightly upset look on his face. Fallen put his hands on his waist. "I'm glad to know my instincts were right about you."

Sinah looked back toward Fallen with a questioning expression, until he continued. "Your combat skills are well beyond the level of a simple novice. Like the rest of my team, you are a reliable soldier." Fallen turned his head toward her. "Sinah, continue to be impressive."

Sinah smiled almost instantly and nodded. The minute the samples were placed in a transport case, Dante called out. "Commander, I'm going to run these over to the ADGL Labs!"

Fallen instantly called back. "NO! Everyone over here! Now!"

Without hesitation, the rest of Fallen's team joined him. The minute they did, he spoke. "Everyone did well today." Fallen turned his head toward Murdoch. "There were only a few minor petty problems."

Murdoch looked toward the ground as if he had been scolded. Bridger glanced toward him with a sympathetic smile as Fallen continued. "All equipment will be returned to Murdoch tomorrow. Bridger, I want you to escort both Sinah and Dante to their homes."

"You got it Commander."

Fallen shifted his attention to Sinah. "Now that you are a permanent member of our team Sinah, be aware that others will start treating you differently."

Sinah's expression shifted to a slight worry. Bridger, who noticed, chuckled. He placed his hand on her head. "It's a good thing. You'll be treated with great respect and a little envy. After all, the Commander's team only has the best."

Fallen locked and unlocked his jaw watching them. Bridger, who noticed, quickly removed his hand. Fallen's lips touched at a slight frown. "Why are you three still here? I've given an order, go!"

Both Bridger and Dante went flush and gave a quick 'Yes Commander.' Sinah on the other hand, smiled and waved good-bye. Fallen barely nodded, watching her join the other two men. "Good-bye Sinah."

Fallen kept his attention locked on Sinah as he spoke. "Murdoch, take the samples to the ADGL Labs then head over to Med for a booster shot. We're going hunting."

After a quick 'Yes Commander,' Murdoch raced toward the samples. As he passed by Bridger, he gave his shoulder a quick squeeze. Bridger couldn't help but to snicker glancing in his direction. Dante looked up at Bridger hearing his slight amusement. "What's so funny?"

"Oh nothing really, mean Helixes don't say thanks."

"What?"

Bridger waved his hand dismissively. "Forget it. Come on let's get you two home."

Forty-seven

Confused Parents

The artificial sky suggested it was late in the evening, when Bridger pulled up in front of the Harmond home. As he turned off the jeep's engine, he glanced up at Dante's reflection in the rear view mirror. "You coming with or-"

Dante cut him off opening the backseat door. "I'll go with you."

Sinah smiled happily walking up the pathway to her house. Once everyone reached the front door, Bridger knocked on it. Sinah smiled even more as Amos answered. A full relived smile instantly took his lips as he snatched her into a hug. "Kid! You're home!! Violet, Kid's back!!"

After almost squeezing the life out of her, Amos let her go. "We were so worried about you. I'm so happy you made it back in one piece." As he stepped back, he noticed her bandaged shoulder and the blood spatter on her face. "Kid, you're hurt! What happened?!"

Before Sinah had a chance to give any response, Violet ran into the room. Her eyes instantly wielded up with tears. "Kid!!" Violet wasn't hesitant in snatching Sinah into an aggressive hug. "You're back! Thank Goodness you're okay!"

Bridger, who was standing just inside the house with Dante, smiled. "Aw, that's so cute."

Both Violet and Amos' eyes darted to him. Amos awkwardly chuckled. "Sorry gentlemen, we didn't notice you."

"That's alright. I figure the return of your daughter is a tad more important than little old us."

Violet placed her hands on Sinah's shoulders as she stepped back from her. "We were so worried about y…" Violet stopped short seeing Sinah's injury. She instantly panicked and cupped Sinah's cheeks with both hands. "What happened?!"

Sinah smiled stepping back from Violet's touch. She quickly shook her head patting her bandaged shoulder.

Bridger crossed his arms. "It was only a minor scratch. Nothing to worry ab-"

"Nothing to worry about!?" Violet hissed cutting him off. "This shouldn't have happened! Kid, shouldn't have even been-"

"Sinah."

Violet's anger shifted to a confused annoyance. "What?"

Bridger gave an upward nod at Sinah. "Her name is Sinah."

Sinah smiled and nodded. Violet's eyes darted toward her. "What is he talking about? Your name is Kid, Kid Harmond."

Both Bridger and Sinah quickly shook their heads. Amos' confusion, minus the anger, mirrored his wife's. "Your name isn't Kid?"

Sinah shook her head while Bridger smiled toward her. "The Commander gave her a new name."

Violet snarled toward Bridger almost instantly. "He has no right to do that!! She isn't his daughter! How dare he!?"

Bridger uncrossed one of his arms. He awkwardly scratched the back of his head and shrugged. "Uh… well… Sinah is a much prettier name. And it does suit her."

Sinah nodded with a full smile and proudly placed her hand on her chest. Amos looked at the beaming with pride Sinah for a few seconds before he barely nodded. "..Sinah."

Sinah turned her smile toward Amos and nodded. Violet's lips were instantly consumed by a frown. "We'll discuss this later Kid. Go get cleaned up then head to bed. I'm sure you must be tired."

Sinah barely nodded as her smile vanished. Violet continued as she reached for Sinah's red scarf. "And let's just return this right n-"

Without hesitation, Sinah pulled the scarf closer to herself. As if having a temper tantrum, she forcefully squeezed her eyes shut and frantically shook her head. Violet drew her hand back in confusion. "Kid?"

Sinah frantically shook her head again before she ran toward her bedroom. Violet held her confused expression following after her. "Kid?!"

Forty-Eight

No Chance

Amos sighed walking toward the kitchen. "Do you gentlemen want some coffee?"

Bridger shook his head. "No thanks. Coffee makes my feet smell and uterus itch."

Amos barely nodded filling himself up a cup. "Oh, alright th…" Amos stopped short actually hearing what Bridger said. He turned so fast he almost took the coffee pot with him. "W… What?!"

Dante, who was giving Bridger a disgusted look, responded. "None for me either, thanks."

Bridger blindly waved his hand behind himself. "Well, we got to get going."

As they turned to leave, Amos raced to the open door. "Wait a minute!"

Bridger glanced back at Amos as he lowered his voice. It was obvious he didn't want Violet to overhear him. "Did Kid..? Did she do okay?"

Bridger turned to Amos with a smile. "From what I heard she did. But what do you expect from the girl who has the top scores in Combat."

Amos placed his hand on his chest releasing a sound of relief. "Good. We were so worried. Combat simulators are one thing but actual battle is a hell of a lot different."

Bridger shrugged. "Well, Sinah obviously can hold her own." Bridger suddenly sighed placing his hands on his waist. "Listen, I know this isn't my place to say anything, but.. Well, you might want to get your wife to understand that Sinah is a member of our team now. I don't care if she likes it or not, that's just how it is. And no matter what, the Commander will make damn sure she remains a member."

"Yeah… yeah I know."

Bridger's tone of voice suddenly shifted to happy. "And she couldn't have a better team! Well, we're off."

Amos was silent as Bridger and Dante left the Harmond property.

As Bridger walked toward the jeep, Dante pointed down the street. "I'm not too far from here. I can walk it."

Bridger barely nodded. "Okay let's go."

Dante pulled his laptop and backpack out of the back seat of the jeep. "I'll be fine by myself."

"The Commander told me to escort both Sinah AND you home. So that's what I'm going to do."

Dante frowned almost instantly. "It's not like I'm going to tell on you."

Bridger snatched Dante's back pack. He began to speak in a sing song like tune as walked away from him. "I'm following orders. I'm following orders."

Dante frowned even more at Bridger's childish chant. "Fine! Fine! Just give me my stuff back!"

Bridger waited until Dante was beside him before he did. "Sinah has quite the protective Mama. Just like someone else I know."

"Well, when Dad died, she had nobody else so… so… uh... You think Sinah would spend some time with me?"

Bridger instantly stopped in his tracks. "Time? You mean alone time?"

Seeing Dante's cheeks touch at a blush, Bridger smirked. "Oh, you mean stand under the artificial stars and whisper sweet nothings?" Dante went red as Bridger continued his train of thought. "Smooch up a storm? Be so passionate that people around you feel uncomfortable seeing such a thing?" Dante went so red it looked like he would spontaneously combust. Bridger giggled. "Enter into the marriage contract?"

Dante frantically shook his head. Both in disagreement and to calm his burning face. "I.. I wasn't talking about the future or marriage contracts or things like that. I was just wondering if you think she'd go to the common social area and watch a film with me or something."

Bridger responded bluntly. "Nope."

Dante's eyes darted to him. "Nope?"

"Yeah. Nope."

Dante couldn't help but to frown. "Gee, thanks for giving it so much thought."

Bridger aggressively pinched Dante's still heated cheek. "I didn't have to."

Dante hissed slapping Bridger's hand away from him. "She obviously liked my scarf and she-"

"Actually, it was the Commander that..." Bridger stopped short. His tone of voice suddenly shifted to astonishment. "You mean, you really haven't noticed? I know Murdoch did, that's why he's so prickly."

Dante rubbed his sore cheek with a frown. "Noticed what? What are you talking about?"

Bridger opened his arms widely and looked up at the artificial sky. "Hell has found his Heaven."

Dante's annoyed expression instantly shifted to shock. "What?! The Commander and Sinah?!"

Bridger lowered his arms and glanced back at Dante. "And I think Hell won't let anyone get in his way. Come on Dante. Let's get you home."

Dante only stood frozen in utter shock.

Forty-Nine

Hunting

Trade had become the main source of currency in the world of the Lost Souls. Food was usually the top item to trade. However, in certain areas the top items were much more gruesome. It wasn't unheard of to offer body parts, blood or even teeth. It didn't matter whose or where they came from. For the right price, a peddler could get a Lost Soul anything their heart desired.

A man with black hair and eyes stood by an alleyway between two tattered buildings. Despite the Lost Souls hope to be unnoticed, this man wore a bright red shirt causing him to stand out like a sore thumb. His particular wares were well known through word of mouth. This trader carried the very rare and forbidden Synthetic D.

As he stretched his arms up to the eclipsed sun and moon, he was greeted by a punch in the jaw. The force of the strike caused him to crash to the mangled pavement. As he scrambled to his feet, he heard a calm masculine voice. "Hello Richard."

The peddler named Richard instantly went flush recognizing the voice. His eyes darted to who had hit him. It was the frowning Murdoch. Richard's eyes then darted beyond him to Fallen. He was leaning against one of the buildings. His arms were crossed and his attention was skyward. Richard lifted his hands defensively stumbling over his words. "C... Commander… uh... It's good to see you still alive. No! I.. I mean.."

Fallen shifted his glowing silver eyes toward him. Seeing the silver out of the side of his sunglasses, Richard went ghost white. Despite the dim blue light covering the world, Richard's flush could clearly be seen. Murdoch suddenly snatched the scruff of his red shirt. Richard instantly forced a smile the best he could. The sweat dripping from his body and his panicked disposition, instantly discredited that smile.

Fallen lowered his head and turned it toward him. "The information you gave me, lead us to an ambush."

Richard awkwardly chuckled. "Oh? Did it? Well… uh..."

Murdoch frowned gripping his sweat soaked shirt tighter. It looked like any minute he was going to bash Richard's brains in.

"Did you really think I would be killed?" Before Richard had a chance to respond, Fallen snarled. "Did you really think I'd let you get away with giving me false information!?!"

Richard instantly began to panic. "I didn't want to! I mean I didn't mean to! I..!"

Fallen's disposition and hostile tone suddenly calmed. "Snap his neck."

Murdoch instantly flipped behind Richard. He hooked his arm around his neck gripping his shoulder. He then placed his other hand on the side of his head. Richard cried out grabbing Murdoch's arm with both hands. "No!! Please!! I.. I can make you a deal! Yeah, yeah I can make you a deal! Just please spare me!! I beg of you!!"

Murdoch glanced up at Fallen awaiting the final command to kill him. Fallen crossed his arms and frowned. "Begging has no effect on me. It's just noise."

Richard tried to swallow but Murdoch's grip was too tight. "Th... That's why I want to make it up to you Commander."

"What's the price?"

Richard tried to shake his head but again Murdoch's grip was too tight. "No price Commander. I'll give you the information for fre-"

Fallen cut Richard off with a snip. "What did they pay you for my ambush?"

Richard began to struggle for air. "S... Synthetic D. A lot of it. M... much more than what you normally trade me."

Fallen's eyebrows were quick to furrow. It was a combination of confusion and disbelief. "Someone from our Lab set it up?"

Richard began to claw at Murdoch's arm feeling light headed. "N... no... the Lost Souls Lab!"

Fifty

Lost Time

Fallen waved his hand at Murdoch. "Release him."

The second Murdoch let him go Richard fell to all fours gasping for air. He rubbed his sore throat as he tried to speak. "Th… they m… make both Synthetic D and A."

Fallen's eyebrows lowered as Richard began to cough. "The Lost Souls are trying to create Synthetic Angels and Demons?"

After getting his breathing under control, Richard slowly got to his feet. "They might be, I guess." Richard instantly went flush as Fallen tossed him a frown. He quickly shook his head continuing. "I... I mean they may be. That's not really what synthetics are used for."

Fallen approached Richard with an ever increasing frown. "What else would they be used for? I always assumed you traded what I gave you to other Labs for supplies."

"No. We use it for… well… You know." Seeing Fallen's eyebrows furrow, Richard could help but to chuckle. "Oh come on. You know."

Not getting a straight answer, Fallen snapped. "Answer me!!"

Richard's amusement was silenced as he cowered like a beaten dog. "G.. Getting high."

Fallen's expression shifted to confusion as he looked toward Murdoch. Murdoch mirrored his expression and shrugged. Seeing that neither of the men understood, Richard spoke. "If you use a few drops of Synthetic D in any liquid and drink it. It makes you forget all about this place. You feel happy, free, you know, euphoric. Your dreams become so vivid and amazing. You truly feel invincible and time just vanishes. For a short time, this lousy world we live in becomes bearable. I sell a lot of them every day."

Murdoch scoffed turning his head in disgust. "The Lost Souls are using something so dangerous for personal amusement."

Richard's tone of voice shifted to defensive. "You don't know how hard it is for us to live out here! We struggle every day just for survival! We..!"

Fallen cut him off. "And yet each and every month, you are given the option to step out of this world and into the safety of our facility. But does your so called struggling kind take it? No. They prefer this way of life so they will have it."

"We don't want to be lab rats! We heard the rumors about the experimentation!"

Murdoch shook his head frowning. "It isn't like that. You get cleaned up, fed, medically checked out then trained in one of our many fields."

Richard's eyes brows lowered slightly. "Yeah and get your reproductive system ripped out."

Murdoch scoffed. "It's not like they're being successfully used out here."

Fallen changed the subject. "And the Synthetic A?"

Richard's eyes darted to Fallen. "What?"

The minute Fallen released an annoyed sigh, Richard quickly nodded. "Uh… Right, the Synthetic A, it helps us sleep." A few sweat beads ran down his forehead seeing Fallen merely staring back at him. "O… Of course if you use too much you might accidently kill yourself. When someone gets too old or hurt or… or… Anyway, a large shot of that and-"

"Where is the Lost Souls Lab?"

Richard nervously looked toward the crumbling cement. "I… If I tell you Commander, will this make things even between us?"

A slight smirk took Fallen's lips. "It depends on the accuracy of the information."

Richard quickly nodded racing back to the alley he normally stood by. "I'll get you the map."

Murdoch kept his eyes locked on him. If Richard made any attempt to escape, Murdoch would be on him like a predator on its prey. After a few seconds of digging in his bag of wares, Richard made a pleased sound. "Aha! Found it!"

He ran back over to Fallen and handed him a piece of paper. Fallen's eyebrows furrowed in confusion looking at it. This particular type of map was unfamiliar to his eyes. Richard pointed at a red dot at the top of a blue path. "It's there."

Fallen gave a slight nod. "Fine."

Richard clasped his hands together like he was begging. He stepped back from Fallen as his expression shifted to pleading. "This squares things between us right? We're good right?"

An ugly grin consumed Fallen's lips. "Of course. After all, you're dealing with..." Fallen zipped his hand across Richard's throat. The motion was so fast only a fine almost invisible blood spray hit the pavement. Fallen turned heel as he finished his sentence. "...Lucifer."

Murdoch quickly followed Fallen as he walked away. Neither of the men glanced back as Richard's head rolled clean off his shoulders.

Fifty-One

Slipping Rank

Bridger smiled childishly at the powder blue bandage on his arm. "My saviour!"

Judith couldn't help but to laugh being snatched into a hug. "I swear you hurt yourself every day on purpose."

Bridger let her go and forced an obvious fake frown. "How rude."

Judith snickered as she walked away from him to return to work. Bridger glanced around at all the female Med Techs. "So Ladies, anyone want to join me for lunch?"

As per usual, his question was answered by many giggles. Bridger glanced over his shoulder toward the Combat area. His expression shifted to confusion seeing Sinah's name still as Kid, rapidly falling from the top scores. "She isn't doing well?"

Bruno approached Bridger with a nervous anxious expression. "Did you talk to the Commander yet?"

"Not yet. The Commander was a little too busy thinking about the Lab mission."

Bruno's sighed as his expression shifted to disappointment. "Oh... Well... maybe, next-"

Bridger cut him off with a dismissive wave of his hand. "As soon as the Commander has a spare moment, I'll talk to him."

Bruno's eyes instantly lit up. He couldn't contain the excitement in his voice. "You will?! Great!! That's great!!"

As Bridger passed through the Med station's exit, he noticed a bunch of folded clothes. His expression shifted to slightly concerned seeing Sinah's red scarf. Bridger turned to the table and looked through the pile. "Who put these here?"

Bruno, who was still in his own happy world, questioned the same. "Who put what where?"

Bridger closed his eyes picking up the scarf. "This is Sinah's combat equipment."

"Who?"

Bridger pressed his ear piece. "Helix 7617 Sinah?" Not getting a response or even expecting one, he continued. "Please report to Medical. I repeat Helix 7617 Sinah, report to the Med station near Combat."

Bruno looked toward Bridger confused. "Who?"

Bridger didn't respond. He merely crossed his arms and leaned against the wall connecting to the Med station exit.

Fifty-Two

A Bridger over Troubled Sinah

The minute Sinah entered the Med. Station, Bridger tossed the red scarf at her. As it flopped over her head and shoulder, she turned quick. Bridger glanced at Sinah's mint green sweater, black pants and sneakers. "Back to your old self I see."

Sinah pulled the scarf off herself. Her features weakened as she gripped it with both hands. Seeing her expression, Bridger's turned sympathetic. "If it means so much to you, why are you returning it?"

Sinah closed her eyes smooshing her face into the scarf. Before Bridger could say anything else, Amos entered the Med station. "Come on Kid, its lunch time. Let's go get something to eat."

Sinah didn't move or react. Amos sighed approaching her. Placing one hand on her back and taking a part of the scarf with the other, he spoke. "Now come on Kid. Your mother and I discussed this with you. Now that the mission is over with, there isn't any reason why you should keep this."

Sinah's grip loosened on the scarf as Amos slowly pulled it away from her. Once it was out of her hands completely, Amos nodded. "Good girl, now let's just-"

"Well, I've seen enough." Both Amos and Sinah's eyes darted to the frowning Bridger. Bridger put his hands on his waist continuing. "That young woman standing there is Helix 7617 Sinah. She is one of the Commander's team. She isn't a simple civilian and shouldn't be treated like one. And she damn well shouldn't have to dress like one."

Amos barely nodded. "I understand that but this morning Violet and I-"

"Neither of you have a say in this."

Amos couldn't help but to frown. "Kid is our daughter and-"

"Sinah!" Bridger said with force. "Her name is Sinah!"

Sinah barely nodded. Amos shook his head noticing her nod out of the corner of his eye. "Now Kid, you shouldn't-"

Bridger cut Amos off with a defeated sigh. "I guess the Commander was right."

Amos looked back toward Bridger. "Right? Right about what?"

"The Commander said that Sinah's new living quarters should be in the Helix Military Residential area. She is one of us after all. I convinced him otherwise. I said she has two loving parents that want what's best for their daughter. But I guess I was wrong." Bridger sighed again, this time shaking his head. "It seems like all you two want to do is keep your 'Kid' a little girl forever. Trap her in the image you see her in. Not even realizing she's obviously miserable. But I guess her parents know what's best."

Amos eyes darted to Sinah. "Kid? You're unhappy?"

Sinah's features weakened as she took the scarf from his hands. Bridger shrugged indifferently. "Oh well. I'll tell the Commander to get the paper work ready for her transfer."

"No! Our daughter isn't transferring anywhere." Amos placed his hand on Sinah's shoulder. "Are you sure about this? Are you sure this is the life you want?"

Bridger's lips touched at a frown. "Uh… The Commander chose her for our team. She doesn't exactly have a choice."

Amos didn't acknowledge Bridger as he questioned again. "Is It?"

Sinah looked at the red scarf momentarily before a soft smile took her lips. Bridger couldn't help but to smile as she gently brushed it against her cheek. "…And Heaven has found her Hell." He quietly muttered to himself.

Sinah looked up at Amos and confidently nodded. Amos closed his eyes releasing a loud defeated sigh. "Okay. Well, we're having lunch with your mother. Let's go try to convince her that this is for the best."

Before Sinah had a chance to nod, Bridger snatched her arm. "Sorry but Sinah's needed to come with me."

"Soldier stuff?"

Bridger forced a full smile. "Thanks for understanding."

Amos placed his hand on the side of Sinah's face. "See you later Ki... Sinah."

Sinah smiled and nodded. Once Amos left the Med station, Bridger let Sinah go. "Grab your stuff and follow me." Bridger suddenly smirked. "Oh and by the way. The Commander didn't say anything about transferring you. I haven't seen him since the mission."

Sinah's eyes darted from the mission equipment up to the chuckling Bridger.

Fifty-Three

Growing Up

The second the 4th building's elevator doors closed, Bridger spoke. "Sorry I stuck my nose in where it doesn't belong."

Before Sinah could give any reaction, Bridger crossed his arms behind his head and chuckled. "I guess I just can't help it. I just can't stand by and watch over protective parents ruin their child's chances at something." Bridger shrugged. "Good or bad, it's the child's life. He or she should have say over their own future." Bridger glanced toward Sinah. "Besides I could see how upset it was making you."

Sinah barely nodded then gave Bridger a questioning look.

"How'd I know?"

Sinah quickly nodded. Bridger smiled answering her expression and his question. "Well, there were a couple of things. First you were falling in the Combat ranks. Which means you're either too upset to focus. Or now that you have experienced real combat, fake ones just seem boring."

Sinah nodded with a smile. Bridger glanced up at the floor numbers as they highlighted one after the other. "I was originally going to snip at you a little for ditching the Commander's gift. I mean you looked really happy with it and-"

Sinah quickly shook her head cutting Bridger off. She pulled the scarf closer to her chest as her features weakened. Bridger glanced toward her out the corner of his eye. He smiled slightly seeing her upset disposition.

"But then I saw how you looked when I tossed it at you and how you look at it now. It wasn't your choice to return it was it?"

Sinah eyes darted to Bridger as she frantically shook her head. Bridger sighed loudly. "Yeah… yeah, that's what I thought. I've seen that look before."

Sinah's expression shifted to confused yet questioning. Bridger forcefully poked the floor selection button again. "I swear this building has the slowest elevator."

Bridger looked toward Sinah as he leaned against one of the walls. "Dante's father was one of the Techs that deliver food and supplies into the World of the Lost Souls." Bridger closed his eyes as his features weakened. "He and two other Lab Techs were killed in a Lost Souls raid. Dante was really young at the time. His mother didn't take news of his death very well."

Sinah's expression shifted to sympathetic as Bridger gave an awkward weak chuckle. "Not that anyone takes death well. Anyway, she became so over protective of him that when the Commander selected him for his team, she had a full out panic attack."

Sinah nodded and tried to motion her hand toward herself, but both were filled with the mission equipment. Bridger nodded understanding her. "Your parents too? Yeah, that's what I thought. And just like you, Dante let his mother try to stop him from growing up. Stop him from becoming a strong, Data, Surveillance and Information soldier. The Helix soldier we need."

Bridger placed his hand on Sinah's head. "Just like you're a Helix soldier we need. We need you to protect the Commander."

Sinah smiled slightly looking up at Bridger. Bridger smiled in return removing his hand. His smile suddenly increased as the elevator doors opened. "Finally!"

Bridger walked with Sinah down the hallway continuing their conversation. "I'll never understand why parents want to trap their child as a child. It makes me happy knowing that Murdoch and I don't have parents."

Sinah ran ahead then stopped short in front of him. Bridger stopped walking as his expression shifted to confusion. "What's wrong?"

Thanks to the combat equipment in her hands, Sinah could only give an upward nod at him. Bridger only held his expression. “Uh… What?”

Sinah gave another upward nod. Bridger scratched to back of his head. “The parents thing?”

Sinah quickly nodded. Bridger indifferently shrugged. “Don’t worry about it. Just like Dante’s mother, your parents will…”

Sinah shook her head with a slight frown. She then gave a full body motion toward Bridger. Bridger placed his hand on his chest. “Me? Oh! What did I mean about Murdoch and I?”

Sinah released a relived sigh before she smiled and nodded. Bridger awkwardly chuckled. “Sorry about that.”

Sinah shook her head then again gave an upward nod at Bridger. Bridger smiled slightly. “Murdoch and I are creation born.”

Fifty-Four

Donation Creation

Bridger gave an upward nod at a fellow Helix soldier as he passed by them. "Do you know how a life is created in the Creation Lab?"

Sinah only stared back at him. Bridger chuckled shaking his head. "What am I saying? Of course you wouldn't. Rumor has it, you were a natural birth." Bridger dismissively waved his hand. "Well, it's really not important or anything. During creation, everyone is given a small amount of Angel blood or Demon blood. I was told the strength of our soul decides how well it takes." Bridger waved his hand again. "Anyway, anyway, the ADGL Labs takes a small amount of the reproductive samples. Our creation is basically the same as in Creation Lab except we get given a mixture of all the special blood samples."

Sinah didn't shift her interested yet confused expression from Bridger. He continued as he began to take the mission equipment from her hands. A smile touched at his lips seeing Sinah pull the red scarf close to her collarbone. "Well, all special blood except the Lucifer blood. Since the Commander's creation, the blood doesn't even try to take to life."

Once all the items except the red scarf were in Bridger's hands, he began to walk down the hall again. Sinah was quick to follow after him. "They pay close attention to our progress. You know to see which blood chooses to blend with the life. A lot of us Helixes are made this way. Sometimes it works, sometimes it doesn't." Bridger smirked, glancing back at Sinah. "And sometimes, really strong, brave, handsome, amazing Helixes are made. You know, like me."

Sinah couldn't help but to smile. Bridger stopped in front of a metal door. "Since the ADGL Labs get a small sample from everyone. It's random who our actual parents are. None of us know or even want to know for that matter. We are raised with others like us."

Sinah barely nodded as Bridger chuckled. "I know that was the boring technical way of explaining it, but did it answer your question?"

Sinah nodded with smile. Bridger smiled himself. "Good, now let's make you look like one of the Commander's team."

Sinah looked down at her mint green sweater in slight confusion. Bridger smirked turning his attention to the metal door. His smirk shifted to a childish grin as he kicked the door open. "Murdoch!!"

Murdoch, who was sitting behind a large counter, frowned lowering a sandwich from his mouth. Bridger snickered approaching him. Sinah walked into the area curiously. On the left side of the room were clip boards and bins of papers. On the right, were different types of guns hanging in display cases. Beyond Murdoch were many closed cabinets and a thick glass door. Beside the door was a lock release panel.

Murdoch indifferently nodded as Bridger placed Sinah's mission equipment on the counter. "Is it all here?"

"Do you still have the proto type of Sinah's battle suit?"

Murdoch bit into his sandwich and mumbled through the mouthful. "Yeah, why?"

Bridger leaned on the counter glancing back at Sinah. She looked very interested in the guns in the display cases. "She needs them."

"Why? They're useless. They're just clothes."

"I know that. The way the Commander tore the shoulder out of her top looked nice. Make sure you have a little of a cold shoulder on each side."

Murdoch lowered his almost finished sandwich from his mouth. "What do you mean 'make sure'? I'm not making her an outfit."

Bridger smiled toward Murdoch. "Oh yes you are. You owe her."

Murdoch instantly tossed Sinah a glare and a frown. "I owe her?"

"Besides, she dresses like a child. She's one of us now. She should look like it."

Murdoch shifted his glare and frown to Bridger. “I’m not some seamstress and I don’t owe her anything.”

Bridger returned his frown. “We shouldn’t have bad blood between us. That’s the last thing the Commander needs.” Bridger began to speak in an ‘As a matter of fact’ tone. “And she did receive an injury protecting the Commander. All of us really should be grateful to her. Even if he can’t die, she did what all of us would have done. And-”

“Fine! Shut it! When does she need it by?”

Bridger shrugged. “How fast can you get it done?”

Murdoch released a frustrated sigh before he began to woof down the rest of his lunch. Bridger turned his attention to Sinah. “Come on Sinah, I’ll show you around and we’ll order up some food.”

Sinah motioned her hand around with a look of confusion. Bridger opened a flap along the counter granting him access behind it. “This is our Military and Helix shooting range. It’s really fun, come on I’ll show you.”

Bridger placed his hand on the door release panel. It made a few beep sounds before the door swished open. Smiling back at Sinah, he spoke. “Come on.”

Sinah didn’t acknowledge Murdoch as she passed behind him then followed Bridger.

Fifty-Five

Director Hart

On the top floor of the 6th building was a singular office. This was the top and most important office there was in the whole facility. Sitting outside the set of double doors was an elderly woman. Her large desk was meticulously organized. It was obvious that she was the receptionist and had been for quite some time. She glanced up from her many green screens as Fallen passed by her desk. "He's in meeting right now Commander! If you would just-"

Fallen ignored her and busted into the office. A man with sandy blonde hair and dark blue eyes, sat behind a very large paper filled desk. His metal walking stick was in his reaching distance. Emma and another ADGL Lab Tech were standing in front of his desk giving their status reports on ADGL failures. Fallen was silent as he walked by all of them to the ceiling to floor windows. The man glanced up at him momentarily while both Emma and the ADGL Tech went flush.

Emma swallowed heavily before she spoke. "We're not sure why there's been a pause in Helix creation, Director Hart. We've been using the same method as we normally do, but nothing seems to take. The samples just simply pass through the life's system."

The Director barely nodded tapping the air accessing the green screens. "And there's yet to be any successful synthetics?"

The ADGL Lab Tech shook his head. "No Director. Those with strong souls seem to have much more aggressive side effects. The resistance of the soul causes them to turn into monsters."

Emma sighed. "They lose their sanity and any signs of humanity."

The Director tapped a few screens. Many unsuccessful Helix progresses appeared. "Lucifer?"

Both Emma and the ADGL Lab Tech's eyes darted to Fallen. Both of their expressions shifted to a nervous discomfort. Fallen merely stared out the window. The Director shuffled through the many failures. "Why do you think there's been a sudden pause in Helix production?"

Fallen crossed his arms and leaned his shoulder and arm against the window. "I wouldn't know."

The Director shifted his attention to the papers on his desk. As he began to search through them, he spoke. "One of your soldiers delivered the Lab mission report early this morning. I've yet to get around to it. Is it safe to assume the rumor of 'God's' creation wasn't true?"

Fallen's lips touched at a frown. "It wasn't."

Emma shook her head in confusion. "Um… Director, what does 'God's' creation have to do with the pause in-"

"You might be a tad too young to remember the sudden halt in Helix creation before the birth of Lucifer."

Emma shook her head. "I was a newbie in the ADGL Labs then. Information like that wasn't given to me."

The Director found the Lab Mission report and placed it in front of himself. "Once Lucifer breathed life, everything returned to normal. It was as if everything had to stop for such an important birth. I thought perhaps Lab 6 had been successful in creating 'God'."

Fallen hissed. "She wasn't God!"

Both Emma and the ADGL Lab Tech flinched at his sudden anger. The Director on the other hand, merely spoke. "The minute you saw her, you should have known that."

Fallen frowned an ugly frown as he stood up straight. His eyebrows lowered. It looked like any minute he was going to rip the Director limb from limb. "I did know it. I felt it right away. I am not flawed."

The Director chuckled a little glancing toward him. "I meant because she was female. 'God' is a male."

Emma quickly protested. "Impossible!"

Both Fallen and the Director's attention shifted to her. Emma could feel a wave of intimidation rush over her from Fallen. She stumbled over her words slightly continuing. "I… I mean… Men can't create. They merely help in the process. It's the woman's body that is the creator and bearer of life. Well, now we just need the eggs but…"

The Director leaned back on his leather bound chair. "God in ancient times was-"

Emma was quick to interject. "Impossible! Only a woman can give birth. God gives birth to life. Women are the carriers and men are the protectors. I mean how can we possibly believe that a skill not possible from the male body can-?"

The ADGL Tech cut her off. "I never once thought God would be a guy."

Fallen shifted his attention back out the window. "My counterpart is female."

Emma didn't hesitate to agree. "She'd have to be. Quoting ancient times: God created in its own image another creator, a bearer of life, a woman."

The Director leaned his elbows on the arms of his chair and tented his fingers. "There isn't any point in continuing this debate. You've been given the samples from Lab 6. I want the status reports by morning."

Once Emma and the ADGL Lab Tech left his office, the Director muttered. "She misquoted the bible." The Director gave a quick shake of his head. "None the matter. Once God is created, its gender will be revealed."

Fifty-Six

Paper Work

After a few moments of silence, the Director spoke. "It's unusual for you to pay me a simple visit."

Fallen's lips were instantly consumed by a frown. "This isn't a simple visit. I need an equipment approval."

"For what purpose?"

"The Lost Souls have their own Lab."

The Director's expression shifted from shock to annoyance. He turned his leather bound chair toward Fallen with a hiss. "They don't have that kind have technology! Who gave them the precious samples!?"

Fallen turned his attention up to the eclipsed sun and moon. "They are only creating Synthetic A and D."

"You need to have access to the original samples to have a base knowledge on where to even start creating synthetics." The Director snatched up the Lab Mission report. As he began to glance through the manila folder, he questioned. "Lab 6 had which Director?"

Fallen merely kept his attention out the window. Once the Director saw Director Courtier's name, he scoffed. "Still trying to save them Carl? Tell me Lucifer, is your source on this information reliable?"

Fallen reached into his pocket and pulled out the map he got from Richard. "Lost Souls never lie when the price is their lives."

The Director flipped to another page in the report. "Then he lost his?"

"To successfully create Heaven and Hell blood must pour."

The Director's lips touched at a smile. "I'm glad to know you didn't ignore everything I said to you."

Fallen approached then flopped the map onto the Director's desk. "This is what I was given."

The Director glanced at it for split second. Actually seeing what type of map it was, he smiled. "Well I'll be damned." Picking it up, the Director chuckled. "Your Data, Information and Surveillance soldier will have trouble with this one."

Fallen's lips touched at a frown as the Director continued. "It's definitely a clever place to hide a Lab."

"Dante will find it."

"I'm surprised you have so much faith in an Angel Helix, Lucifer."

Fallen's response was to increase his frown. The Director dropped the map back onto his desk. "Well unless he looks underground, he won't find it."

Fallen furrowed his eyebrows a little. It was obvious he had no idea what the Director meant. Seeing his confused expression, the Director explained. "It has many names. It depends on your location in the world. The subway, the metro, the rocket, the-"

"Dante will find it. Now I need equipment approval."

The Director turned his attention back to the Lab Mission report. "Without proper research, you'll be stepping into a potentially dangerous situation."

Fallen's many levels of frowns were replaced with a slight smile. "That doesn't concern me in the slightest."

The Director flipped to the next page. "It may concern your men."

"We have dealt with optional missions before. I will lead and my men will follow."

The Director's eyebrows furrowed a little. It appeared that something in the report had caught his attention. "Just like the leader of Hell should."

Any momentary smile that had touched at Fallen's lips was once again taken by a frown. His tone of voice had become impatient. "I need an equipment approval."

The Director didn't glance up at him as he responded. "You have a fourth member on your team?"

Fifty-Seven

Hell's Team

Fallen's lips were consumed by a full frown. "I don't need your permission to collect more members for my team."

The Director's eyebrows lowered slightly looking up at Fallen. "If it wasn't for me Lucifer, you wouldn't even be here."

Fallen wasn't shy in releasing a disbelieving scoff. "My creation was inevitable. Just like my counterparts is."

The Director couldn't help but to chuckle. "Arrogance isn't a sin but it really should be." The Director glanced back at the report. "Sinah Harmond. Harmond? That name isn't familiar. I assume with a name like Sinah, she's a woman."

Fallen turned his head before giving a slight nod. The Director nodded himself before he chuckled. "You're definitely different from your predecessor that I've read so much about. In ancient times-"

"It doesn't matter what Lucifer was in the past. I am what I am now." Fallen sent a full frown toward the Director. "Now I need an equip-"

"And you'll get it. But first I want to know why you choose a woman to join your team."

"Gender had nothing to do with it."

The Director tapped the air in front of himself. Once many green screens appeared, he began accessing the Helix files. Fallen's eyebrows lowered watching him. "Her scores in Combat were too impressive to ignore."

The Director switched his search over to the Combat files. As he began to check the past top scores, he noticed Sinah's name appear as Kid. "Kid Harmond? Is this the same person?"

Fallen gave a slight nod. The Director shrugged looking at her ever increasing scores. "That is impressive but there are other Helixes more-"

"The people I want for my team is my choice. As long as we complete our missions with minimal damage, what does it matter who I choose?"

The Director glanced toward Fallen as he lowered his hands from the screens. Once they vanished he spoke. "I suppose you're right. As long as we don't lose too many Helixes it shouldn't matter. I don't care how it gets done as long as it gets done."

Fallen's lips were consumed by a full frown as he nodded. "Then stop wasting time and leave my team to me."

The Director tapped the air in front of himself again and began to access the equipment approval release forms. "Tell me, what type of Helix is she?"

Fallen wasn't hesitant in his response. "A."

The Director shook his head releasing a laugh. "Another disposable A Helix, Lucifer? Surrounding yourself with Helixes that will only obey you as long as God isn't created is quite risky. The minute he breathes life, all of them will abandon you."

Fallen's tone of voice suddenly turned colder than ice. "And that will be just fine."

The Director glanced up at Fallen but remained silent.

Fifty-Eight

The Shooting Range

Bridger couldn't help but to cheer every time Sinah hit her target. Any other regular or Helix soldier standing near her tried their best to out shoot her. Unfortunately for them, all of Sinah's shots were dead on target and dead perfect.

Murdoch walked onto the shooting range with a pile of clothes in his hands. As he walked by the other training soldiers, he could clearly hear their annoyance with her. Once he stepped beside Bridger, he spoke. "Is she any good?"

Bridger smirked glancing toward him. "She's killing everyone here. It's no wonder she got the top Combat score. She could probably even whip our old ones."

Murdoch handed him the clothes. "Yeah well, you might want to get her out of here soon. The last thing we need is a bunch of pissed off soldiers."

Bridger couldn't help but to chuckle. "Who cares about them? We're the Commander's team. We're supposed to be amazing."

Murdoch glanced toward the annoyed soldiers then Sinah. "Yeah but I don't think she'd want everyone hating her for it."

Bridger looked toward them himself. Seeing their dispositions, he nodded. "You're probably right. Sinah!"

Sinah's eyes darted back to him. Bridger gave an upward nod. "Come on let's get you out of those 'Kid' clothes."

Sinah looked down at herself with a look of confusion. As Bridger began to walk toward an unnoticeable door near the last shooting point, he called back. "Thanks Murdoch!"

Murdoch didn't respond as he turned heel and left the shooting range. Bridger glanced toward Sinah as he opened the door slightly. "Okay take these and change in here."

Sinah looked down at the clothes he was offering her then toward the open door. Bridger smiled opening the door wider. Inside the small room was a set of bunk beds and a dresser. Upon the walls were various types of pictures. The severely differing content suggested this room was shared by two people with very different tastes. Bridger gave an upward nod. "It's not much but it has its uses."

Sinah's eyes darted to Bridger as she pointed at him then into the room. Bridger smiled handing her the clothes. "Murdoch and I share this space. Now hurry up and change."

Sinah quickly nodded. As she passed by Bridger, he chuckled. "Then I'll show you the Commander's office."

Sinah instantly smiled nodding again. Bridger couldn't help but to smile as she closed the door behind herself.

Fifty-Nine

From Kid to Sinah

Bridger, who was leaning against the wall near the room, stood up straight hearing the door open. Sinah nervously stepped out of Bridger and Murdoch's room. Not only did Bridger's but all the other male soldier's eyes dart toward her. Sinah looked like she was in her battle suit. Except Murdoch had made Sinah's black shirt a cold shoulder with a medium sized key hole on her chest. The key hole exposed a small amount of her cleavage. Her red scarf rested attractively down her back as did her hair she had taken from its ponytail. Thanks to this outfit, Sinah looked more like a proper young woman rather than a mere child.

Bridger gave Sinah a smile and a nod. "You look much better."

Sinah nervously looked down at herself then shrugged. Bridger chuckled at her nerves. "Trust me you definitely look like Sinah, one of the Commander's team."

Sinah blindly motioned her hand behind herself toward the room. Bridger gave her a confused look until she pinched her shirt then waved again. Bridger shook his head. "Forget about your old clothes. That's your old self. This is the new you. Come on. Let's go see the Commander's office."

Sinah nodded in excitement as a full smile took her lips. As they passed by the other soldiers, Bridger noticed them all staring at her. Bridger instantly shot them a slight frown. "Don't shoot yourselves in the foot!"

Hearing that, all the soldiers looked down at their guns in confusion.

Bridger followed Sinah out of the shooting range. As he passed by Murdoch, he spoke. "Leave it to a D Helix to try and make an A Helix look sexy."

Murdoch glanced back at Bridger then over to Sinah. After giving her outfit a quick once over, he questioned. "What are you talking about?"

Bridger approached Sinah and pointed at the medium sized key hole. "I didn't say anything about this."

Murdoch indifferently shrugged then loudly yawned. "I really wasn't paying too much attention when I cut it. I guess I cut the wrong spot. I told you I'm not a seamstress."

Bridger chuckled shaking his head. "And Dante calls me lazy."

Murdoch's eyes instantly darted then sharpened toward him. "What did you say?"

Bridger smiled defensively lifting his hands. "Nothing mean Helix, I swear. We were just leaving."

Sinah smiled and nodded toward Murdoch. Bridger, who noticed smiled himself. "I think Sinah says thanks for the shirt." Sinah nodded until Bridger continued. "Even though, it's a tad too sexy for a sweet little A Helix like me. But you did your best. …I guess."

Sinah quickly shook her head. Murdoch gave Bridger a slight frown. "Yeah, fine. Bridger if you're not going to do any work, Get the hell out of here!"

Bridger snatched Sinah's hand as he mockingly saluted him with the other. "Yes sir mean Helix sir!"

Murdoch only frowned even more as Bridger pulled Sinah out the room. The minute the door slammed shut, Murdoch released a sigh full of annoyance. "I guess I better make another shirt for her."

Sixty

Sneaking Around

Bridger knocked on Fallen's office door as he glanced up and down the hallway. There wasn't a single person wandering around the 10th floor in building 6. Bridger knocked again slightly louder as he called out. "Commander? Are you in there?"

The only response he got was silence. Bridger clapped his hands together like an excited child. "Alright! I finally get to try Dante's trick!"

Sinah looked toward Bridger with a questioning expression. Bridger lifted his index finger into the air. "Okay. Step 1: Check to see if the door is actually locked." Bridger grabbed the door knob and tried to turn it. He smiled feeling the locks resistance. "Okay it's locked. Step 2: Check to see if the lights are on in the room."

Sinah watched Bridger flop to the ground and peek under the door. The only light illuminating Fallen's office was the dim blue light from the windows. Bridger leapt back onto to his feet. "Okay lights are off. Step 3: Distract computer by asking for a security sweep of the building." Bridger glanced back at Sinah. "That will lower the security on all the floors except the top. That's the Director's floor."

Sinah barely nodded with a look that suggested she was really curious about what Bridger was trying to do. Bridger called out. "Computer, run a security sweep on building 6 please."

The computer beeped a response. "Commencing sweep. Floor 1 in progress…"

Bridger smirked. "And now the fun part, Step 4: Bust the lock." The second Bridger was finished his sentence, he grabbed the doorknob. With a quick yet aggressive jerk, the lock broke open. Bridger quickly opened the door then gave an upward nod inside. "Get in! Hurry!"

Sinah quickly raced into the office. Bridger followed close after then closed the door behind them. Bridger smiled slightly. "Step 5: Stop security sweep and act like it was a minor problem."

Sinah walked toward the ceiling to floor windows as Bridger called out. "Computer, there was a stupid accident on floor 10. Please restore lights to the Commander's office. Also repair broken door lock."

The computer beeped a few times. Sinah didn't shift her attention to Fallen's desk as the lamp flicked on. Bridger smiled proudly hearing the lock re-secure the room. "Dante says about 2 out of 3 times this works. If it doesn't it's because of higher security codes, whatever that means. But... hey! It worked, we made it in!"

Sinah looked up at the eclipsed sun and moon. Bridger held his beaming pride as he approached her. "The good thing is, Dante says the computer actually covers your tracks for you. He said the system will reset itself if someone opens the door. The lights will turn off then-"

The desk lamp suddenly flicked off. Bridger instantly went flush. "Uh-oh."

The door opened and the lamp flicked back on. Once Fallen walked into his office, his attention instantly darted to Sinah and Bridger. Bridger awkwardly finished his thought. "Turn back on when someone opens the door."

Fallen's lips were instantly consumed by a full frown. "What are you two doing in here?"

Sixty-One

Busted

Bridger awkwardly chuckled as he defensively lifted his hands. "Uh… Hi Commander. We… We were just-"

Fallen's full frown didn't decrease. "Any particular reason you wanted to break into my office?"

Bridger glanced toward Sinah. Her attention was still skyward. "Well… uh… I just wanted to show Sinah where your office was. I'd hate for you to call a meeting and for her not to know where she needs to go."

Fallen shifted his attention toward Sinah. "That doesn't explain why you broke in."

Bridger tried his best to hide his awkward expression with a pleasant smile. "W… Well no, it doesn't. But…"

Fallen approached his desk and sat down. As he began accessing the green screens, he spoke. "A memo will be sent out the minute I'm finished writing it. Tonight we have a volunteer mission."

Bridger's tone and disposition instantly shifted to serious. "Has something happened Commander?"

"It was discovered last night, that there is a Lost Souls Lab." Fallen quickly began to write out the mission itinerary. "They're only creating synthetics. This has to be dealt with as soon as possible."

Bridger was quick to nod in agreement. "Synthetics are dangerous, especially in the wrong hands. I can't think of hands any more dangerous than the Lost Souls. They've got nothing to lose."

"Unfortunately we don't have time to prepare."

Bridger couldn't help but to respond with a chuckle. "For volunteer missions we never have time to prepare Commander. That's what makes them so much fun."

"We don't know how far the Lost Souls have evolved the synthetics. This could very well be one of our more dangerous missions."

Bridger made a loud dismissive sound. "Pssha!! We can handle anything Commander."

Bridger watched Fallen work on the itinerary for few seconds before he spoke. "Don't bother sending me a memo Commander. I'm with you and I'm positive Murdoch is too."

Fallen lowered his hands from the green screen slightly. "And Dante?"

Bridger smiled almost instantly. "We never refuse to follow you into any mission Commander. I'm sure he won't have any problem following you either."

Fallen leaned back on his chair and turned his attention to Sinah. "And you, Sinah? Will you be joining us on this mission?"

Bridger was quick to answer for her. "She'll probably have to ask her parents first."

Fallen shifted his silver eyes toward Bridger from out the side of his sunglasses. "That will be all Bridger."

"Oh! Okay Commander. Come on Sinah, I'll walk you h-"

"I'll walk her home."

Bridger couldn't help but to smile. "Yes Commander."

Fallen removed the map he got from Richard from his pocket. "Take this to Dante. Tell him it's called a subway or something. Apparently it's underground."

Bridger gave Fallen a look of bewilderment as he approached and picked up the map. "Underground? Okay."

"Also tell Dante if he isn't joining us on this mission, I need to know right away."

"Yes Commander. Although, I don't think he's going to say no."

Fallen shifted his attention back to Sinah. "That will be all Bridger."

Bridger gave a quick 'Yes Commander' then approached the exit. As he opened the office door, he glanced back at Fallen. He had stood up and approached Sinah. Bridger couldn't help but to smile as he left closing the door behind him.

Sixty-Two

In The Dim Blue Light

Fallen stood silently beside Sinah as they both stared up at the eclipsed sun and moon. After a few very long moments, Fallen finally spoke. "I often stare up at the sky and wonder what it was like before the fall? This is the only sky I've ever known. Would I even want to know a different one?"

Sinah looked toward Fallen and shrugged. Seeing her out of the corner of his eye, he continued. "This is the only sky most of us have ever known. Only the Director has-"

Fallen stopped short noticing Sinah's outfit. Sinah gave him a slightly confused look. Once Fallen saw her expression, he quickly shifted his attention back out the window. "You look breath taking. I'm sorry I didn't notice it sooner."

Sinah smiled as much as she could toward Fallen. She opened her arms widely and did a spin, showing him the outfit in its entirety. Watching her out the corner of his eyes, Fallen allowed his lips to reveal a slight smile. "Even though it isn't in my place to say anything..." Fallen turned his head toward her as he finished his sentence. "This look suits you far better than the sweat shirts you are always in."

Sinah placed her hand on the side of Fallen's arm. Her full smile didn't wavier in the slightest as she nodded. Fallen reached his hand out and gently moved a few strands of hair from her face. "...You're welcome."

As he drew his hand back, her smile softened a little. She then removed her hand and turned her attention back out the window. Fallen studied the side of her face for a few moments before he released a slight sigh. Sinah's eyes darted back to him.

Fallen turned from the window and crossed his arms. As he leaned his back against the glass, he spoke. "Sinah, will you be joining us on our volunteer mission?"

Sinah nodded with a smile then suddenly stopped. Her smile vanished as she weakly shrugged. Fallen gave a slight nod. "Bridger mentioned you needed to have your parent's approval first."

Sinah lowered her head as if her feelings had been hurt. Fallen turned his attention to his closed office door as he stood up straight. "So let's go get it."

Sinah's head shot up and to Fallen as he began to walk toward the exit. "You are a member of my team. Your skills are needed." As Fallen opened his office door, he continued. "And even if they weren't, I want… No, I need you with us."

Sinah smiled slightly as Fallen glanced back at her. "…I need you with me."

Sixty-Three

Permission Denied

Amos stood just outside of the Combat area. His expression was a combination of awkward and shock. Fallen's lips touched at a frown. "As you already know a volunteer mission isn't mandatory."

Amos barely nodding looked toward Sinah. She had pleading look on her face. "K… S… Sinah, are you sure this is what you really want to do?" Seeing her almost instant nod, Amos sighed loudly. "You'll have to get your mother's okay."

Sinah nodded as did Fallen. "What Lab does she work in? We'll deal with this right now."

"A… actually, she's at home. After our lunchtime conversation, she was too upset to go back to work."

Sinah's expression instantly weakened. Before Amos could say anything else, Fallen turned from them and began to walk away. "Let's go then."

Amos frantically opened the door to Combat and yelled out. "Uh… Lu! Cover for me!!" Without getting a response, he chased after Sinah who had followed after Fallen.

Amos and Sinah trailed just slightly behind Fallen walking through the grassy field leading to the Residential area. Amos couldn't stop himself from sighing. "Your mother is having a hard time excepting our Kid as Sinah."

Sinah barely nodded. Amos awkwardly motioned his hand toward her outfit. "I don't think she's going to be too happy about seeing you dressed like this either."

Fallen frowned almost instantly hearing him. Amos glanced up at the artificial sky. It was a decent midday sky with minimal cloud coverage. "I really should have grabbed my jacket." Even though Sinah shook her head, Amos only sighed louder. "This isn't going to go well."

Sinah's features weakened to a sad disappointment. Fallen, who had stopped just outside the Harmond home gate, noticed her expression. Fallen reached out and softly placed his hand on her shoulder. Both Sinah and Amos' eyes darted toward him as he spoke. "I need you with us, Sinah."

Sinah smiled confidently, shaking off any and all doubt she had. Amos' expression instantly shifted to awkward as Fallen hesitantly removed his hand from her. "...Oh boy, this is going to be more than a mess." Amos opened the gate to their home. "Come on Sinah, let's get this over with."

Sinah nodded racing through the gates toward her house. Fallen, waited for Amos to the pass the gate before he followed after. Sinah smiled busting into the house. Violet, who was sitting on the couch, looked toward her in surprise. "Kid?! What-"

Violet's sentence was cut short as Amos and Fallen entered her home. Violet wasn't shy about tossing a frown in Fallen's direction. "Whatever you want the answer's no!"

Fallen returned her frown with one of his own. "She isn't a child. This should be her decision."

Violet shook her head approaching Sinah. "She is our child and-" Violet stopped short looking at Sinah's outfit. "What are these? Where is your sweat shirt?"

Sinah motioned her hand toward her outfit with a pleased expression. Violet quickly shook her head. "Kid, these type of clothes aren't for-"

Fallen suddenly cut her off with a hiss. "Her name is Sinah!"

Violet responded back with her own hiss. "What makes you think you have the right to re-name our daughter?!"

"Sinah herself gave me that right!"

Violet's eyes darted to the smiling and nodding Sinah. Violet shook her head in disapproval. "Kid, this isn't okay. I know you think you're ready for-"

"I don't have time for this parental nonsense. I want Sinah to join our volunteer mission tonight."

Violet hissed toward Fallen. "Well I don't care what you want! She's not going anywhere!"

Sinah quickly shook her head clasping her hands together in a pleading manner. Violet spoke in a forceful parental tone as she looked back at Sinah. "No Kid! Go to your room and get out of those clothes! We'll return them tomorrow and be done with this."

Sinah frantically shook her head. Her expression looked like she was begging. Fallen's lips were consumed by a full frown. "Sinah, will-"

Violet hissed toward him cutting him off. "Volunteer means choice! And she chooses not to go!"

Sinah squeezed her eyes forcefully shut as she continued to plead. Violet looked back at Sinah with a slight frown. "That's enough Kid! Go to your room!"

Sinah stopped shaking her head as she unclasped her hands. She frowned as much as she could toward Violet before she stomped down the hallway to her room.

Sixty-Four

Threats and Truths

Violet frowned turning her attention back to Fallen. "You're turning our daughter against us!"

Fallen's lips touched at a smirk. "Is that how you see it? It looks more like you're turning her against you, yourselves."

"You have no idea what's best for her! Stay the hell away from our daughter!"

Fallen's expression suddenly shifted to ice cold. Amos stepped back a little feeling the overwhelming air of intimidation. Fallen's tone mirrored his expression. "And if I don't?"

A few nervous sweat beads formed on Violet's forehead as she fumbled over her words. "She… she shouldn't… she…"

"Whether you want it to be true or not, Sinah is now a part of my team. You may have the choice to let her go on volunteer missions, but not on Lab ones. She and I will always be a part of one another's life. So go ahead and keep her trapped in this 'Kid' prison all you want." Fallen's eyebrows suddenly lowered as much as they could. Even though his whole demeanor just screamed hostility and danger, his tone remained calm. "Even if I have to claw her out myself, she will be free of it."

Violet's voice shook, any anger or confidence she once had, was now replaced with fear. "G… get out of m… my house."

Fallen wasn't hesitant to turn heel and leave. Nor was he shy about slamming the door behind himself. Violet looked at her trembling hands. "Oh my god, Amos I'm shaking."

Amos quickly approached his wife. He began to rub her upper arms in an attempt to calm her down. "You just yelled at the devil. I'd be shaking too."

Violet closed her eyes as she released a defeated sigh. "I wish he'd just leave her alone."

Amos was silent as he weakly nodded.

The force Fallen used to slam the gate closed caused the hinges to snap. As he stomped passed the broken gate then Harmond home, he heard odd clicking in his ear piece. Fallen stopped short glancing around the mostly empty Residential area. As his attention shifted back to the Harmond home, he noticed Sinah. She was half flopped on the ground tapping her ear piece. Fallen's eyebrows furrowed in confusion approaching her.

Sinah had climbed out her bedroom window. As she was making her escape, her window slammed shut on her ankle, which in turn caused her to fall face first onto the ground. Fallen's look of confusion didn't fade as he spoke. "Sinah?"

Sinah tried her best to look up at him, lowering her hand from her earpiece. Fallen opened the window setting her free. Sinah sat up and began to rub her ankle. Fallen watched her for a few moments before he spoke again. "Your mother was quite vocal on her refusal to let you go."

Sinah quickly nodded as she stood up. She smiled up at Fallen placing her hand on her chest. Fallen gave a slight nod. "But you still want to go?"

Sinah held her smile and nodded again. Fallen turned his attention to the closed window. "I feel like I should question your need to openly defy your parents. And yet, I-"

Sinah cut Fallen off placing her hand over his mouth. Once Fallen turned his attention back to her, she smiled softly lowering it. Fallen gave another slight nod. "Then let's go."

Sinah snatched Fallen's hand and nodded in excitement. A slight smile took Fallen's lips as she tightened her grip and pulled him away from the Residential area.

Sixty-Five

Quick Prep

Bridger placed the final metal case down beside the lone hummer. As he stood up, he glanced toward Murdoch. He was double checking all the Combat gloves. Dante, who was sitting on one of the cases hissed in frustration. "I hate these stupid volunteer missions! I feel so unprepared!"

Bridger chuckled stretching his arms up to the dim blue sky. "Are you kidding me? I love these missions. You have to think on your feet and-"

Dante rapidly clicked on his laptop. "That's all fine and well for fighting. For me, getting maps, codes, passwords and releasing all sorts of locks really fast is a pain. It can take a while, which leaves us at a constant disadvantage. Not to mention the pressure the Commander puts on you."

Once Dante was in reaching range, Bridger gave his arm a nudge with a snicker. "You can handle it Data, Surveillance and whatever soldier."

Dante hissed but didn't lift his attention from his laptop. "Whatever soldier?! I'm a-"

Murdoch cut Dante off standing like a soldier awaiting a command. "Shut it both of you! the Commander's here."

Bridger looked toward one of the large hangers. He couldn't help but to smile seeing Sinah and Fallen walking hand in hand. Once in ear shot, he questioned. "Sinah, your parents actually said you can go?"

Sinah let Fallen's hand go as her expression shifted to slightly awkward.

Fallen watched her give a slight shrug before he spoke. "We'll be leaving much earlier than expected. Sinah will be put on the missing person's report very shortly."

Dante's eyes darted toward her. "You ran away from home?"

Before Sinah had a chance to have a reaction of any kind, Fallen responded. "She did what any of you would have. She stayed with our team."

Bridger couldn't help but smile seeing her smiling up at Fallen. "Well let's get you suited up and ready to go."

Sinah's expression saddened a little looking down at her shirt. Fallen, who noticed shifted his attention to Murdoch. "How long will it take to alter her battle suit to look like her current outfit?"

Sinah's disposition instantly became happy as Murdoch answered. "5 minutes max, Commander."

Fallen motioned his hand toward one of the Launch Pad area Techs. "Make it happen."

Murdoch picked up Sinah's battle suit from one of the metal cases. "Yes Commander."

As the Launch Pad Tech approached Fallen, his expression shifted to confusion as a mechanic raced passed him over to Dante. Fallen's lips touched at a frown noticing the Tech's empty hands. "Have orders been sent down from the Director?"

The Launch Pad area Tech quickly nodded. "Yes Commander. We just need a few of your signatures then you're good to go."

Fallen barely nodded so did the Tech. After a split second of silence, Fallen snapped. "Get the forms!"

The Tech instantly jumped then ran to get the paperwork. "Oh! Yes Commander!"

The mechanic that had run passed them was Alex. He nervously glanced around as he whispered. "So, I've left three messages with your mom. Did you get any of them?"

Dante nodded but didn't glance up from working on his laptop. "Yeah, sorry about that. I was going to get back to you but then this mission came up."

"I understand. But when you get some free time, you really need to check out what you recorded."

Dante's eyes darted up to Alex. "Something's there, isn't it?"

"It took a long time to clean it up and restore the image, but..."

Dante looked toward Sinah. She was trying her best to help Bridger load the hummer. Not being as strong as him, she basically just dragged the metal cases over to him to load. "But there was definitely something there."

Alex nodded looking toward her, himself. "It was hard to slow down but I managed it. You really need to see it for yourself."

"The minute I get back from this mission."

Alex barely nodded as Dante went back to work. "It doesn't matter what time you make it back Sir. This is far too important to wait on."

Dante looked back at Sinah as Alex ran back toward one of the large hangers. "I wonder what I saw." Dante shook his head returning his attention to his laptop. "I can't think about this right now. I've got to focus."

Sixty-Six

To the Underground

Bridger chuckled looking at Sinah in her battle suit. It looked exactly like the outfit she had on before. "Be careful A Helix, looking too sexy isn't proper for us."

Sinah shook her head pointing at Bridger. Bridger smiled standing up tall and statuesque. "Well of course I look sexy. I always look sexy."

Dante frowned opening the hummer door to the back seat. "I think she meant, that's just your opinion."

Sinah quickly nodded toward Dante. Bridger snatched his arm around Sinah's shoulders. She couldn't help but to smile as he cooed. "Admit it, you think I look sexy."

As Bridger glanced toward the hummer, he caught the glare tossed at him by Fallen. Bridger quickly removed his arm then spoke in a forced serious tone. "Alright everyone, pile in so we can get out of here."

Murdoch snickered getting into the passenger's seat. "Oh yeah, that sounded real forceful."

Bridger stuck his tongue out at Murdoch's sarcasm before he climbed into the back seat himself. The minute Fallen was in the driver's seat and everyone was buckled up, Dante spoke. "Okay Commander, you're heading east."

Fallen wasn't hesitant to turn on the engine and gun out of the Launch Pad area. Dante opened his laptop and began to click away. "I've tapped into the Lost Soul's city surveillance. It's been functioning for I don't know how long. There are many accesses to the underground in block based intervals. I suggest we take a more hidden route."

Murdoch glanced back at Dante. "Giving us the surprise advantage."

"That and since the passages are so openly available. I'm not sure if they're even useable. Who knows what the Lost Souls could've done. Is that alright Commander?"

"Fine. As per all volunteer missions, be prepared for anything."

All three men nodded. Sinah on the other hand, merely kept her attention out the window. Fallen glanced up at her through the rear view mirror. "Sinah?"

Sinah looked up at his reflection. Fallen gave a slight nod. Sinah smiled nodding in return. Bridger, who was watching him couldn't help but to smile. Dante frantically clicked on his laptop. "Okay, there's a hidden route in a place known as an amphitheatre."

Not understanding what Dante had said, Bridger questioned. "A what? I've never even heard that word before."

Dante flipped over to another file. "Uh... Amphitheater: Oval or circular unroofed building with tiers of seats surrounding central space for spectators. Apparently there's an underground access path just under the stage."

Murdoch lips touched at a frown. "Tiered seats for spectators means, a very large space. We need to be very cautious."

Bridger nodded in agreement. "It sounds like we'll also have to ditch the hummer quite a ways from destination point."

Murdoch watched the wreckage of the world whisk by his window. "Do you have any trap equipment?"

Bridger responded with a childish giggle. "But of course! I always have some of that. Don't worry, our way back will be nice and protected."

Fallen momentarily shifted his attention to the side view mirror. "A place like that also sounds like a perfect meeting point for Lost Souls to gather. It looks like we'll have to wander directly into their world."

Bridger hooked his arm over Dante's shoulders. "That's alright Commander. When they see our tough little A Helix here, they'll run for the hills."

Dante frowned toward Bridger. "Or they'll see your face and-"

Bridger cooed rattling Dante a little. "Fall madly in love."

Murdoch couldn't help but to chuckle. "Shut it both of you."

Bridger smiled. "Yes mean Helix."

Fallen shifted his attention to each mirror before looking back to the road ahead. "Let's just be on our guard."

Sixty-Seven

The Amphitheatre Grounds

Bridger smiled proudly hooking the final wire to the hummer. "That should do it."

Murdoch glanced toward the intercut wire work and hidden activation points. "How high is the voltage?"

Bridger snickered turning all the activation points on. "It won't kill anyone if that's what you're asking. Just stun them."

"Stun them enough to keep them away from our way back?"

Bridger chuckled with a shrug. "Well, we'll probably have to step over a few on conscious Lost Souls but, yeah our ride will be safe."

Dante sighed closing his laptop. "There's more than a hundred active life signs near our entrance point." He continued as he put his laptop into his backpack. "Even if we wanted to, we can't avoid them."

Fallen glanced around the destroyed parking lot. Cars, trucks and so on had long been stripped down and torn apart. "Unless given a reason, we won't waste our time bothering with them. The Lab is our mission, not wiping out the Lost Souls. Let's go."

Everyone nodded and followed after Fallen. As Bridger passed, Dante spoke. "Should I have my gun ready?"

Bridger shook his head stepping over some cement rubble. "No, if we look like we're going to attack, the Lost Souls might panic."

Murdoch, who was walking beside Dante, nodded. "Bridger's right. If we go in unarmed, they might just ignore us."

Fallen shifted his attention up toward a shell shaped dome in the slight distance. "Dante, is that our destination?"

Dante's eyes darted to Fallen then where he was looking. Seeing the dome himself, he nodded. "Yes Commander, the stage should just be under that."

Fallen didn't show any sign of caution as he jumped the turnstile onto the amphitheatre grounds. He glanced back at Sinah as she did the same. Murdoch was quick to follow after them. Dante shook his head pointing at the passage bars. "You know, you can just walk through there."

Bridger placed his hand on the bar and tried to push them. They were locked into place. Bridger chuckled, glancing back at Dante. "Looks like you'll have to hop it too. Just as well, I'm sure this thing would have made some sort of noise that would tell the Lost Souls we're here."

Dante's lips touched at a frown. "Instead of all this talking you're doing?"

Bridger kneeled down beside the turnstile and cupped his hands by his knee. "Alright Data, Surveillance and whatever soldier, up you go!"

Dante instantly began to fume. "I'm not a whatever soldier and I can do it myself! I don't need your help!!"

Bridger stood up while defensively lifting his hands. "Alright tough guy, have it your way."

Dante frowned as much as he could as he stomped toward the turnstile. He placed his hand on the bar and tried to push it. It was locked in place.

Bridger crossed his arms. "It's locked."

Dante tossed Bridger a glare. "I know that!"

"Just saying."

Dante tried his best to climb over. Every few seconds, he would either slip or almost fall off completely. Fallen, who had stopped walking a few feet from them called out. "Pick up the pace! I want this dealt with today!"

Dante went flush almost falling off it again. "Uh… y… yes Commander!"

Bridger chuckled watching him struggle. "You know there's an easier way."

Dante snorted loudly. It was a sound very unbecoming of an A Helix. "I don't need your help!"

Bridger uncrossed his arms and released an exasperated sigh. "Okay fine. You want to move out of my way then? I don't want to keep the Commander waiting."

Dante frowned stepping a few feet back. Bridger smiled approaching it. He spoke turning completely toward him. "Thank you."

Even though Bridger could easily hop the turnstile like everyone else, he just hooked his butt on the edge. Dante gave him a questioning look until he swung his legs over the bars. Dante barely nodded watching him easily shift himself through the entrance. Once Bridger hopped off, he glanced back at Dante. "Want me to wait for you?"

Dante quickly shook his head. "No, that's okay."

Bridger gave a slight nod before he walked toward Murdoch. Once he reached him, he spoke. "Is he doing it my way?"

Murdoch looked toward Dante. He was entering the amphitheatre grounds the exact same why Bridger had. "You know he is."

Bridger smirked. "Now do I rub it in? Or do-"

Bridger was suddenly cut off by a booming loud male voice. "Brothers and Sisters today is the day of Judgement!!"

These words were greeted by many excitable loud cheers.

Sixty-Eight

Offerings

Bridger's eyes darted to the shell shaped dome. "Is that coming from there? It sounds like our Lab's announcement system."

Dante, who was walking toward them spoke. "That makes sense. I figure whoever's on the stage would want even the furthest person back to hear them. I guess they kept their announcement system up and running."

The male voice boomed again. "The fall of Heaven and Hell meant nothing to us!!"

Again, those words were greeted by cheers. Fallen's lips touched at a frown. "Let's find out just what's going on."

Both Murdoch and Sinah nodded. As they moved in the direction the voice was coming from, Dante quickly shook his head. "Wait a minute Commander."

"What is it?"

Dante unhooked his backpack from his back to retrieve his laptop. "I just want to check something."

Before Fallen had a chance to respond, the male voice boomed again. "Without God, we are free!! Free to control our own destinies!!"

Fallen frowned even more, hearing the responding cheers. "And just look at what you have done with your destinies."

Dante glanced up from his laptop. "Commander, there seems to be a side entrance. It's really close to the stage. Uh… Apparently it's a standing room area for concerts."

Bridger scratched his head not understanding. "What's a concert?"

Dante shrugged flipping over to another file. "It says here its musical entertainment by usually several performers, combination of voices or sounds working together. There were a lot of them here before the fall."

The male voice boomed again. "And with this freedom we are the Gods!!"

Many happy cheers instantly followed. Fallen clinched his fists with a full frown. "Where's this side entrance?"

Dante quickly flipped back to his original file. "It's on this path Commander. If we keep heading this way we'll see signs for section A. That's the area we're looking f-"

"Then let's move out."

Before anyone could respond, Fallen raced down the path. Without even blinking, both Sinah and Murdoch gave chase. Dante hastily stuffed his laptop back into his backpack. Bridger smiled watching him. "There's no need to panic Dante. The Commander will reach a certain point then wait on us."

Dante spoke hooking his backpack over his shoulders. "Then he'll get ticked off he had to wait on us. I don't want to be a weakness on the team."

Bridger quickly shook his head as Dante ran passed him. "But you're not!"

Dante ran as fast as he could in the direction the others had gone. Bridger effortlessly caught up then jogged alongside him. He snickered a little seeing Dante put all his effort into running. "I think you're out of shape Info, Surveillance and whatever soldier."

Dante panted out of breath as he hissed. "Sh- Shut up!"

Bridger snickered again until he looked ahead of himself. Fallen and the others were standing cautiously near an entrance leading sideways. The male voice boomed again. This time his voice sounded only a few feet away. "And those who dare to enter a God's world will be punished!!"

The crowd cheered loudly. Only this time their cheers could clearly be heard. "That's right!"

"Burn them all!"

"Kill them!!"

Once Dante and Bridger reached the others, Dante spoke through gasps. "I… In here, w… we should see the side… of… of…"

Fallen lifted his hand cutting him off. "Is everyone ready?"

Everyone, even the gasping for dear life Dante, nodded. Even though the entrance ran along the side of the stage, Fallen didn't have to step too far in to see it clearly. His eyes darted to two severely injured people lying in front of five armed men. The man in the middle was holding a microphone and a shot gun.

Murdoch, who had stepped beside Fallen, glanced toward the audience. The Lost Souls had managed to make this area into a makeshift town. Some of the original seats were still in there designated spots but most had been ripped out to provide more space. Every single Lost Soul had their eyes locked on the stage. Their focus was so held on the man with the microphone, they didn't notice Fallen or his soldiers.

Bridger whispered trying to look beyond them. "What's going on?"

Sinah moved closer to Fallen so that she could see the Lost Souls 'shanty' town. The man with the microphone spoke. "Today we spill the blood of those who dared to step into our world! Today we cast Judgement upon them!"

The excited crowd instantly cheered as loud as they could. "Rip their hearts out!"

"Slaughter them!"

"Cut their heads off!"

Bridger awkwardly glanced toward Dante. "Well… They're a lot more savage than I thought."

Sinah glanced toward the stage. The minute her eyes caught sight of the two wounded people, she gasped and tried to get passed Fallen and Murdoch. Fallen shifted his attention back to her. "Sinah, what's..?"

Sinah cut him off pointing toward the stage with a panicked expression. Murdoch glanced toward her then to the two wounded people. One was a woman. She was wearing shreds of a bloody lab coat and looked like she had been repetitively beaten. The other was a man. He barely moved and looked like one of his eyes had been gouged out. "It looks like a couple of Lab Techs. They're not ours are they?"

Dante shook his head answering. "I don't think so. We haven't had any reports of any missing Techs and our next trip into the world of the Lost Souls is…"

Dante stopped short seeing Sinah try to get around Fallen. Fallen shook his head, turning to her and placing his hands on her shoulders. "Sinah, they're not from our Lab. We don't have any reason to help them. We…"

Sinah frantically shook her head forcefully squeezing her eyes shut. Fallen watched her upset disposition for a few moments before he released an annoyed sigh. "Fine, I'll handle it."

Sixty-Nine

Unlikely Saviour

Everyone's eyes darted to Fallen. Murdoch was quick to question. "Are you serious Commander?"

Fallen frowned slightly looking down at Sinah. "I am. Now Sinah…"

Sinah stared up at him with a shocked yet somewhat apologetic expression.

"I will handle it. Stay here with the others."

Sinah barely nodded as Fallen lifted his hands from her shoulders. As he turned and began to walk toward the stage, Sinah snatched his wrist. Fallen glanced back at her holding his frown. Sinah's features weakened as she looked toward the ground. Fallen's angry disposition faded a little as she slowly shook her head.

"They're blocking our passage to the underground anyway."

Sinah looked up at him but her expression didn't change. Fallen softly placed his free hand on the side of her face. "…It's alright."

The minute Sinah let his wrist go, Fallen left them. Bridger clasped his hands over his chest. "Ohhhh. Isn't it so sweet?"

Dante looked up at Bridger slightly baffled. "What is?"

Bridger's eyes glossed over in a misty lust. "It's like those books the women from our Lab giggle about. The ones we have in the Archives Lab. You know the ones where the guy is all buff and his shirts wide open or he's not wearing one. And the woman's in an elegant dress or about to take it off."

Dante went bright red in embarrassment. "Are you talking about romance novels?!"

"Yeah that's them." Bridger brought both hands to the side of his face and cooed. "Ah sooo romantic."

Murdoch snipped back at them. "Shut it or we'll be noticed."

Bridger couldn't help but to snicker. "Yes, mean Helix."

The man with the microphone motioned his shotgun toward the wounded man. "This one didn't even put up a fight! He fell the minute we..."

The woman forced herself to her knees cutting him off. "Bastards!! You flanked us!"

The microphone man flipped his shotgun upside down. Without hesitation, he cracked her in the mouth with the butt. The force was aggressive enough to slam her to the ground, breaking a few of her teeth, but not aggressive enough to break her jaw.

"Silence!" The microphone man hooked his shotgun over his shoulder like a soldier. "They come into our world and act like we're the enemies!"

The crowd instantly responded with 'boos and hisses.' The microphone man smirked. "It looks like this bitch has a lot more fight in her than we thought! Maybe a few more rounds of beat down will break her! Maybe blowing her head clean off her shoulders will-"

The wounded woman cut him off with a mutter. "B... bastards..."

The microphone man glanced back at his armed friends "It's time to end this!"

The four other men approached the two wounded Lab Techs. One had a machine gun and the other three had handguns. All four of them pointed their armed weapons down at their victims. The wounded man remained still while the wounded woman forced a defiant frown up at them.

The microphone man returned his attention to the audience. He raised his shotgun in triumph as he spoke. "Brothers and Sisters, tonight we end these intruders! Tonight they'll get our justice!"

The crowd exploded with wild excitement. They cheered and screamed as loud as they could, jumping up and down. The microphone man flipped his shotgun back down to the woman. "There's no point in begging for mercy. Without God your prayers won't be answered."

Suddenly four gunshot sounds were heard. The microphone man's eyes darted to each of his comrades as they flopped to the ground dead. All of them had a bullet hole clean through each of their skulls. The microphone man as well as everyone in the audience looked in the direction the shots came from.

Fallen stood on the stage a few feet away from them, smoke escaped his raised gun as a slight smirk took his lips. "God may not hear your prayers but Lucifer sure did."

Seventy

Utter Shock

The microphone man instantly went ghost white. He shook his head in disbelief stepping back from the dead and wounded. "N… no, there… there is no God or Satan! There is no Heaven or Hell! There's… there's…"

Fallen scoffed, cutting him off. "Why doesn't it surprise me that the Lost Souls think they're the ones who should cast judgement."

The microphone man kept backing up as he stumbled over his words. "The… there is no Heaven or Hell. There… there…"

The wounded woman stared up at Fallen in shock as he passed by her. Fallen gripped his gun a little as he spoke. "You're right there is no Heaven or Hell. Which makes me wonder, where will your worthless soul go?"

The microphone man yelled as loudly as he could into his microphone. His voice was full of panic and terror. "Brothers and Sisters, save your-!!!"

Fallen cut him off racing toward him. The minute he was in reaching range, Fallen effortlessly slammed his hand clean through the microphone man's chest. Blood shot from his mouth as his eyes widened. Fallen lips touched at a cold grin. "Nobody can save you."

Fallen held his grin ripping his hand out of the man's chest. Blood sprayed across the stage and against the two wounded Lab Techs. The microphone man's expression just screamed shock and agony. Both the microphone and shotgun fell from his hands as he dropped to the ground dead.

The second he did, the audience went into a full blown panic. They either ran for their shacks or tried to escape the area completely. Anyone who ran toward the side entrance screeched seeing Fallen's soldiers. Bridger watched the Lost Souls run about in a full fledge panic screaming in terror. "I guess without a leader, they're just lost sheep running around."

Murdoch frowned shaking his head. "He wasn't a leader. Just some mouth piece with a shotgun."

Fallen carelessly flicked the blood and guck from his hand and arm as he called out. "Dante!"

"Yes Commander!"

Fallen glanced toward Sinah, she had a slightly relieved look on her face. Seeing her expression, he released an annoyed sigh. "Deal with the wounded."

Dante gave a quick 'Yes Commander' then moved passed his fellow soldiers.

Bridger whispered toward Sinah as he watched Dante climb onto the stage. "Remember to thank the Commander Sinah. Acts of kindness are very hard for him."

Sinah, who had her eyes locked on Fallen quickly nodded. As she walked toward the stage, a Lost Soul yelled out. "S… stop right there!"

Everyone's including Fallen's eyes darted to the Lost Soul. She had picked up a hand gun that fell from one of the dead man's hands on the stage. She trembled shifting the gun from Fallen to Dante. "T… those traitors are ours!"

Seventy-One

Disbelief

Sinah's expression turned sympathetic as she approached the traumatized armed Lost Soul. The woman's eyes darted from Fallen to Dante. The minute she noticed Sinah in her peripheral vision, she quickly turned the gun toward her. The gun trembled in her hand as she spoke. "Stay bac-"

The Lost Soul didn't get a chance to finish her sentence before a bullet zipped straight through her brain. As she flopped to the ground dead, Sinah's eyes darted to Fallen. He had his gun raised and a full frown sprawled across his lips. "I don't have any mercy for the Lost Souls Sinah, not a drop."

Sinah barely nodded looking down at the dead woman. Bridger approached her with a slightly sympathetic expression. "Sinah, we better get on the stage before we get trampled."

Sinah responded with a weak nod. Bridger softly placed his hand on her shoulder. "Come on."

Sinah looked toward the freaking out Lost Souls. Bridger looked toward them himself as he spoke. "They made their choice. As A Helixes we can't help but to want to save them." Bridger removed his hand from her shoulder and turned toward the stage. He went a little flush seeing Fallen's full frown greet him. He glanced back at Sinah as he continued his thought. "But we'd be wasting our time. Those who don't want to be saved won't be. No matter what we say or do. Come on."

Sinah closed her eyes before she turned toward the stage.

Dante placed the last bandage on the wounded man's large thigh gash. The wounded woman's eyes never once left Fallen. "W… Why are you helping us? We're not from your Lab."

Dante looked at the wounded man's very pale face. His one eye stared back at Dante with an almost vacant expression. "I wouldn't be worrying about that right now. Just be happy you're alive."

"S… Satan saved us?"

Dante picked up the wounded man's wrist checking his pulse. It was much slower than normal. "Your friend here has lost a lot of blood. I don't know how long he's going to last."

The wounded woman closed her beginning to water eyes lowering her head. "They ripped us right off the supply truck. Those bastards just kept laughing. There was so many of them. It was a mob attack." A saddened laugh escaped her throat. "Thank god for small miracles."

"What do you mean?"

The wounded woman looked toward her Lab Tech partner. "They tried to rape us, both of us. With the reproductive system not working correctly, they couldn't. And when they couldn't, they beat on us more. They… They are the monsters. Even when a synthetic turns on us, they're nothing like these bastards. These monsters, these people, they are the reason we lost Heaven and Hell."

Dante looked at the woman in sympathy. "I'm sorry this happened."

The wounded woman weakly smiled looking back at Dante. "Thanks but we all know the risk for trying to help them." Her smile faded looking toward Fallen. "But I… I never thought it would be the Devil that would save us."

Fallen turned his attention to Dante. "Once they're fixed up, get them out of here."

Seventy-Two

Helping Hand

Dante removed his laptop from his back pack. "I'm going to send a S.O.S out to your Lab." As he clacked on the keys, he questioned. "Which Lab are you from?"

The wounded woman closed her eyes. "Uh… 3. It's quite a ways from here. I think anyway. We've had sacks over our heads and was dragged all over the place."

Dante reached down his shirt and removed his heart bomb. As he placed it on his laptop he barely nodded. "Okay. We need to get you two to the main road. My heart bomb will act as a tracker for your rescue team."

"Y… you're actually going to help us get out of here? B… but we were told the Lab with the Devil is a traitor Lab, the one that kills everyone for their samples."

Murdoch kneeled down to the wounded man. "We are."

The wounded woman's eyes darted up to Murdoch. "Th… Then why?"

Murdoch hooked the wounded man's arm over his shoulders then stood up with him. The wounded man could barely stand on his own feet. As Murdoch wrapped his arm around his waist, he spoke. "The Commander commands and we obey."

Dante handed the wounded woman the heart bomb. "Now don't fiddle with this. It's a bomb. One wrong move and…" Dante shrugged at the obvious result.

Bridger looked at the barely conscious wounded man. "Murdoch, need any help?"

Murdoch shook his head looking toward one of the dead men on the stage. "Give the girl the machine gun." As Bridger walked toward it, Murdoch turned his attention back to her. "Shoot anyone who comes close. He's pretty much dead weight and won't be able to help you."

The wounded woman barely nodded getting to her feet. Bridger smile handing her the machine gun. "Don't think about it just shoot."

Fallen shifted his attention to the almost completely empty area. Any Lost Soul that did stay tried their best to keep quiet in their shacks. "Get a move on Murdoch."

"Yes Commander."

The wounded woman looked nervously toward Fallen as she approached him. Fallen kept his attention on the audience area until she stepped in front of him. Once his attention shifted to her, she went flush feeling an air of intimidation. "I… I don't know why you saved us but…thank you Satan."

Fallen turned his head toward Sinah. She was watching the last remaining Lost Souls running around disorientated. "It was her sympathy, not mine. Murdoch, get them out of here. Flop them by the main road then come back."

Murdoch began to drag the wounded man toward the back of the stage "Yes Commander."

"Wait! Wait!"

Murdoch glanced back at Bridger slightly. "What's the problem?"

Bridger smiled toward the wounded woman. "There's a hummer parked in the parking lot. Unless you want to get fried, I suggest you steer clear of it."

Murdoch looked toward the wounded woman. "Got that?"

She quickly nodded while Fallen gave an upward nod. "Get them out of here."

Murdoch gave a quick 'Yes Commander' before leading them away.

Seventy-Three

Under the Stage

Fallen, who was staring straight ahead, frowned as much as he could. Bridger glanced toward him then Dante. "Stay close to us Dante. Without a heart bomb…"

Dante nodded putting on his backpack. "I know. If I'm captured, I'll be experimented on or worse."

Fallen didn't shift his attention to Sinah as she stepped in front of him. She smiled softly as she placed her hand on his chest. After a few moments of silence, Fallen sighed looking down at her. "More Labs will be destroyed. Many more people will be killed. Any more moments of mercy and-"

Sinah quickly shook her head before motioning her second hand toward the front of the stage. She then placed her second hand on his chest with the other. Fallen placed his hand over hers. "Let's just forget about this. We have a mission we need to complete."

Sinah nodded with a full smile. Fallen removed her hands from him but only released one.

Dante clicked and clacked on his laptop. "The entrance isn't too far away from where the Commander and Sinah are. It's a simple manual trapdoor. No electronic lock codes or passwords needed."

Bridger walked to the back of the stage looking toward the ground. "A manual trap door? That seems a little careless. Didn't they have any security for these ampy-things?"

"Basic locks and-"

Bridger cut Dante off seeing an unnoticeable square on the stage. "I think I found it."

Bridger kneeled down and grabbed the flattened handle. Fully expecting it to be stuck, he pulled hard on it. Ripping it clean off the hinges, he gasped stumbling backward. Bridger couldn't help but to chuckle lifting the trapdoor in his hand. "Uh… I think I broke the lock."

Sinah pulled Fallen by the hand over to the hole with a curious expression. The entrance under the stage was so dark it was impossible to see just how deep the hole was. The only thing that could be clearly seen was a metal ladder leading downward. Fallen tapped the side of his sunglasses turning on the thin light. Even though he shone the light into the hole, the darkness was so thick it was still impossible to see the bottom.

Bridger chucked the trapdoor aside before checking his basic supply pack. "Do we have any light sources?"

Dante chuckled hooking his laptop into his backpack. "Your Combat gloves."

Bridger's eyes darted down to his gloves. He chuckled himself as the microchips produced flash light beams. "I only use my gloves for explosives. I always forget they have basic uses too."

Sinah released Fallen's hand and looked at her gloves. Once she activated the same flash light beams Bridger did, she pointed the light into the darkness. Even with hers, Fallen's and Bridger's light, it still wasn't enough to completely illuminate the path downward. Sinah looked up at Fallen shaking her head. Fallen shook his head in return. "It doesn't matter how deep it goes. This is our passage and we can handle anything."

Sinah nodded with a confident smile. Both Bridger and Dante's eyes darted to Murdoch as he raced back onto the stage. Bridger looked toward the Lost Souls 'shanty' town. Those hiding kept nervously peeking out. "Was there any trouble?"

Murdoch spoke once he caught his breath. "Nothing a few gun sprays couldn't handle. I left them by the main road where I was supposed to. If their Lab sends help, they won't be missed."

As Fallen climbed onto the ladder, he spoke. "Stay here. I'll check this area out." As everyone nodded, Fallen glanced toward the nervous looking Sinah. He gave her a quick nod before he climbed downward vanishing into the darkness.

Seventy-Four

To the Subway

Fallen lifted his hand in front of himself, forming a medium size red orb within his palm. Once completed, he carelessly tossed it a head of himself. Upon contact with the floor, a bright blinding light was released. Thanks to his sunglasses, the flash didn't affect his vision. As the orbs light simmered down to a soft illuminating glow, Fallen glanced around. He was surrounded by many different types of pipes, random tools and other repair items. It was obvious he was in a maintenance tunnel. Fallen glanced back at the metal ladder as he called out. "All clear!"

Murdoch wasn't hesitant to climb down. Dante was quick to follow after. Bridger glanced toward the uncomfortable looking Sinah. "Sinah."

Sinah's eyes darted up to him. Bridger confidently smiled before he spoke. "We can handle anything."

Sinah swallowed heavily before she nodded. Bridger held his smile watching her climb into the darkness.

Dante spoke glancing back at Sinah as she placed her feet on the ground. "It should be only a short walk before we reach the passage to the subway."

Sinah nervously looked around as she stepped closer to Fallen.

Bridger, who had stepped onto the ground himself, touched one of the pipes. His expression shifted to disgust as dirt, dust and grime transferred onto his hand. As he wiped his hand against his pants, he spoke. "Gross. I'm guessing this place hasn't been used in quite a while."

Everyone, except Fallen flashed their flash light beams all over the small area. As they made their way through the passage, Fallen's lips touched at a frown seeing a lone door ahead of them. "Murdoch, deal with it."

Murdoch's eyes darted to Fallen then in the direction he was looking. Seeing the door himself, he quickly nodded. Murdoch grabbed the doorknob and gave it a slight jiggle. It was locked. Bridger chuckled turning his flash light beam toward him. "Be careful, doors around here aren't too sturdy."

Murdoch gently placed his palm on the door and gave it a light push. The door easily popped off the hinges and flopped to the ground. As huge amount of dust was kicked up, Bridger couldn't help but to chuckle again. "See."

Murdoch cautiously looked around the doorframe. To the left was the exit and entrance from the subway station to the street. All the windows had long been smashed. To the right were turnstiles and the passage ways to the subway. The area was illuminated only by the emergency lighting systems.

Murdoch glanced back at Fallen and his fellow soldiers. "All clear Commander."

Fallen gave a brief nod before he left the maintenance area. Once everyone else followed after, Dante noticed the turnstiles. A slight whine instantly coated his voice. "Another one?"

Bridger cautiously approached the stations open but destroyed doors. Looking around the streets, he didn't see a single wandering Lost Soul. Dante knelt down as he removed his laptop from his backpack. After a few seconds of working, Dante sighed. "Damn. We're going into another Lost Soul populated area."

Fallen effortlessly jumped the turnstile as he questioned. "Is the Lab far away?"

"No Commander, I'm picking up tons of computer activity, maybe about a mile to the east."

Fallen glanced back at Murdoch and Sinah as they hopped the turnstile as well. "Then we're heading east."

Bridger glanced at Dante who was putting his laptop away. "Need help?"

Dante instantly through Bridger a frown, as he zipped the zipper shut with authority. Bridger chuckled hopping the turnstile himself. "Just kidding."

Seventy-Five

Subway

The minute Bridger stepped onto the Platform, his eyes darted to the subway train. It was pulled half way into the station and all the doors were wide open. "Wow! What is that thing?!"

Everyone's eyes darted in the direction Bridger was looking. Like two excitable children, both Murdoch and Bridger ran toward it. Dante quickly retrieved his laptop as Murdoch cautiously stepped into one of the subway cars. Bridger peered through the windows at the uncomfortable looking seats. "It looks like some sort of travelling vehicle."

Murdoch glanced up at the long expired ads. "An underground vehicle? I didn't even know there were such things."

Bridger chuckled walking into the same car as Murdoch. "I didn't know there was anything except ground under the Lost Souls world."

Dante spoke, approaching them. "This is a subway. It drives along a track that goes from one station to another."

Fallen shifted his attention from the subway to Sinah. She was nervously looking down the darkened tunnel. Dante clicked on his laptop looking at the subways schematics. "There's a door in the front and back of each train piece." Dante was quick to correct himself. "I mean subway car." Dante continued as he closed his laptop. "We just need to pass through them then through the tunnel."

Fallen, glanced toward the damaged and spray paint covered walls. "Sinah?"

Sinah's eyes darted to Fallen. He spoke walking toward his men. "Let's go."

Sinah quickly nodded and raced after him. Bridger walked to the back of the first car. He smiled easily popping the door open. "There doesn't seem to be any locks."

Murdoch watched Bridger easily pop the door to the next train. "Those are probably emergency doors."

Fallen glanced back at Sinah as he spoke. "It doesn't matter what they are or were, we just need to pass through them."

Bridger cautiously stepped into the next car. "Hopefully we can pass through them smoothly. These subway car things would be a bad place to fight in."

Murdoch wasn't shy about hiding his amusement. "You only say that because you only fight with explosives."

Bridger cooed glancing back at him. "Is there any other way to fight?"

Murdoch couldn't help but to laugh.

Seventy-Six

Entering The Lost Soul's Lab

Sinah was the last to jump off the final car deep in the darkened tunnel. She swallowed heavily approaching Fallen and the others. Dante clicked on his laptop before he spoke. "There seems to be only one access point to the Lost Soul's lab." Dante gave a slight upward nod at the tunnel as he continued. "We need to follow this passage until there's a split in the subway tracks. Then we'll be heading down the right tunnel. That will lead us right to it." Dante sighed closing his laptop. "Unfortunately, again we won't be able to avoid a Lost Soul populated area."

Bridger gave an indifferent shrug. "That's alright we can handle anything."

Murdoch glanced toward Fallen and Sinah as they passed by him. "More than likely they won't even glance twice at us down here."

Bridger looked toward Murdoch as they began to follow after them. "How do you figure?"

"Synthetic D is being used in a weird way. The Lost Souls down here could be failed experiments or simply in a euphoric state."

Bridger's expression shifted to confusion as he glanced around the dark, rat and bug infested area. "Euphoric state?"

Fallen began to walk down the right tunnel at the split in tracks. "Without any chit chat it will be easier to enter unnoticed."

Both Murdoch and Bridger went flush. Almost in unison they said 'Yes commander.'

Once through the tunnel, the area opened up. Another Lost Soul 'shanty' town had been created. This one was quite different from the amphitheatre one. Despite the filth and infestation of the subway tunnels themselves, this seemed like a fully functioning town.

Lost Souls wandered around without any fear or panic. Many gathered and socialized at the multiple sets of the steel drums used as fire pits. Others chatted with the many peddlers that had set up booths. A much better selection of food and supplies were offered here rather than the surface. It was more than obvious these Lost Souls took care of one another.

Fallen shifted his attention to the ceiling. Despite being surrounded by cement and having only small simple fire pits, the area was overly warm. The smell of moisture and dirt overwhelmed the senses. Fallen closed his eyes as a sigh fell over him. "My ancestor's blood truly runs through my veins. I feel very comfortable in the darkness of-"

Fallen was cut off as someone bashed into him. His eyes snapped open as he quickly turned his head. Sinah had not only bashed into him but also had an overly tight grip on his basic supply pack. Her expression just screamed uncomfortable as her eyes darted around. Fallen's expression shifted to slightly sympathetic. "And yet for those whose blood runs from the Heavens, this place much be torture."

Fallen offered his hand back to Sinah. Once she noticed it, her eyes darted up to him. Fallen turned his head slightly eyeing her out the corner of his eye. Sinah stared at his silver eye for a few moments before she hesitantly let his basic supply pack go. The minute she placed her hand in his, Fallen tightened his grip. Sinah smiled slightly as he began to walk with her.

Bridger, who had watched them couldn't help but to smile. He nudged Dante's arm and whispered. "Sooo cute."

Dante shifted his attention from the Lost Souls to Bridger. "What is?"

Before Bridger had a chance to respond, Murdoch spoke. "Shut it both of you. There's a lift."

Both Dante and Bridger's eyes darted in the direction Murdoch was looking. There was a medium size caged lift at the end of the tunnel. Dante quickly nodded opening his laptop. "That's what we're looking for. That's the only way in or out of the Lost Soul's Lab."

Fallen and Sinah walked straight toward it. As he reached his hand out to open the cage part, a woman spoke. "You have to register here first."

Seventy-Seven

Silver Tongued Angel

Everyone's eyes darted to a woman wearing a lab coat, sitting at a small desk. She had an open laptop on her desk and a novel in her hand. She spoke not lifting her eyes from her book. "I need your names so the people upstairs can expect your arrivals. After that, take the lift then pass through the small sewer area. Don't touch the water. To your right there's a set of stairs. That will lead you to a really short hallway. After you turn the corner, you'll see two soldiers. Don't worry about them. Since you registered, they'll be expecting you."

The woman released a sigh before she continued her speech. It was more than obvious she had given this run down before. "They'll let you in without any problem. Then go to the big reception desk, they'll give you what you need there."

The woman indifferently flipped to the next page in her book. "Or you can just wait for tomorrow's shipment. Peddlers down here will be stocked by the afternoon hours. The surface peddlers will be by the evening. It's a lot less of a hassle if you wait."

Bridger glanced toward the frowning Fallen. "I'll handle this Commander."

Fallen gave a slight nod as Bridger approached her desk.

Bridger displayed his most friendly smile as he pinched the top of her book and leaned it toward her. The woman's eyes instantly darted up to him. Seeing his pleasant smile, her eyes weren't shy about exploring the good looking built man in front of her.

Bridger smiled even more getting a good look at the book cover. It was called 'The Love of Spring.' A beautiful woman dressed in delicate robes and adorned with many different types of flowers was on the cover. She was smiling sweetly at a man dressed in dark shadowy robes. He stood at a distance and gazed at her with such longing in his eyes. Bridger glanced back at Fallen and Sinah. "Sooo cute."

The woman shook her head not understanding what he was talking about. "Uh… What?"

Bridger shifted his smile and attention back to the woman. He spoke letting the top of the novel go. "Wow. I've never read this one before."

The woman's cheeks touched at an embarrassed flush. "M… men don't usually read these."

Bridger placed his hand on the table and leaned his weight against his arm. "I think it's really a shame that they don't. I mean you discover a lot of wonderful things from those books. Maybe even learn a few tips you may not have known."

The woman only stared up at Bridger as he continued. "Such as treating a lady like a lady, the way she deserves." Bridger's eyes flirtatiously explored the woman as he gently bit his lip. "…Delicately. …Sweetly."

The woman's cheeks caught a bright blaze as she pressed the book against her chest. "N… not all women like that."

Bridger stood up straight as he gently took her hand. "I said a lady."

The woman went so red she looked like she would spontaneously combust. "Oh, of… of course, a lady."

Bridger brought her hand to his lips softening his smile. "It's really a pity that seduction has been lost over the years."

The woman slowly nodded with her eyes fixated upon him. "I think so too."

Bridger sighed as he took the novel from her second hand. "It's also such a pity I used a seductive moment for such wrong intentions."

The woman quickly drew her hand back from him. "What do you-?"

The woman's sentence was cut off as Bridger smacked the novel against her forehead. The force caused the woman's head to bash against the cement wall behind her, knocking her unconscious. Bridger expression shifted to awkward and apologetic as he lifted his hands defensively. "Oops! Sorry! Sorry!"

Murdoch, who had watched them just like everyone else, chuckled. "Why are you apologizing? You didn't kill her."

Bridger gently pulled the woman forward and rested the side of her head upon the desk. He shrugged dropping the book next to her. "It's still mean."

Murdoch glanced back at Fallen as he opened the cage to the lift. "Tons of people die in your explosions."

Bridger walked toward his fellow soldiers as he spoke. "Yeah but I don't chat with them first."

Dante followed Sinah and Fallen onto the lift. Right before Bridger followed after them, he glanced back at the woman. Murdoch gave him a confused look as he ran back over to her. A chuckle instantly caught his throat as Bridger scooped up the romance novel. Once everyone was inside, Bridger showed Dante the novel. "Wanna read it when I'm done?"

Dante looked toward it, then instantly went red in embarrassment. "N… No! I don't read those things!"

Murdoch glanced toward the cover himself. "I'll read it after you."

Bridger smiled hooking the book into his back pocket.

Seventy-Eight

Infiltration

Dante kneeled down and placed the microchip pieces of his Combat gloves above his laptop keypad. Typing as fast as his fingers could hit the keys, Bridger questioned. "What are you doing?"

Dante didn't glance up as the short lift ride ended. Nor did he when Fallen opened the cage for the exit. "I'm programming my Combat gloves to respond as if they were my laptop. We don't know what we're up against and it will take too much time to-"

"But doesn't that mean you won't be able to use your Combat gloves for actual Combat?"

Before Dante could answer, Fallen spoke. "For this mission we won't be separating. Within the group, he'll be more than fine."

Bridger chuckled, poking Dante's leg with his foot. "Don't worry Information, Data and whatever soldier, I'll protect you."

Dante's lips touched at a frown as his voice filled with sarcasm. "Gee, thanks."

Fallen cautiously approached the lone set of stairs leading upward in the small sewer area. "How long will programming the gloves take?"

Dante rapidly typed on his lap top keys. "Minutes, Commander."

Fallen shifted his attention to Murdoch. "Stay with Dante until he's done, then both of you follow after. Sinah, Bridger and I will handle the soldiers."

Murdoch gave a quick 'Yes Commander' while Dante protested looking up at him. "But Commander-"

"Hurry up!"

Dante went flush before he went back to work. Fallen shifted his attention to Sinah then Bridger. "Let's go."

The three of them quickly yet silently raced up the stairs. Once at the top, there was about five feet worth of hallway ahead of them then a turn. Fallen withdrew his gun pressing himself against the wall. With a quick peek around the corner, he could see two armed soldiers guarding a closed door with a complicated control panel beside it.

Fallen stepped back and turned to Bridger and Sinah. He pointed at both of them then to his sunglasses. As he gripped his gun preparing to strike, Sinah tugged his hand. Fallen quickly turned his head back to her. Sinah smiled pointing at herself then upward. Both Bridger and Fallen looked up at the ceiling with a slightly bewildered expression.

The ceiling was made out of various matching panels. Bridger looked back to Fallen with a questioning expression. Fallen shifted his attention back to Sinah. She confidently nodded before pointing upward again. Fallen gave a slight nod letting her hand go. Bridger kneeled down and cupped his hands together. Once she hooked her foot into his palm, Bridger effortlessly lifted her to the ceiling. Sinah quickly and quietly moved a panel aside so she could climb inside. Sinah glanced downward at Fallen with a smile. Fallen kept his attention locked on her as she hopped up into the ceiling.

Bridger didn't glance toward Murdoch and Dante as they quickly ran up the stairs. Murdoch's expression shifted to confusion seeing both Bridger and Fallen simply standing in the small hallway. "What are-?"

Bridger quickly turned to him pressing his finger to his lips. Murdoch shifted his confusion to Fallen. Though he couldn't see the exact location of Sinah, he kept his attention on the ceiling.

Sinah quietly crawled through the dusty cobweb infested ceiling. She glanced through the cracks of each panel connection for her location. Once she was right above the two soldiers, she made a dagger appear in each hand. Sinah's eyebrows lowered slightly as she slashed the panel below her in an X pattern. She and the panel fell toward the floor.

The minute she hit the ground, she sweep kicked one of the soldier's legs out from under him. She then kicked her second leg upward slamming the soldier against the wall. The force of the kick caused his neck to snap and blood to spray from his mouth. Before the second soldier could react, she whipped both of her daggers into his jugular. It took mere seconds for him to bleed out and die.

Sinah smiled as she calmly tapped her earpiece. Fallen smiled slightly seeing the blood spray across the wall as he walked toward her. Bridger chuckled looking at it himself. "I think you're faster than all of us in Combat skills Sinah."

Sinah smiled proudly looking toward the dead. Fallen shifted his attention from the complicated control panel to Dante. "Dante."

Dante quickly nodded stepping over the bodies. He looked at it momentarily before he recognized the system. "Palm and retina scanner, Bridger can you help me out?"

Bridger nodded scooping up one of the dead soldiers. "No problem."

Once the soldier's palm and eye were used, the electronic locked door swished open. Sitting behind a large reception desk was a woman dressed in a lab coat. Not expecting any Lost Souls toady, her eyes darted up to Fallen and his soldiers in surprise. "Who the-?!"

The woman never got a chance to finish her sentence before Murdoch shot her. The bullet hit her in the forehead, instantly killing her.

Bridger smiled walking toward the desk. "Nice shot. Now isn't killing without causing suffering so much better?"

Murdoch gave a blunt emotionless response. "Nope."

Bridger couldn't help but to snicker. "You're cold mean Helix."

Seventy-Nine

Protected

Dante loaded all the information from the reception's computer into his Combat gloves. He smiled finding a map of the facility. "Good, now we won't be just dangerously wandering around."

Both Murdoch and Bridger stood on either side of another set of stairs leading upward. Besides the large reception desk and a few chairs, nothing else was in this room. It was obvious these small simple areas were used just to deal with Lost Souls.

Dante clinched one of his fists. A small green screen lifted from his Combat glove. With his other hand he began to scroll through many files. "It looks like every other Lab besides ours knows about the synthetic production here. Files and progress reports have been sent to all of them."

Fallen lips hinted at a frown. "Any successes?"

"Nothing confirmed. However, there seems to be some promising results coming from this Lab."

"Lab location?"

Dante flipped over to the map. After a few seconds he answered. "Upward."

"Then that's where we're heading. Let's move out."

Murdoch was quick to lead the way. Bridger waited until Fallen, Sinah and Dante passed by him before he followed after.

Once they stepped on the main floor, everyone cautiously looked around. The walls all once made out of glass, were now boarded and barb wired up as were the three original entrances on the main floor. Gatling guns had been perched and aimed directly toward each of the old passages. Needless to say, if anyone broke in, they would be instantly be gunned down. As Dante tried to take a step forward, Bridger stuck his arm out stopping him. "This area isn't soldier protected."

Murdoch's eyes shifted around the empty area. There was only one set of escalators on the main floor. His eyes then shifted to the ceiling. There were different wires and cords wrapped around the buildings many artistic metal beams. Something appreciated before the fall. "It's rigged."

Bridger nodded pointing toward the scanner near the stairwell they had just walked up. "I'd say heat and motion sensor. It's actually quite impressive. Even our Lab don't use these type of things. Well not that I know of anyway."

Dante lifted his Combat glove to scan the area. "If its heat and motion sensor activated, why hasn't it attacked?"

"We're not really moving. Not aggressively anyway. Obviously Lab Techs and soldiers have to pass through his area. If it was trigger happy, they'd be in trouble too."

Dante looked at the green screen as it finished its scan. "The defensive weaponry outside is much higher. Downstairs really is our only way in and out of here."

Bridger glanced back at Fallen. "Murdoch and I can trigger the traps Commander." Murdoch nodded in agreement as Bridger continued. "While the defensive system is focused on us, you, Sinah and-"

"I'd rather us enter unnoticed. Decoys will cause too much of a panic."

Bridger placed his hand on his chin. He looked like he was thinking of a new plan. After a few moments he shrugged toward Murdoch. "Frost Bomb?"

Murdoch instantly closed his eyes releasing an annoyed defeated sigh. "I just knew you were going to suggest that."

Dante gave both Bridger and Murdoch a look of confusion. "How will a Frost Bomb help?"

Bridger closed his eyes reaching his hands far out in front of himself. "It will mess up the heat sensors, freeze the motion detector and screw with all the mechanical devices the area. Guns, laser triggers and everything else ends up with a massively slower reaction time. The only problem is the damn thing doesn't last too long."

Murdoch stepped in front of Bridger reaching his hands far out in front of himself as well. "So when we activate it, run or skate as fast as you can up that escalator."

Fallen quickly snatched hold of Sinah's hand. Bridger smiled as a large blue orb began to form in his palms. "I haven't yet mastered these things."

Murdoch's lips instantly touched at a frown. "Yeah, I know! I can't stand frostbite and yet every time-"

Bridger squinted his eyes shut, the blue orb quickly turned white. Ice rapidly began to crystalize around it. "I really should practice more with the things I create, shouldn't I?"

Murdoch's eyes sharpened a little. "Damn lazy A Helix."

Fallen locked his attention on the escalators. "Everyone get ready."

Both Sinah and Dante quickly nodded. Dante tightly gripped the straps of his backpack in anticipation. Murdoch frowned watching the orb become larger and more frozen looking. "Come on! Come on! The larger that damn thing is the harder it is to get in the air."

Bridger's features suddenly relaxed. "Ready?"

Murdoch's frown increased. "Do I have a choice?"

Bridger's eyes snapped open as he tossed the orb to Murdoch. Murdoch volleyed it off his forearms high into the air. Any part of the orb that had touched him instantly caused frostbite. Bridger quickly leapt into the air and spiked it downward. The orb zoomed toward the ground. The second it made contact, it shattered. Ice rapidly coated the floors, walls, sensors and everything else in the area. Bridger glanced back at his fellow soldiers. "Go!"

Everyone wasn't hesitant in running toward the escalators. Despite being a completely frozen floor, it was only Murdoch that kept slipping. As Bridger passed him, he snatched Murdoch's wrist and dragged him up the escalator with everyone else.

The minute they were on solid ground, Murdoch tore his wrist back from Bridger and hissed. "Frostbite!!"

Bridger watched as Murdoch raised the sleeves of his battle suit. His skin looked very red and irritated. Bridger awkwardly chuckled as Murdoch began to rub his sore arms. "Well, they aren't too frosty."

Murdoch frowned lifting his fist. "I ought to punch your lights out."

Bridger glanced into the main area noticing smoke rapidly covering everything. The frost was quickly dissolving. "Damn. I can't seem to figure out how to make them last longer."

Murdoch shifted his attention toward Fallen. He was cautiously looking up and down the empty hallway. "You never work on it."

Bridger chuckled dismissively waving his hand. "I'm too busy with other stuff."

Murdoch shook his head in disappointment.

Dante stepped close to Fallen and whispered. "The Lab area is down the right side of this hallway. Most of these other rooms seem to be meeting rooms."

Fallen didn't glance back at Dante as he responded. "Life signs?"

"Each room has about 20 or so. There's a great deal of computer activity triggering my Combat gloves."

Fallen gave a brief nod before shifting his attention to his soldiers. "Let's go."

Eighty

Synthetics Lab

Dante scanned the electronic lock panel beside the door leading to the Labs, while everyone else kept guard. Not a single soldier or Lab Tech was seen or even heard wandering around. Murdoch gripped his gun and leaned close to Bridger. "Where the hell is anyone?"

Bridger glanced down the empty hallway to the right of them. "Maybe because this Lab is a Lost Souls Lab, they figure nobody would bother to attack it. I mean our Lab didn't get any reports from the others to even know there was one."

Murdoch lips were instantly taken by a smirk. "Would you send a message to a Lab that's eventually going to blow you up?"

Bridger snickered looking back down the hallway behind them. "Not unless I wanted everyone dead."

Dante frowned quickly tapping on the green screens from his Combat gloves. "I hate card key locks. There such a pain to override. I swear they take forever."

Fallen tossed him an instant frown. "We don't have the time to waste Dante."

Dante went flush. "Yes Commander."

Sinah approached the panel with a curious expression. Once she was in Dante's peripheral vision, he turned his head toward her. Sinah looked at Dante then made a fist. Dante's expression shifted to questioning until she pointed at the machine with her other hand. Dante quickly shook his head. "Electronic locks can't be broke or forced open. Not only do they set off alarms but it triggers the emergency security systems. Mind you that is if they even have one. That system puts everything on lock down. It's almost impossible to override anything when that happens."

Fallen began to impatiently tap his foot. "Hurry up. They longer we stand here, the higher our chances of being caught."

Dante tapped a couple more green screens then suddenly smiled. "Okay, I think I got it." Dante looked toward the panel, he smiled even more as the lock flashed green and the door swished open. "No problem Commander."

Without hesitation, Fallen entered the dimly lit Lab with his gun raised. Everyone was quick to follow after him.

Within the Lab were many walls of large tanks filled with bluey green fluids. Each tank had a different creature varying in size and stage development. Most of them were unrecognizable to anyone's eyes.

Fallen lips touched at a frown as he reached his hand out toward one of the tanks. Right before contact, a male voice spoke. "Perfection, aren't they?"

Both Fallen and Murdoch were quick to turn their guns toward a rather plain looking dark haired dark eyed man wearing a lab coat. He stood a few feet from them and had his attention locked on the creations. Bridger protectively moved in front of Dante. The man didn't shift his attention as he spoke. "I assume you're Lucifer."

Fallen gripped his gun as he frowned. "And if I am?"

The man glanced at the development status pad beside one of the tanks. "You must be. Why else would you break into a Lab without any pure samples? It would be pointless for anyone else." The man looked at the next tank pad as he continued. "Director Courtier said it would only be a matter of time before you'd find this location, and then come here."

Fallen's eyebrows lowered as the man turned toward them. He glared at Fallen as he gave an indifferent shrug. "And I said let him come here. Let him see our creations, our work."

Fallen didn't shift his attention as his tone of voice became hostile. "And let me see for myself a successful Synthetic D."

Eighty-One

A Twisted Success

The man's lips touched at a condescending smirk as he turned completely toward them. "Impressive. I was created to look forgettable just like everyone else. Yet even in this so called human shell you knew. Now I know for sure that you are Lucifer."

Fallen stepped a few steps forward away from his soldiers. "I also know when someone or rather something isn't alive, Synthetic D."

The man chuckled, noticing Fallen's team send him looks of utter shock. "Oh please call me Kadin."

Murdoch glanced up and down Kadin with a slight frown. Looking at his dark hair and eyes he shook his head. "It's impossible to-"

Kadin scoffed toward Murdoch cutting him off. "This is too much for your puny little mind to comprehend soldier. Just stand there and be quiet. I'm sure intelligence isn't you're strong suit."

Both Murdoch and Dante instantly began to frown. Before Murdoch had a chance to snap, Dante stepped out from behind Bridger. "Well it is mine! The Synthetic D needs a strong soul to latch onto. Death causes the soul to abandon its flesh."

Kadin's eyes darted to Dante as a full smile took his lips. "I'm surprised soldiers would bring a Lab Tech with them. Considering the dangers of-"

Before Dante had a chance to cut off Kadin, Bridger chimed in. "He isn't some simple Lab Tech! He's our Surveillance, Intelligence and hand to hand Combat expert!"

Dante's eyes darted to Bridger. Seeing his confident disposition, he forced one himself. "That's right!"

Kadin held his smile toward Dante. "It's nice to speak to someone intelligent. Now I won't have to dumb things down for your group."

Dante wasn't shy about exposing his full frown. "It's impossible to successfully use Synthetic D on someone soulless or even someone with a weak soul. It either causes insanity or it simply passes through."

"No, you're wrong! We've discovered how to make it work. The first attempt, we used synthetic A. Unfortunately, in a body with or without a soul the results were the same."

Bridger's features instantly broke. Murdoch, who noticed, hissed. "Focus!"

Bridger's eyes darted to Murdoch. Murdoch tossed him a slight frown and gave a confident nod. As if slapped across the face, Bridger features instantly returned to normal.

Kadin chuckled a little. "Then you know what happens with synthetic A. We can only use very small doses to put ourselves or humans to sleep. Too much and they don't wake up. We don't have any real use for it, so what's the point in making something that causes so many problems."

Dante gave a look of confused intrigue. "Then how?"

Kadin shifted his attention back to Dante with a smile. "With a pure sample of the A blood. We don't carry any of that here, so A Helixes are created in Director Courtier's lab. Well they were before it was blown up. Afterward they're sent here."

Dante, who felt perplexed by the whole conversation, shook his head. "That doesn't make any sense. Why would you make an A Helix unless you..." Dante paused for a moment before his entire disposition turned hostile. It was as if everything Kadin was talking about suddenly became clear. "You bastard!!"

Bridger and Murdoch looked toward Dante in shock. Neither was expecting Dante to snap. Dante hissed toward Kadin. "You sick bastard!!"

Fallen didn't shift his attention back to Dante as he questioned. "Dante?"

Dante pointed an accusatory finger toward Kadin. "They create A

Helixes so the soul becomes intact! The A Helix latches itself onto the soul thus protecting it. During the beginning stages when an A Helix is developing, they add Synthetic D. The synthetic will attack the soul and because the A Helix isn't fully developed, it can't resist long. The A Helix and soul are eaten by the synthetic. Basically, causing the body to become soulless, but since it had a soul to begin with, technically it's undead."

Kadin clapped his hands together in excitement. "I knew someone with intelligence would understand!"

Bridger shook his head in disbelief. "Wait a minute. We have the soulless in our Labs. They're not undead."

"No, we have creations born without souls. That's why they seem like there's nothing inside, like they have no life within. They're void." Dante frowned toward Kadin as he continued. "But as you can see, he seems like he has a soul. They murdered one of our brethren to create this creature."

Bridger hissed toward Kadin. "That's sick!"

Kadin opened his mouth to say something but Dante hissed first. "We die so you can create synthetics?!"

Kadin smiled turning his attention to the frowning Fallen. "They just don't understand the value of us. Synthetic's don't have to follow you or your choices. We are not bound by Helix to serve you, Lucifer. We do as we please and we carry all the strength and capabilities that pure D Helixes do. We just don't have the restrictions of a Master."

Fallen's eyebrows lowered slightly. "You're committing a sin against God."

Kadin chuckled shaking his head. "Luckily for us, he doesn't exist."

Dante suddenly withdrew his gun. Without hesitation, he pointed it at Kadin and pulled the trigger. "Bastard!!!"

Eighty-Two

Disagreement

Dante's eyes darted down to his gun confused. Though he had indeed pulled the trigger, nothing happened. "What the hell?"

As he lifted and aimed to shoot again, Bridger spoke. "Dante, you don't think straight when you're upset."

Dante's eyes darted to Bridger. "What?!"

Bridger smiled slightly glancing toward him. "Combat."

Dante went flush realizing since his computer was installed into his Combat gloves, the Combat function wouldn't work. Dante suddenly hissed. "Fine then!"

Bridger couldn't help but to chuckle as Dante whipped his gun at Kadin.

Kadin hissed smacking it out of the air. "How rude! Now I understand why they brought you along. You're just as savage as the rest of them."

Murdoch chuckled a little. "Look who's talking synthetic D. Born by killing another? What's wrong with you? Synthetics are dangerous and stopping there production will make this world a better place."

"Heaven and Hell abandoned us so long ago, that time is over! Don't you understand that with synthetics we can create super humans." Kadin's tone of voice became defiant. "We don't need God or the Devil. We are beings that can live and make this world a better place on our own!"

Bridger closed his eyes slowly shaking his head. "A soulless world filled only with synthetics? That's too horrible to even think about."

Fallen's lips touched at a cold smile. "How unfortunate for you and your Synthetic kin, that I was created." Kadin's eyes shifted to Fallen as he continued. "And I won't allow your filth to taint my world!"

Kadin protested almost instantly. "We weren't asking for your permission! We are a new breed of..."

While Kadin continued his speech, Dante felt a gentle poke in his back. He quickly turned with a full frown. His frown instantly vanished seeing Sinah. She had many different types of syringes with different samples in her arms. Dante's eyes darted down to them then up to her as he whispered. "Where did you get those?"

Sinah glanced behind herself toward the large tanks. Dante looked in the direction, she was looking. "There's a passage?"

Sinah looked back at Dante narrowing her eyes. Dante looked back toward her. Seeing her expression, he instantly understood. "It's hidden."

Sinah nodded relaxing her features. Dante removed his backpack from his back and zipped it open. As he began to put all the samples Sinah had collected inside, he spoke. "I'm going to go check it out. Cover me."

The minute Dante put the last sample away, Sinah quickly stepped behind him. She gently pinched Bridger's battle suit sleeve and pulled him slightly closer to herself fully hiding Dante. Not shifting his attention from Kadin, Bridger didn't give any resistance.

Dante swiftly yet quietly began to search the tanks looking for the passage. Without specifically looking for it, the passage could easily be overlooked. Once found, Dante glanced back at Sinah and Bridger, before walked down it.

The pathway led to a decent sized area filled with computers and lab equipment. Dante's eyes darted down to the eight Lab Techs unconscious on the floor. He smiled slightly approaching one of the computers. "Sinah managed to knock everyone out in silence. That's pretty good." Dante began to click on the key pad. "Hopefully that things blabbing will buy me enough time to collect all the info we need."

Kadin hissed. "...And furthermore..."

Fallen suddenly cut Kadin off. "I've had just about enough of this and enough of you. Without my counterpart, the world belongs to me! And only me, I-" Fallen suddenly stopped short as his brows furrowed a little. It was as if his own words didn't make any sense to his ears.

Murdoch was quick to question. "Commander?"

Fallen gave a quick shake of his head before he continued. "No. It's nothing. Synthetics will rule over my dead body."

Kadin smiled a grim smile. "I was hoping you'd say that."

Kadin suddenly leapt toward Fallen. Without hesitation, both Fallen and Murdoch began to shoot their guns. Bridger glanced toward Sinah. "Dante, we need to-" Bridger chuckled seeing Sinah. "You're not Dante. Come on we need to set up some bombs."

Not having ever dealt with bombs before, all Sinah could do was barely nod. Before they had a chance to start setting up, Dante raced out from the back area. "We've been discovered! Security's closing in fast!"

Kadin gurgled laughed. Reddish grey liquid gushed out from every bullet hole. "Nobody leaves here alive."

Eighty-Three

Trapped

Murdoch's eyes darted to Dante with a look of annoyance. "Why the hell didn't you give us any warning?"

Dante looked at the green screen from his Combat glove. His alarmed expression suddenly shifted to confusion. "That's not right. My gloves aren't picking up any other life signs besides the ones I first detected. And they haven't moved from their spots."

"Then what are you talking-"

"The security cameras in the back Lab are showing soldiers moving in fast."

Kadin gurgle laughed again only much louder. "Even failed synthetic D's when on a leash can be useful."

Dante swallowed heavily. "And since they are basically undead, they don't register on my Combat gloves."

Kadin tilled his head back as his loud liquid filled laughs shifted to sounding insane. "I wonder how much synthetic D we'll have to inject into you before you're A Helix panics then dies."

Fallen lowered his gun. "I won't allow that to happen."

Kadin smirked lowering his head. Reddish grey liquid oozed from his mouth down his front. "Oh, I wouldn't be worrying about them Lucifer. For what we have in store for you is-"

Kadin didn't get a chance to finish his sentence before Fallen raced over to him and slashed his head clean off his shoulders. As if having a reaction to the deathblow, Kadin's entire body began to melt. Fallen flicked the reddish grey liquid from his hand watching Kadin's liquefying body turn into a puddle then melt into the floor.

Dante made a sound of frustration, checking the map. "Damn it! This place is too damn straight forward."

Murdoch gripped his gun looking toward him. "So then there isn't a backdoor to this place."

"No, unfortunately the way in is the way out."

Fallen turned back to his soldiers as he spoke. "Dante collect the samples."

Dante motioned his hand toward Sinah. "Sinah already got them. She dealt with the Lab Techs back there too."

Fallen's eyes shifted toward the proudly smiling Sinah. "Has all the information been collected as well?"

"Yes Commander, we have everything we need."

Fallen moved his attention to Bridger. "I want enough explosives to destroy this entire place."

Bridger quickly questioned. "Are you sure Commander? That much will cause the underground to collapse destroying the 'town'."

Fallen gave an indifferent shrug. "We got what we need here. The Lost Souls shouldn't be allowed to continue with this abomination."

Bridger glanced toward Murdoch. "Give me a hand?"

Murdoch responded with a quick nod.

Dante began to scan each of the large tanks with his Combat gloves, while Fallen cautiously approached the exit. Sinah watched as Fallen gripped his gun pressing his ear against the door. His lips touched at a frown hearing quiet whispers of instructions. He frowned even more clearly hearing. "Director Courtier wants the one with sunglasses only. The rest are to be eliminated."

Those words were followed by many 'Yes Sirs.' As Fallen lifted his head, he felt a hand on his back. Fallen glanced back to see who it was. Sinah, who was standing beside him, lifted her fist and gave a confident nod. Fallen gave a slight nod in return. "We're going to have to fight our way out."

Sinah removed her hand from Fallen then clinched both of her fists.

Sinah nodded again displaying her most ready for combat expression. Fallen shifted his attention to Dante. He was looking at the completed scans. "Are they synthetics Dante?"

"Most of them are. The Synthetic D has been combined with animal Helixes."

"And are they successful?"

"Apparently so Commander, I guess animals have less resistance then humans or Helixes"

Fallen frowned slightly looking toward the creatures in the many large tanks. "Or they are adapting for survival. I highly doubt the reproductive issues just affected humans."

Bridger smiled hooking a few clusters of bombs onto each tank. Dante watched him for a few seconds before he muttered. "It seems a little cruel of us to destroy them, even if they are Synthetic D creations."

Fallen held his slight frown shifting his attention back toward the exit. "We have our orders."

Dante barely nodded. As Murdoch passed by him with more bombs, Dante pointed. "There's a passage to the back of the room over there."

Murdoch looked in the direction he was pointing then nodded. "I'm on it."

Eighty-Four

Escape Plan

Bridger placed a large orange orb in the middle of the Lab. The minute he released it, he frantically waved his hands. "Ow! Ow! Ow! Son of a bitch, that burns!"

Murdoch snickered glancing toward him. "You should have had me make it."

Bridger blew on his gloved hands before he spoke. "You wouldn't have been able make one strong enough."

Murdoch's amused disposition instantly shifted to annoyance. Bridger, who noticed smiled. "I haven't taught you this combination yet. And it isn't something you can perfect on the fly."

Murdoch's eyes darted from Bridger to the orb. "You mean you actually worked on something long enough for it to be dangerous? What's the combination?"

Bridger began to wave his hands again. "Come on rapid healing skill, my hands are barbequed." He looked toward Murdoch as he answered his question. "Corrosive, which as you know eats through everything. Splatter effect, which as you know causes a full blown spray and toxic gas. This little Lab has one of my many nastier bombs. Let's just say, not only will everything be destroyed but it's enough to topple a city."

"But we don't want to-"

"Don't worry its isolated enough to only destroy the Lab and collapse a large part of the underground. Nothing here will survive. Probably not too many Lost Souls either. I used a long timer with a manual over ride activation."

Fallen gripped his gun. "Long timer or not, we need to get out of here. Dante stay close to the team."

"Yes Commander."

Murdoch looked toward the exit door. "Why haven't they busted in to attack?"

Bridger shrugged peeking under his Combat gloves to see if his hands were damaged. "Maybe they don't want to risk accidently shooting the tanks?"

Dante swallowed heavily looking toward the floor. "That could be one reason. Another could be they know we're pretty much trapped in here. Eventually we're not going to have any choice but to fight our way out. Nobody's escaping this battle unharmed."

Fallen glanced back at his soldiers. "That's why I'm going to lead the way. I overheard a soldier say I'm to be captured. So they won't open fire right aw-"

Sinah cut him off snatching his arm and quickly shaking her head. Fallen shook his head in return. "I won't be captured Sinah."

Sinah let Fallen go then made two small thick blades lift from her hands. She then leapt against the door slamming the blades into and pinning herself against it. Fallen's eyebrows furrowed slightly not understanding what she was doing. "Sinah?"

Sinah lifted one of her feet that were helping to brace her then touched it against the door. Bridger crossed his arms. "I'm guessing she wants you to hit the door into the hallway. She'll act as the decoy."

Sinah quickly nodded while Fallen began to frown. "I'm not sending you directly into danger. Since I'm the one they want, they won't simply open fire. We'll have the advantage of their hesitation."

Sinah shook her head before she lifted then lowered her foot again. Bridger looked toward the ever frowning Fallen. "Well they'll definitely be surprised by her."

"I won't put her in harm's way."

Bridger uncrossed one of his arms and put his hand on his chin. "Right after we can send out a flash bomb. That will-"

Dante cut him off. "No good. The cameras showed soldiers with gas masks. Those are usually flash and blind protected."

Fallen quickly hissed back at them. "I will be going out there first!" Fallen shifted his hiss to Sinah. "Sinah, get down, that's an order!"

Sinah stared back at Fallen for a few moments before she hesitantly shook her head. Fallen's eyebrows lowered slightly. "Sinah I know you heard my order. Now get-"

Fallen was cut off by a loud repetitive warning sound flooding the Lab. Dante instantly went into panic looking at the green screen from his Combat gloves. "Oh hell!"

Fallen looked at Sinah, she smiled confidently back at him and nodded. Fallen released an annoyed sigh before he spoke. "Status Dante?"

Dante tapped the screens before he answered. "The emergency system has been activated. We have to get out of here now or we're going to be beyond screwed."

Fallen sighed annoyed again. "Then we have no choice. Be careful Sinah."

Eighty-Five

Scramble

Fallen slammed his fist into the wall close to Sinah's hip. The sliding mechanism snapped as the door went flying into the hallway. The force caused any soldiers in its path to be knocked off their feet. Those still standing immediately opened fire.

Sinah's eyes darted upward to another paneled ceiling. Without hesitation, she did a handstand then thrusted herself upward through the panel into the ceiling. The soldiers shifted their weapons upward continuing to shoot.

Fallen and Murdoch left the Lab opening fire on the soldiers. Bridger calmly tossed one small acid bomb after another. Any soldier hit, had their gun and most of their protective gear rapidly melt. Murdoch wasn't hesitant to use their lowered defenses to his advantage and shoot vital areas.

As Bridger began to form another, the panel just inside the Lab was opened. Bridger's eyes darted upward almost instantly. Sinah smiled reaching her arms down to him through the hole. Bridger smiled up at her as he tossed his barely formed acid bomb aside. He then turned to Dante. He was anxiously tapping on his green screens muttering. "I have to slow it down! I have to do something! Everything's locking down! Every-"

Bridger cut Dante off by scooping him off his feet. Dante went flush as his eyes darted to him. "Bridger, what the hell are you doing?!"

Bridger lifted Dante toward the open panel. "I'm getting you out of harm's way."

Sinah grabbed Dante's arms then backpack effortlessly pulling him up into the ceiling with her. Once Bridger couldn't see him, he instantly went back on the attack. Dante released a defeated sigh. "Without a weapon I'm so useless. Not that I'm any good in Combat anyway."

Sinah quickly shook her head pointing at his Combat gloves. Dante sighed again. "Don't try to make me feel better, I-"

Sinah shook her head then pointed downward then began to count on her fingers. Dante, who understood, shook his head. "I don't how many. My system can't track the undead. We never even thought that the undead could-"

Sinah looked around the area in a searching manner. She smiled seeing a ventilation shaft on the wall to her right near the spot she first busted in. She patted Dante's shoulder before she crawled toward it. Dante gave her a look of confusion as she kicked it open then crawled inside. He spoke quickly following after her. "Sinah, where are we going?"

Once he made it through the shaft himself, he looked toward Sinah. She was pointing downward. Dante shook his head holding his look of confusion. "I don't understand."

Sinah mirrored his expression lifting her hands looking around. Dante barely nodded lifting his Combat glove. "Where are we? Okay, uh… We're above a meeting room. They're 20 life signs just below us."

Sinah smiled and gave a quick nod before she made two blades appear in her hands. Dante gave her a look of shock as she slashed the panel directly under her and fell. The minute Sinah's feet hit the large conference room table she released a wave of throwing knives. Not a single person in the room had a chance to react before they were killed.

Sinah smiled jumping to the floor. Dante nervously looked down the hole before he hang dropped onto the table with a flop. Once he accessed the Lab's map, he spoke. "The escalators aren't too far from here."

Sinah leaned her head close to the wall. She could clearly hear the rapid gunfire and screams of battle. Sinah approached another wall, this one led to the hallway just left of the Lab. She nodded hearing the exact same sounds. Dante climbed off the table giving an upward nod toward the closed door. "It's not locked. Come on, let's-"

Sinah shook her head returning to the first wall. She looked toward Dante and closed her hand. Dante looked at her hand as she suddenly opened it. Dante, who understood shook his head. "Only Bridger can make bombs."

Sinah looked back toward the wall momentarily before she suddenly snapped her fingers. Dante gave her a look of confusion as she climbed back onto the table then leapt back up into the ceiling.

Eighty-Six

Sinah's Insane Plan

Bridger continued to toss his acid bombs as fast as he could create them. "Is it just me or do these soldiers seem endless?"

Murdoch shot as fast as he could pull the trigger. "I swear I keep shooting the same ones."

Fallen frowned rapidly shooting as well. "It's the Synthetic D's rapid healing capability. At this rate, we're going to be caught up in the explosion."

Bridger's eyes darted up to the ceiling as a thick metal blade poked halfway through one of the panels. His expression shifted to confusion as a blade poked through many different spots above the soldiers. Sinah shifted one of the panels aside then sent a wave of metal blades downward. Instead of hitting any of their enemies, the blades slammed into the floor all around them. Sinah smiled shifting the panel back closed.

Bridger's expression remained confused until Fallen hissed. "Enough of this!"

Before Fallen could step into action, Bridger called out. "Commander, wait!" Fallen's eyes darted back at him then to the blades Bridger was pointing at. "I think Sinah is working on our way out."

Sinah landed on the conference room table again. Dante, who was standing by the exit, looked toward her. "Sinah, let's get-"

Dante stopped short as Sinah hopped off then pushed the table onto its side. She then pointed at Dante then behind it. Dante shook his head not understanding her. Sinah raced over to the wall and began to shoot metal blades on angles halfway through many spots. Being utterly lost at Sinah's actions, Dante questioned. "What are you doing?"

Sinah reached down her battle suit and removed her heart bomb. She then pressed it against the middle of the wall. She smiled as it attached. She nodded then looked toward Dante. He hadn't moved from the doorway. She instantly frowned and ran toward him. She quickly snatched his wrist and dragged him behind the table. After letting him go, she kneeled down and covered her head. Dante gave a slight nod before he copied her.

Sinah nodded before she suddenly stood up and shot a throwing knife toward her heart bomb. She barely had a chance to duck for cover before it was hit and set off. Bridger smiled slightly as the electrical blast went off. Acting as a conductor the electrical current struck each and every one of Sinah's metal blades. Every soldier in the area of the blast were instantly stunned.

Bridger couldn't help but to chuckle. "That's pretty clever."

The heart bomb suddenly exploded destroying the wall and burying the soldiers. Without hesitation, Fallen raced passed the huge hole in wall and called out. "Sinah! Dante! Let's go!"

Sinah looked out from behind the table. She instantly smiled at the destruction she caused. Dante raced toward the exit. As he glanced back at Sinah, he saw both Murdoch and Bridger race passed the hole as well. "Come on!"

Sinah quickly nodded before she gave chase.

Eighty-Seven

One Left Behind

Dante looked toward the escalators, they were moving so fast it would be impossible to step on them. Bridger looked toward them then to Murdoch. He was shooting the remaining advancing soldiers. "Is this because the emergency thing was set off?"

Dante nodded. "Yeah the emergency system is trying to protect the facility."

Bridger smiled reaching down his battle suit. "That was a really good idea Sinah." Sinah looked toward Bridger in a questioning manner until he removed his heart bomb and continued. "You gave us a way out."

Fallen, who was shooting the soldiers as well, frowned. "Well let's not let her efforts go to waste."

"We won't Commander. Murdoch, I need your heart bomb."

Murdoch didn't shift his attention from the battle. "What?! Now?! Why?!"

Bridger smiled and began his explanation. "If I toss them toward the main floor area then set them off, the electrical current will zap everything. It will not only mess up all the censors but stall everything for a couple of minutes. I'm sure in that time we can-"

Murdoch quickly reached down his battle suit and removed his heart bomb. He hissed thrusting it toward Bridger. "Just use it already and get us the hell out of here!"

Bridger nodded taking the heart bomb. As he began to attach them together, he spoke. "Sinah, Dante get behind me. One wrong move and I could accidently fry you both. This way if I screw up, I'll be the one to take the hit."

As Sinah and Dante did as Bridger asked, he quickly removed a few wires from the heart bombs. "Okay. I think that should do it. I disassembled the bomb part. We just need the electrical-"

Murdoch hissed back at him. "Stop yapping about it and hurry up!"

Bridger snickered. "Alright mean Helix alright. Helix 7923 Bridger heart device…" Bridger glanced toward Murdoch. "Your turn."

"Helix 3421 Murdoch heart device…"

Bridger tossed them toward the center of the main floor. "Now! Activate!"

Murdoch wasn't hesitant to call out afterward. "Activate!"

Instantly being triggered, the heart bombs released a bright blinding blue light. Bridger turned his head as the electrical blast hit everything on the main floor. The moment the escalators came to a screeching halt, Bridger snickered looking at his success. "Aha! It worked! Alright, let's go!"

Before anyone could react, Bridger turned and tossed Dante over his shoulder. Dante went flush almost instantly. Before he had a chance to resist or even question, Bridger carried him half way down the escalator then hopped over the side. Murdoch wasn't hesitant to follow after them. Sinah looked in the direction they went then back toward Fallen. He was still shooting every soldier in sight.

Sinah ran over to him and snatched his free hand. Fallen didn't shift his attention toward her as he spoke. "Get out of here Sinah! I'll catch up!"

Sinah shook her head tugging his hand toward the escalators. Fallen gave a quick shake of his head. "Go Sinah! We're running out of time!"

Sinah looked toward the advancing soldiers. They seemed endless and didn't show any signs of retreating. Sinah let his hand go then pressed her palms together. She closed her eyes lowering her eyebrows. She looked like she was concentrating as hard as she could. After a few seconds, Sinah slowly parted her hands. A large curved blade began to form between her palms. Once complete, Sinah opened her eyes then thrusted the blade forward. It zipped by Fallen and sliced the soldiers closing in on them clean in half. Sinah then snatched Fallen's hand.

Before she had a chance to coax him toward the escalators again, Fallen gripped her hand and raced passed her. Having such a tight grip, Sinah was dragged behind him. Once half way down the escalators, Fallen leapt over the side. Since Fallen still had her hand in his, she didn't have any choice but to follow. The moment they landed, they raced through the main floor, down the stairs, through the reception area toward the stairs leading to the sewers.

The loud warning emergency system blared louder and louder. Sinah glanced behind herself hearing loud slamming and banging sounds. Steel doors were rapidly shutting the facility down attempting to protect it. Fallen and Sinah raced toward the lift, where everyone else stood awaiting them.

The minute Fallen stepped onto the lift, something snapped around Sinah's ankle. Before she could react, she was ripped away from Fallen's grip. As he quickly turned back to her, steel bars slammed down right in front of him.

Eighty-Eight

Panic, Pain and Sacrifice

A greyish red tentacle had grabbed hold of Sinah. As it lifted her high off the ground, Fallen yelled out. "Sinah!!"

Before it had a chance to slam her into the cement below, she made her boot blades appear and swung her free foot upward, slashing through it. The minute she hit the ground, Sinah ran toward her fellow soldiers.

Fallen gripped the steel bars hissing back at Dante. "Get this open now!"

Dante quickly tapped the green screen from his Combat glove. "I don't know if I can Commander. The emergency system has-"

Fallen cut him off with a snarl. "Now!"

Dante instantly went flush and began to frantically work. "Y... yes Commander."

Bridger glanced down at his own Combat glove. "Commander, we're running out of time!"

Fallen reached through the bars and placed his hand on the side of Sinah's face. "I won't leave you behind."

Sinah's features weakened as she slowly shook her head. Right before Fallen opened his mouth to say something, he noticed tentacles slowly crawling up from the sewer water. His eyebrows lowered as he growled. "Dante get this open!"

Anxious sweat formed then fell from Dante's panicked face. "I'm trying Commander, I'm trying!"

Bridger leaned toward him and whispered. "Can you do it?"

Dante glanced up at Bridger with an awkward worried look in his eyes. Bridger mirrored his awkwardness barely nodding.

Murdoch suddenly withdrew his gun and stepped beside Fallen noticing what was crawling out of the water. "Commander!"

Fallen nodded not shifting his attention from them. "Be on your guard."

Sinah stared at Fallen's angered expression for a few seconds. She barely nodded before she reached her hands through the bars then placed them upon the sides of his face. Fallen eyes instantly darted back to her. Sinah weakly smiled before she pulled him down to her and firmly pressed her lips against his. Before Fallen could have a reaction of any kind, she stepped back from him and his grip. Sinah's features broke as she slowly shook her head.

Fallen shook his head with a hiss reaching his hand out to her. "No! I won't leave you behind!"

A loud chuckle flooded then echoed through the small area. "Aw, isn't that cute? Lucifer won't leave his little A Helix behind."

Quickly turning toward the voice, Sinah's eyes darted to the tentacles. Without hesitation, she made two blades appear in her hands and shifted into an attack stance.

Many of tentacles suddenly rushed up and out of the sewer water, lifting a being with it. "I told you. Nobody leaves here alive."

Fallen frowned instantly recognizing the creature. It was Kadin. His skin colour was a greyish red as were his eyes. The only part of him that resembled anything human was from the waist up. Everything below, were just tentacles.

Kadin chuckled looking toward Sinah. "And once I kill this girl, I'm going to kill the rest of you."

Before Sinah had a chance to react, Fallen began to shoot. Murdoch quickly followed his lead and began to shoot as well. Kadin chuckled again blocking each and every shot with his flailing tentacles. Even though the bullets had made contact and hit their targets, the wounds rapidly healed.

Kadin wasn't shy about basking in his utter amusement. "Is that the best you can do Lucifer, silly little gun shots?" Pointing toward Sinah, he continued. "Now let me show you a real attack."

Many of his tentacles darted toward her. With Sinah's amazing reaction time, it didn't take any real effort for her to slash all of them within her range. Just like the bullet holes, the wounds rapidly healed. Fallen snarled, shooting as fast as he could pull the trigger. "Dante!"

Dante swallowed heavily, frenetically working on the green screen. "I'm trying Commander!"

"Stop trying and get it done!"

Bridger looked toward the panic soaked Dante in sympathy.

Kadin looked up at the cement ceiling listening to the alarm. "Hear that beeping? Soon the whole facility will be sealed. Then there won't be any way to escape."

Sinah's eyes darted to Fallen as her features weakened. After a few seconds of simply watching him shoot, her expression suddenly shifted to firm and determined. She gave a quick confident nod as she turned her attention back to Kadin. She opened her hands releasing the blades. As they fell then vanished, she leapt on top of some of the tentacles and raced toward Kadin's main body.

Any part that swung toward her, Murdoch and Fallen shot clearing her pathway. Once Sinah was in range, she slammed her hand deep into Kadin's chest. As she ripped her hand out, she grabbed onto a lump of something. Before Sinah had a chance to even glance at the black lump resembling a heart, acidic black liquid gushed from the hole in his chest. Sinah's body instantly phased protecting her from damage.

Kadin snarled snapping a tentacle around a hanging piece of her red scarf. "You think you can kill me?!"

Before Sinah could react, Kadin aggressively whipped her toward the cement wall. Sinah smashed into it then weakly flopped to all fours. Fallen instantly screamed out. "Sinah!!"

Sinah's breathing shook as she gave a slight nod in acknowledgement.

"Get it open!!"

Dante closed his eyes, hesitantly lowering his hands. The green screens vanished as he slowly shook his head. "I… I can't Commander. The lock down system has sealed-"

Fallen hissed, tossing his gun aside. "Fine! I'll do it myself!!"

Both Bridger and Dante's eyes darted to him as he grabbed the bars. They could hear the back of his battle suit snapping and ripping from his strength.

Sinah slowly got to her feet. The second she did, the tentacles snapped around her body. Kadin chuckled watching her struggle. Kadin shifted his body toward her. A cold smile took his lips as he wrapped his hands around her throat. "Watch as I kill your pathetic little A Helix."

Fallen snarled. "Get your filthy hands off of her!!"

Sinah struggled for breath as she tried her best to get free. Kadin laughed at her pointless attempts in amusement. "They get to watch you die before they're trapped here forever. I can't wait to experiment on their bodies. I wonder what they'll become."

Sinah turned her head toward Fallen. Her expression broke seeing him use all his strength trying to break through the steel bars. The thick bars only seemed to slightly move under his force. Sinah then looked toward Bridger.

The minute he made eye contact with her, he heard a soft voice whisper from within. "*Please, save him.*"

Eighty-Nine

Fallen Angel

Bridger's expression instantly shifted to shock and confusion. Sinah's features weakened even more. Bridger gasped placing his hand on his chest hearing the voice again. "*Please. Please save him.*"

Bridger stared at the choking Sinah for a few more seconds before he gave a quick nod. Dante's eyes darted to him as he snatched his backpack. "What are you doing?!"

Bridger unzipped the top and pulled out six of the Synthetic D syringes. "I'm doing what A Helixes do. We save as many as we can."

As Bridger approached Fallen, Murdoch noticed him out of the corner of his eye. Once he turned, his eyes darted down to the samples. A full frown instantly took his lips as he spoke. "What the hell?"

Bridger looked toward Fallen. The back of his battle suit and sleeves had become shreds from the force he was using. "We're going to get caught up in the explosion Murdoch. For how much explosives we used, only the Commander will survive. Barely but he'll survive."

Murdoch looked toward the struggling for life Sinah. She had her eyes squinted shut but she was still trying her best for freedom. "What about her?"

Bridger closed his eyes and turned his head as his features weakened. "…Sacrifice."

Murdoch's eyes darted back to Bridger. "B… but I can't just let y-"

"Just look away Murdoch. I can't let us all be killed."

Murdoch frowned shaking his head. "And I-"

"Damn it mean Helix!" Bridger hissed looking toward him. "Don't let her sacrifice be for nothing!"

The second Murdoch closed his eyes and turned his head, Bridger slammed all six syringes into the back of Fallen's neck. Fallen made a loud sound of discomfort as all the samples were forced into his blood stream. He tossed his head back as blood and saliva sprayed form his mouth. His breathing rapidly became laboured as he seemed to crumble over. Both Bridger and Dante watched his distress in sympathy.

A thick clear mucus like drool oozed from Fallen's mouth as he groaned. "Sin… ah…" He reached his shaking hand through the bars out toward Sinah before he lost consciousness.

Thanks to Bridger's quick reflexes, he caught him before he hit the ground. "Murdoch! Little help!"

Murdoch turned his head back toward them. His expression instantly broke seeing Fallen's condition. Bridger hooked one of Fallen's arms over his shoulders. Murdoch quickly went to his other side and did the same.

Bridger removed one of his Combat gloves looking toward Sinah. She had gone very pale and her resistance had become slight to almost nothing. Bridger tossed the glove toward her calling out. "Sinah!"

Sinah weakly shifted her dimming eyes toward him. Bridger pointed at the glove that landed only a few inches away from her. "The manual activation button!"

Sinah's eyes shifted from it back up to Bridger. He closed his hand into a fist then suddenly opened it. Sinah, who understood weakly nodded. Kadin snarled tightening his grip on her throat. "Snap damn you! Snap!!"

Bridger's features weakened as he spoke. "Dante, press the lift."

Dante's disposition was so upset, he could barely speak. "…Y…yeah…"

Bridger closed his eyes and lowered his head. "Good-bye Sinah. …I'm sorry."

As they vanished, Sinah looked back at Bridger's Combat glove. Her eyebrows lowered as she aggressively began to struggle again.

Bridger and Murdoch dragged Fallen off the lift. As they began to move through the underground, Bridger glanced back at Dante. He was removing his Combat gloves and back pack. Bridger's expression shifted to confusion as pulled out his laptop and tossed everything else aside. Once Dante noticed Bridger watching him, he quickly shook his head. Bridger barely nodded returning his attention back to escaping.

As they passed through the 'shanty' town, Dante kept an eye out for any Lost Soul in the area. Luckily for them, the Lost Souls simply ignored the soldiers and went about their business. They quickly passed through the subway cars then up the stairs. Bridger hooked Fallen onto his back as he climbed up the ladder leading to the stage. Murdoch and Dante quickly followed after them.

Bridger frowned toward the Lost Souls in the amphitheatre 'shanty' town. Most had returned to their homes. Murdoch hooked Fallen's arm back over his shoulders. "Just keep moving. I have a free hand." As Murdoch lifted his gun in his hand, he continued. "Dante, you're our eyes."

Dante nodded paying closer attention to his surroundings. A few of the Lost Souls nervously looked toward them but kept their distance. As they left the amphitheatre grounds, Bridger couldn't help but to snicker seeing a few fired Lost Souls near their hummer. As Bridger leaned Fallen more on Murdoch, the bombs went off.

Everyone's eyes darted to the shell like dome as it collapsed. Bridger's features broke as he closed his eyes. "Good-bye fellow A Helix."

A few tears escaped Dante's eyes. His expression shifted to confusion as he touched them. It was as if his emotions had not only overpowered him but also overwhelmed him.

Murdoch listened to the many screams of the Lost Souls. "We don't have time to stand around here. Bridger, deactivate the electrical traps and let's get out of here."

Bridger barely nodded opening his eyes.

Ninety

A Broken Team

Murdoch anxiously paced Fallen's office. Both he and Bridger had laid the unconscious Fallen on his leather couch. Dante, who was standing by the desk, glanced toward Bridger. He was leaning against the ceiling to floor windows with his arms crossed.

Murdoch suddenly hissed. "He better recover!"

Bridger barely nodded. "He will. Being such a large sample, it probably just needs time to work its way through his system."

Murdoch frowned pacing even faster. Bridger looked toward Dante. He looked like he was drained from crying. "Why'd you ditch the samples and info Dante?"

Murdoch instantly stopped short and questioned. "You ditched them?" Before Dante had a chance to answer, he questioned again. "So she died for nothing?"

"No! We were sent to deal with the Lost Soul's Lab and we did. We destroyed that place!" Dante's angered tone broke as he continued. "A… And we lost a member of our team for it."

Bridger's features weakened a little. Murdoch shook his head. "But we-"

Dante hissed regaining control over his emotions. "If we would have brought back the information and samples, the ADGL Labs will start testing and creating some themselves." Slamming his fist onto the desk, he continued. "And I won't let our Lab create creatures like them! I don't care what my punishment will be!"

"It's not like anyone is going to find out there were any samples."

Both Bridger and Dante's eyes darted to Murdoch in shock. Murdoch snickered at their expressions. "Don't look so surprised. I think the synthetics are dangerous and nobody should have it. We lost the info and samples in the explosion and that's all anyone needs to know."

Dante barely nodded. "Yeah."

Fallen suddenly made a loud gasp sound as he sat up. Everyone's eyes darted toward him. Murdoch's eyes instantly lit up. "Commander!"

Fallen shifted to the edge of his couch and leaned over. As he began to make retching noises, Murdoch's features weakened. Blood, black guck and a greyish red tar like substance poured from his mouth onto the floor. Dante watched him with a slightly disgusted look. Once all of the synthetic was out of his system, he spat on it. Dante's expression shifted to shock as the vomit caught flame. As it burned to ash, Fallen spoke. "…You left her to die."

Bridger stood up straight quickly responding. "It was my call Commander."

Fallen growled, getting to his feet. "Your call?! Since when do my commands get over turned by an A Helix?!"

Bridger's lips touched at a slight frown. "If we would have stayed Commander, we would have been killed as well."

Fallen hissed, clinching his fists. "The only A Helix that mattered was killed!"

Bridger's features weakened a little. "I understand how you felt about Sinah, Commander. But-"

"You understand nothing! I've had my fill of A Helixes! All you've done is caused me nothing but trouble! I don't need any more disposable soldiers!"

Bridger snapped advancing on Fallen. "Disposable soldiers?! That's all we are t-"

Fallen cut Bridger off with a fist slam to his jaw. The force knocked Bridger clean off his feet. Frowning down at him, Fallen spoke. "And I don't need traitors who disobey my commands."

Dante quickly ran to Bridger's side and helped him to sit up. "But Commander-"

"Has the clean-up crew been dispatched yet?"

"No Commander, your recovery was more important."

Fallen turned his attention to Murdoch. "Get a booster shot and send them out. We're going to find her." As Murdoch nodded, Fallen glared back at Bridger. "And you. You're not on my team any longer. I won't tolerate traitors."

Both Bridger and Dante were silent as Murdoch and Fallen left the office.

Ninety-One

After All's said and Done

Bridger slowly got to his feet as he rubbed his jaw. "Thank goodness for my rapid healing skill. I'm glad he didn't break any teeth or jaw for that matter."

Dante looked up at Bridger sympathetically. "I… I'm sure the Commander didn't mean it. He's probably still disorientated from the Synthetic D."

Bridger smiled slightly. "Thanks Dante, but we both know he meant every word. The Commander never says what he doesn't mean."

"But… but…"

Bridger smirked putting his hands on his waist. "Well good luck finding anyone who can handle explosives like I do. Murdoch's only learned a few of my tricks. But he doesn't realize how much strength and energy it takes to make multiple ones. And I'm the only one that knows how to fine tune the heart bombs."

"Isn't there creation in the Combat files?"

Bridger snickered with a shrug. "Well, the basics are, yeah. But did you really think I'd go into detail about them? Do you know how much work that is?" Bridger waved his hand dismissively. "Forget that!"

Dante couldn't help but to weakly laugh. "You're so lazy." His expression shifted to upset as he continued. "I'm going to miss you on our team."

"Yeah, it's going to be boring around here but you know…" Bridger lowered his tone of voice. It was as if he didn't what anyone else to hear him. "Something inside me feels like it couldn't care less."

"What do you mean?"

Bridger scratched his head as his expression shifted to confusion. "It's hard to explain. It feels almost as if I want to tell the Commander, I'm an A Helix and I don't have to obey-" Bridger stopped short as his bewilderment increased. "But that would mean-" Bridger suddenly gasped in shock. "Oh my god!"

"What's wrong?"

"Test my blood!"

"What?"

Bridger unhooked one of his suspenders. As he began to wrap it around his forearm, he spoke. "I need you to test my blood. Check my A Helix status!"

Dante's lips couldn't help but to touch at a frown. "Do I look like an ADGL Lab Tech to you?"

"Just do it!"

Dante walked behind Fallen's desk and tapped the air activating the green screens. "I don't know if I can even access those tests up here."

Bridger grinned tapping one of his veins. "Ah. This one's nice and juicy."

Dante placed his open laptop below the green screens as he continued. "I guess I could try to use them through a back door. That way we won't be noticed."

"Got a syringe or something?"

Dante opened the drawer to the desk. There were papers, pens, paperclips and other random office supplies inside. Since almost all work was done on the green screens, everything was covered in dust. Dante smiled finding a thumb tack. He spoke picking it up and offering it to him. "Here you go."

Bridger looked at it as if he wasn't sure what it even was. "What's that for?"

Dante placed a piece of paper on the desk top. "Poke yourself then wipe it on this. I only need a smear."

Bridger's suspender made a loud snap sound as he let it go. "That's all? Then how come whenever I'm normally tested I need to give a syringe full?"

Dante shrugged tapping on his laptop keys. “Your Lab Tech is an idiot? All you ever need is a smear.”

Bridger smiled poking his index finger with the tack. “Maybe he just likes spending time with me.”

Dante continued working as he called out. “That reminds me, computer, location of Alex the mechanic.”

Bridger questioned wiping his blood on the paper. “Who?”

The computer beeped. “Mechanic with the first name Alex is located in Launch Pad area, hanger number-”

“Call location.”

Bridger put his bleeding finger into his mouth as a voice spilled through the green screens. “Mechanic station, how can I-”

“This is Helix 2341 Dante. Please Send Alex to the Commander’s office. Inform him that he needs to bring what I had him work on.”

“Y… Yes Sir.”

Once the call was disconnected, Bridger cooed. “Ooo you sound so dominate and macho, Info, Surveillance and tough guy soldier.”

Dante frowned as he snatched up the paper. “Shut up.”

Bridger childishly giggled. “Yes Sir tough guy Helix.”

Dante only continued to frown.

Ninety-Two

A Helix Blood

Alex nervously knocked on the closed office door. He was caught off guard as Bridger opened it and offered him his hand with a full smile. "Hi there, are you Alex? I'm Bridger."

Alex nervously took then shook his hand. "Uh… Yes, I know sir."

Bridger chuckled pulling him into the office. As he closed the door behind him, he spoke. "Relax the Commander isn't here. And call me Bridger."

"Uh… I… I know that Sir, uh Bridger. The Commander went with the clean-up crew."

Bridger pulled Alex over to Dante. "Alex's here."

Dante barely nodded not shifting his attention from his laptop. "Give me a minute." After a few moments of working in silence, he hissed. "Damn it!"

Alex walked behind the desk to Dante's side. "What are you trying to do?"

Dante released a sigh full of frustration. "We need to check Bridger's Helix status and I'm having a hell of a time entering the Helix files undetected."

"Of course anyone who tries to enter would be noticed. They're some of our more protected files."

Dante instantly tossed Alex a slight frown. Noticing it, Alex spoke. "Maybe you can check his Helix outside the Helix files."

Dante's slight frown suddenly shifted into a full smile. "By doing a room sweep! Of course!"

Bridger smiled toward Alex. "You should be a Lab Tech."

Alex chuckled a little. "I am a Lab Tech. I'm just temporarily working as a mechanic."

"Now that I'm free, maybe that's what I should try to do."

Dante looked up at the green screens. "Computer, scan room for blood samples, excluding the Commanders."

A green wave scanned the room. The minute it hit the blood smear, it beeped. "Blood sample detected, Helix 7923 Bridger."

"Display sample."

The minute the computer made Bridger's Helix appear on the screen, both he and Dante gasped. Alex's eyes widened looking at it as well. Bridger's Helix which was normally a high A Helix was now a midrange double Helix. Dante shook his head in disbelief. "H… How is that possible?"

Bridger only stared at his developing double A Helix in shock. Alex shook his head questioning. "Aren't double Helixes supposed to have some sort have physical change?"

Dante quickly wiped Bridger's blood from the tack then jabbed his own finger. The second he smeared his blood sample on the paper, he spoke. "Computer, scan room for blood samples excluding the Commander's and Helix 7923 Bridger's."

The green wave scanned the room again. Once it hit his blood sample, the computer beeped. "Blood sample detected, Helix 2341 Dante."

"Display sample!"

Once Dante's Helix appeared on another green screen, he stared at it like it didn't belong to him. Dante's once midrange Helix was now almost at the same level as Bridger's originally was.

Bridger looked at it then nodded. "Yours changed too. I knew it."

Dante's eyes darted to him. "Knew what?"

Bridger placed his hand on his chest. "Something inside me changed when we were on the lift. And something feels different now."

"What are you talking about?"

Bridger's tone and disposition became very serious. "Dante, do you still feel loyal to the Commander?"

Ninety-Three

Hard Drive

Dante stared at Bridger in shock and disbelief. "Of course I do! Don't you?"

Bridger looked at his developing double Helix. "No."

Dante shook his head as if he didn't understand what Bridger was saying. "But the Commander is-"

"Lucifer."

Dante opened his mouth to say something but Bridger suddenly gasped. "Oh my god!"

Dante gave him a confused look. "What? What's wrong?"

Bridger pointed at their Helixes displayed on the green screens. "That's why our Helix's have changed. That's why I don't feel loyalty to the Commander like I once did. That's why I heard that voice inside me! It's Sinah!"

"What's Sinah?"

Bridger quickly responded. "She's God!"

Dante held his look of confusion, shaking his head. "What are you talking about? Sinah's not-"

Alex cut Dante off as he pulled a microchip out of his pocket. "That would explain what I saw." Both Bridger and Dante's eyes darted toward him as he continued. "I've been carrying this around since I got it off of your laptop. I was so worried someone might find it."

Dante took the microchip from Alex then quickly hooked it into his laptop. Bridger went to his side to look at the screen aswell. "What are we watching?"

Dante instantly went flush as his expression shifted to awkward. "Uh… Remember when Sinah first joined us?"

Bridger snickered a little. "And someone tried to take a peek at an innocent girl."

"Uh… Well… I… I recorded…"

Bridger's disposition instantly shifted from amused to a disappointed disbelife. "You did what?"

Alex quickly shook his head. "Forget about that! Play the recording!"

Dante tapped on his keys to begin the recording. The image of Sinah changing into her battle suit appeared on the screen. As she turned toward the computer, she phased. Right after the recording shut off.

Bridger crossed his arms shaking his head and closing his eyes. "You know that was wrong, right?"

Dante looked toward the desk with a slightly ashamed look on his face. Alex pointed at the computer, shaking his head. "If he didn't, we wouldn't have this. I didn't notice it at first. I've never seen anyone phase before so I watched it again."

Bridger spoke in a voice full of disapproval, looking toward them. "You mean you just wanted to watch a pretty girl take off her clothes again."

Both Alex and Dante went bright red. As Alex shook off his embarrassed flush, he spoke. "Slow the recording down."

Dante tapped on his laptop slowing the image down and also clearing it up. Bridger's eyes darted to just below Sinah's ribcage seeing very heavy scarring. They looked like terrible burns that had long healed. "What happened to her?"

As the image of Sinah slowly began to phase, both Dante and Bridger's eyes widened. Within the phase it looked like another form of herself appeared right behind her. This Sinah was surrounded by a weak golden light with a large ethereal golden circle floating directly behind her back. Bridger couldn't help but to smile softly at the heavenly image. "…I knew it."

Dante stared at the second image of Sinah in shock and disbelief. "Wh… Why didn't we notice it? We're both A Helixes, why didn't we sense it or something?"

Bridger held his soft smile. "Maybe her Helix wasn't developed either."

Dante quickly began to tap on the green screens. Alex looked toward him then at the green screens himself. "What are you doing?"

"I'm accessing Sinah's Helix file."

"They'll be able to detect you if-"

"Her file was put in the Commander's personal files." Dante gave a quick shrug as he continued. "Normally, I'd need his voice to unlock the voice recognition but I personally put it in there myself, so…" Sinah's Helix appeared on one of the green screens. Dante's eyes instantly locked on the shadow behind it. "There, that shadow."

Bridger looked toward it himself, before he spoke. "So that's why her parents hid her. If an ADGL Lab tech would have noticed that, they would have kept Sinah in the Labs nonstop. She'd be the next perfect experiment A."

Alex looked toward Bridger then Dante. "How come a Tech hasn't noticed it? What about in the booster shot lines? Surely, they-"

Dante shook his head a little. "She wasn't a registered Helix. We believe her parents stole the samples to maintain her sanity."

Bridger slowly shook his head. "Or maybe they didn't. She is the Commander's counterpart. She, like the Commander may not have even needed them."

Dante released a saddened sigh closing his eyes. "What are we going to tell her parents? How can we possibly explain that not only was Sinah God but now she's dead."

Bridger walked toward the ceiling to floor windows. "That explosion would have killed everyone but the Commander. What if…? What if Sinah's Helix jumped to protect her? That would explain why our Helixes jumped as well."

Dante's eyes darted to him. "Are you saying Sinah might be alive?"

Bridger put his hands on his hips. "If I'm right then, yeah barely but yeah."

Alex began to smile. "Then that's good. That means the clean-up crew or the Commander will find her."

"I'm a high A… No, a developing mid-level double A Helix. It's my duty to find God. So Dante…" Bridger turned his attention back to him as he continued. "I'll ask you again. Do you still feel loyal to the Commander?"

Ninety-Four

Loyalty and Friendship

Dante sighed closing his eyes. "I know you want me to say no. But I just don't feel that way. What I am I owe to him. I really do owe him everything."

"I do too. If it wasn't for him, I wouldn't be standing here." Bridger forced a laugh through a weakened expression. "I'd be in a cell right now or maybe even worse."

Both Dante and Alex's eyes darted toward him. Bridger glanced at their shocked and questioning expressions. He released a defeated sigh before he spoke. "Remember when that Kadin thing or whatever it was, talked about Synthetic A's reaction?"

Alex held the same expression, while Dante nodded. "And Murdoch told you to focus."

Bridger turned from them and walked toward the ceiling to floor windows. "When too much Synthetic A is put in a body, with a soul or without, it... well, it..." Bridger turned his head as if he didn't want anyone to see his upset disposition. "It attacks them. It melts the living flesh clean off their bones and those poor beings feel every part of it. It's so awful and because it's formed from an A helix, it screams out for help. It cries out to other A Helixes in a state of panic. And as fellow A Helixes we feel all the suffering, all the pain. We feel the agony of the snapping of the veins, the heat of our eyes boiling, the-"

Dante tossed Bridger a look of disgust. "Okay, we get it. Gross."

Bridger looked up at the eclipsed sun and moon. "I still can't believe something created from something so pure, so innocent and so good could do such a horrible thing." Bridger awkwardly chuckled. "Murdoch was already a part of the Commander's team then. The ADGL Lab Tech's didn't know how things were going to go, so he was asked to be there for safety. When it happened, it caused my Helix to go into a frenzy. I felt like I wanted to rip everything and everyone apart. I wanted them to feel what that poor soul was feeling. Then suddenly everything went white. Blank. My Helix snapped."

Bridger closed his eyes. "When I came too, I was pinned on the floor by the Commander. When I looked around, the Lab was trashed and all the ADGL Lab Tech's were huddled in the corner. They were staring back at me traumatized. And I had seriously hurt Murdoch."

Dante's expression shifted to shock and disbelief. "Murdoch was hurt? Aren't you two basically evenly matched?"

Bridger began to rub his upper arm, it was as if he was trying to comfort himself or warm up from a sudden chill. "Yeah but when a Helix goes into a frenzy-"

"It takes someone much stronger to stop you."

"Seeing what I had done, I couldn't apologize enough. I wanted so bad to get to my knees and beg for forgiveness. But obviously I couldn't, I was still pinned. I broke down and before I began to cry..." Bridger indifferently waved his hand. "I was really upset and couldn't control my emotions. Anyway, the Commander said 'Strength and anger like this for a fallen fellow Helix shouldn't be wasted guarding some Lab experiments. You're on my team now.' He then let me up and left. That was that, I was a part of the Commander's team. Normally if a Helix snaps-"

Date was quick to finish his thought. "They are put into a cell as a failed Helix. After that-"

"I try not to think about that." Bridger suddenly smiled pushing back any upset feelings he had of the past. "Thanks to the Commander, I didn't receive any punishment and my Helix never snapped again." Bridger's smile shifted to proud. "And now that I'm a developing double A Helix, obviously I wasn't a failed Helix to begin with."

"If you owe him so much, how can you turn against him?"

Bridger chuckled shaking his head. "I'm not turning against him. I just don't feel like obeying him anymore. The Commander may be Lucifer and Sinah may be God and all but I care about both of them." Another chuckle caught his throat. "It's silly I know but I think of them as my friends. So not only do I want to find Sinah out of friendship, but I also want to bring Heaven back to her Hell."

Dante sighed closing his eyes. "But there's nothing we can do. Without any equipment we-"

A smirk instantly consumed Bridger's lips. "Well gentlemen, I think it's time for a rebellion."

Ninety-Five

The Rescue Plan

Before either Dante or Alex could question, Bridger spoke. "It's a good thing we didn't take off our battle suits or we'd be screwed on defense."

Dante looked toward Alex then back to Bridger. "Are you serious?"

"About what? The rebellion?" Bridger made a fist then confidently lifted it into the air. "Damn right! We have to save Sinah! She could have been blown a distance from the blast zone." Bridger lowered his fist as his tone of voice became impatient. "She could be lying in some ditch just bleeding and waiting for us. She could-"

Dante lips touched at a frown. "Okay, you made your point."

Bridger walked in front of the office desk. "So, are you with me, Info, Surveillance and tough guy soldier?"

Dante released a defeated sigh before he gave a confident nod. "Proper protocol, be damned. We protect our friends."

Bridger slammed on his hands on the top of the desk. Both young men jumped as he yelled out. "Damn straight!!"

"I'd like to help." Alex went flush as Bridger's and Dante's eyes darted toward him. "I know I'm just a simple human and I can't fight or anything but-"

Dante quickly shook his head as he began to work on his laptop. "No, no Lab Tech help is great. You can follow the surveillance and be our eyes. I'll hook up a line of communication from my laptop to our ear pieces."

Bridger put his hands on his waist and grinned. "Okay, we'll need some weapons. And since the Commander took Murdoch with him, I highly doubt he had a chance to deactivate the Combat gloves."

Dante didn't glance up from working. "Will they still work?"

Bridger shrugged. "I don't see why not. The last thing Murdoch does after all the equipment is returned is remove the chips. The Commander was his priority so he probably just tossed them into the shooting range without thinking."

"If you think Sinah could have been blown somewhere, I don't think taking a hummer will be able to find her."

Bridger shook his head. "No, we can't cover enough ground. We'll probably be caught by other soldiers before we even-"

"We have helicopters."

Bridger awkwardly chuckled looking toward Alex. "That's the one thing I can't use."

Alex looked toward Dante. "Can you?"

Dante gave a brief shake of his head. "No and I can't drive either."

Bridger placed his hand on his chin like he was thinking. "If we're going to make a break for the 'copters, we're going to need one hell of a decoy."

Alex suddenly smiled. "I can override the hanger doors in the Launch Pad area. Most mechanics work inside so I can trap them in there."

Dante clicked slightly faster on his keypad. "That's not a bad idea. How about also causing a blackout? Lock as many people in the dark as you can. It's a bitch to reboot everything and until a Lab Tech makes it out there, they won't be able to do anything."

"That means we'll have to access the Launch Pad area through Residential. The problem is there are a couple of security issues along the way."

Dante looked up at Bridger. "I can handle all of them except the soldier manned security booths."

Bridger smirked. "Oh I can handle those. All I need is Combat gloves."

"We still have the helicopter prob-"

Bridger suddenly snapped his fingers. "Bruno! He can fly one."

"He can?"

Bridger chuckled shaking his head. "I swear you and Murdoch are so rude. You two just hear nagging and nothing else."

Dante indifferently shrugged. "Well, he's annoying. Do you think he'll join us?"

"If he thinks this will increase his chances of joining the Commander's team, he will."

"Alex, I'll be done here in a few moments. I'll then hook you over to the Launch Pad systems."

"Okay then I'll take your laptop to-"

"I think it's best to work in here. This is the last place anyone will catch you."

Alex nervously looked around the office. "B… but what if he comes back?"

Dante lifted his hands up to the green screens. He responded flipping through them. "I'll access the Commander's life sign. It will make a beep sound once he's in the area. The faster the beeping, the closer he is you. Try to stay as long as you can. Since this is the Commander's office and you're using my laptop, it's going to take them a hell of a long time to locate exactly where the problem is coming from."

As Alex nodded, Bridger walked toward the closed office door. "I'll go get the Combat gloves and give Bruno a call. The last thing I want to do is run into Amos. Dante meet me down at the jeeps."

"Okay, contact me if the Combat gloves have been deactivated. If I have to, I'll make a side trip to equipment and steal some."

Bridger lifted his finger and shook it in disapproval. "Ah, ah, ah, we don't steal fellow A Helix. We borrow."

Dante couldn't help but to snicker. "Okay then, I'll borrow some."

Ninety-Six

Tricks and Lies

Bruno was so excited it looked like any moment he was going to jump out of his skin. "I can't believe it! This is going to be great!"

Bridger smiled as the microchips on his Combat gloves instantly lit up. "Now remember, this doesn't mean you're a part of the Commander's team. This is like-"

"Like a test or something to see if I'm good enough?"

Bridger couldn't help but to chuckle at Bruno's happy tone and ecstatic disposition. As he left the shooting range, he spoke. "Yeah sure, something like that. The Commander left it up to me to see if you'll be a good team player."

"I am! I'm a great team player!"

Bridger waited until Bruno got onto the elevator with him before pressing the floor button. "Well that's what we're going to find out. I'm the lead on this mission, so whatever I say goes, got it?"

"I'll obey your every Command." As Bridger nodded, Bruno glanced down at the second set of Combat gloves in his hands. "Are those for me?"

Bridger didn't shift his attention from the elevator floors being highlighted. "No, this isn't a Combat based mission. It's a rescue mission. Your job is to drive then fly us where ever I tell you."

Bruno quickly nodded with a confident smile. "I can do that!"

Once the elevator doors opened, Bridger and Bruno stepped into an area designated for facility use only jeeps. Soldiers or maintenance crews were the main groups who drove them. Mostly everyone else accessed different points of the facility on foot.

Once Bruno's eyes caught sight of Dante, he called out. "I'm so happy to be finally working with you Dante!"

Dante didn't make a single attempt to pretend he was glad to see Bruno. "Yeah okay, did the Combat gloves work?"

Bridger nodded handing him his pair. "Yup, I told you Murdoch wouldn't bother with them right away."

Dante put on his Combat gloves, once the microchips lit up, he spoke. "Get in the jeep. I'll let you know when you can drive through the exit."

Bridger nodded opening the driver's side door. "Hop in Bruno."

Like an excited dog going on a much needed walk, Bruno raced over to him. "Okay!"

Bridger couldn't help but to chuckle while Dante rolled his eyes. As Bridger approached the passenger side, he spoke. "Where are you headed?"

"To override a few systems, it has to be done manually. Pick me up when I tell you." Not waiting for a response, Dante raced toward the exit. Once a few feet near it, he pressed his ear piece. "Alex, can you turn cameras A and B away from the exit panel."

Alex was quick with his response. "On it, how long do you need?"

"As soon as I'm done here, the cameras won't be a problem."

"Should I cause a blind spot in Residential?"

The second the cameras turned away from the exit, Dante accessed the green screens at the panel. He responded as he went to work. "We won't need one. I'm activating the maintenance systems. I'll just load them into my Combat gloves and whenever I need a blind spot, I'll just make one."

"And nobody will think anything of it. Maintenance causes temporary gaps in the systems all the time, great idea!"

Dante's lips touched at a pride filled smile. He smiled even more as the garage doors began to open. "That was too easy."

Alex smiled seeing all the codes coming up on Dante's laptop. "Cameras down. Maintenance codes displaying, you're good to go."

Dante pressed his ear piece. "Ready."

Bridger pointed towards the exit. "Let's head out!"

Ninety-Seven

The Rebellion

The minute Dante climbed into the jeep, he activated the maintenance files from his Combat gloves. "We don't have much time."

Bridger smiled and pointed ahead of himself. "Bruno, get us through Residential to the Launch Pad area and step on it!"

Bruno calmly drove out of the garage exit then into the Residential area. At each intersection he approached, he cautiously looked in each direction before moving through. Bridger glanced toward the homes as they slowly passed by. "Uh… What part of step on it didn't you get?"

Bruno glanced toward his side view then rear view mirror. "But they're could be people walking around."

Dante who was frantically working on his green screens, frowned. "We don't have time for a leisurely drive."

Bruno glanced up at Dante's reflection. "But-"

Bridger glanced toward him with a slightly disappointed expression. "You know questioning a leader of a mission is very defiant. The Commander wouldn't tolerate that. Now-" Bridger pointed ahead of himself again. "Floor it!!"

Bruno went flush before he did as he was told. Despite being rattled from Bruno's zipping around corners, Dante didn't shift his attention from working. "Hurry up! The passage has been momentarily unlocked."

Bruno's erratic speeding came to a shrieking stop at the dead end. As the jeep began to lower, he placed his hand over his racing heart. "I've never driven that fast before in my life."

"Well once we hit the surface road, I want you to gun it as fast as you can again. Drive past the security booth and right through the boom gates."

Bruno's eyes darted to Bridger. "Go through the-"

Bridger made a disapproving noise. "Tsk, tsk, there's that questioning a leader again."

Bruno instantly went flush. He barely nodded driving onto the second platform. "O… Okay. I'll handle it."

The moment the jeep was on the road leading to the Launch Pad area, Bridger stood up in his seat. Bruno's eyes darted up at him in a panic. "What are you doing?! That's dangerous!"

Bridger clapped his hands together. "Focus on the road! Gun it!!"

Bruno nervously nodded as he stepped on the gas. Bridger locked his attention on the security booth being rattled around. "When in range, both of you close your eyes. Bruno, just keep driving straight."

Dante nodded pressing his earpiece. "Alex, the minute we are through activate the blackout lock down."

"Okay."

Bridger opened his hands forming a large greenish white orb. Bruno swallowed swerving the speeding car a little. Bridger kept his eyes transfixed on the booth as he whispered. "Stay calm Bruno. You can do this. Get ready… get ready…"

Once in throwing range, Bridger whipped the orb. A bright blinding light enveloped the entire area. Bridger forcefully squeezed his eyes shut as they plowed through the boom gates. "Sorry about that!!"

The security booth soldiers could only helplessly rub their eyes trying to regain their vision. Without being able to pay attention to the road and the startle from the destruction, Bruno's driving became erratic.

Bridger, who was almost tossed from vehicle, quickly leaned down and grabbed the steering wheel. "Careful now, I have this thing about dying!"

Bruno's eyes snapped open. Going a little flush, he took back control of the jeep. "Sorry!"

Alex spoke through Dante's earpiece. "Everything's down! Go for it!"

Bridger pointed toward the helicopters. "Go! Go!"

Bruno anxiously forced the gas petal to the floor. Once they were close enough, Bridger yelled out. "Stop!!"

Bruno stomped the breaks. The jeep swerved so wildly, it spun clean around and almost flipped over. Dante covered his head with both arms crying out. "Don't kill us!!!"

Bridger gripped whatever he could, being tossed about. "Hang on and don't puke!!"

Once jeep finally came to a complete stop, Bruno went ghost white. "Oh my god, we-"

Bridger cut him off snatching his arm and dragging him out of the vehicle. "No time for whining! Let's go!"

As the three of them ran toward the helicopters, Alex spoke. "Security has been alerted! Good luck you guys!"

Bridger smiled pressing his earpiece. "Thanks for the help Alex. See ya!"

Bruno didn't wait for Bridger or Dante to get buckled in before he started up the engine and took flight.

Ninety-Eight

Blast Zone Confusion

Fallen carelessly tossed chunk after chunk of the Lab aside. Thanks to Bridger's type of bomb, most of it broke apart in his hands. As he reached to grab another piece, his eyes darted to a piece of red material. He wasn't shy about shoving anyone of the clean-up crew aside as he raced toward it. His eyebrows furrowed slightly instantly recognizing the material as a piece of Sinah's scarf. It had become caught on a large blood covered rock.

Fallen's hand trembled a little as he reached out for it. Once in his grip, he clenched it in his fist. Thick red blood oozed from the scarf over his knuckles. He lowered his head and turned it away from the others. His entire disposition just screamed upset as he whispered. "…Sinah."

A member of the clean-up crew spoke approaching. "Do you want me to put that in a UV for you Commander?"

Fallen's eyebrows lowered as he turned a full icy frown toward him. The clean-up crew member instantly went flush feeling an almost suffocating wave of intimidation rush over him. He defensively lifted his hands and began to back away. "S… Sorry Commander."

Fallen stared him down until he rejoined the others working. His features then weakened again as he looked back at the bloody scarf. "I shouldn't have left you behind."

As he reached into his basic supply pack for a UV, Murdoch approached him. "Commander?"

Fallen didn't shift his attention as he spoke. "What?"

Murdoch glanced toward the many shocked and baffled looking clean-up crew members. "We seem to have a situation."

Fallen's lips touched at a frown. "What kind of situation?"

"There's been an attack on our Lab."

Fallen's eyes darted up to Murdoch. "Our Lab is under attack?" Before Murdoch had a chance to respond, Fallen advanced toward the crew. "Report!"

One of the crew quickly responded. "Yes Commander! Someone from inside the Lab has stolen-"

Before he could finish his sentence, a helicopter flew overhead. It was flying low enough to cause massive wind turbulence and drown out any sounds of conversation. Everyone except Fallen and Murdoch ducked for cover. Fallen frowned up at the helicopter as it circled the area a few times then hovered. Murdoch stared up at it in confusion as the helicopter door was pushed open. His expression instantly shifted to shock as Bridger stepped into the opening. Bridger smiled down at them and happily waved. Murdoch held his expression as he slowly lifted his hand in acknowledgement.

Fallen pressed his earpiece and began to yell something. His whole demeanor was annoyed. Bridger shook his head pointing at the helicopter blades spinning above him. It was impossible for anyone to hear anything. Fallen only yelled again, this time he looked like he was getting angrier by the second. Bridger glanced back at Bruno then nodded. Bruno gave a slight nod himself as he lifted the helicopter back up into the sky.

As Bridger began to get comfortable in his seat again, he could clearly hear Fallen's voice through his earpiece. "Get back to Lab!!! Now!!!"

Bridger chuckled a little, looking toward Dante. "My, my, someone's a little pissed off."

Dante, who was tapping on the green screen from his Combat glove, spoke. "What do you expect? We did steal a helicopter."

Bridger was quick to correct him. "We borrowed it."

Fallen's yelled again. "Don't make me repeat myself!! Bridger get-"

Bridger pressed his earpiece cutting Fallen off. He spoke in a mocking a childish tone. "I'm not on your team anymore so I don't have to listen to you. If you want this 'copter back why don't you come up here and get-" Bridger stopped short seeing a mangled body lying on the edge of a dilapidated building. He quickly grabbed Bruno's shoulder then pointed toward it. "There!"

Bruno looked where he was pointing then shifted the helicopter in that direction. Dante looked toward the body himself. "By the amount of explosives you set up, if that's her, she's in the range of where she could have landed."

The second Bruno safety landed, Bridger jumped out and ran toward the body.

Ninety-Nine

Left for Dead

Bridger's expression instantly broke recognizing the mangled bloody body of Sinah. She had sustained many brutal injuries and looked more like a shattered doll, rather than a person. Bridger couldn't help but close his eyes in utter despair. Dante climbed out of the helicopter, the minute he saw Sinah, his eyes welled up in tears. Trying his best to fight them off, he spoke. "I… Is she dead?"

Bridger slowly approached her. As he kneeled down, Bruno hopped off the helicopter himself. He looked toward Sinah with a slight look of confusion. "We were looking for her?"

Bridger gently moved a few bloody strands of hair from Sinah's colourless face. His features weakened as he slowly slid his finger tips to her jugular. Dante quickly wiped the tears from his cheeks, hoping nobody would notice. "Is she…?"

Bridger barely nodded not feeling any sign of a pulse. "…Yeah. Yeah, she's gone." Bridger suddenly shook his head in disbelief. "But I was so sure. I mean what about the change in our Helixes and what about that video? That has to mean something!"

Before Dante could respond, Fallen hissed through his earpiece. "Dante, Location, Now!!"

Dante looked toward Bridger. Without wanting them to, his eyes shifted to Sinah. He quickly turned away from them as he spoke. "The Commander wants to know where we are."

Bridger barely nodded again as he pressed his earpiece. "Commander, we… we've found Sinah."

"Alive?"

Bridger closed his beginning to water eyes before he hesitantly answered. "…No." Before Fallen could respond back, he spoke again. "Please return to our Lab. We'll be there with her body shortly, over and out."

Bruno, who had heard what Bridger said, nodded. "I'll get the 'copter ready."

Bridger delicately crossed Sinah's arms over her chest, like she was very frail rather than dead. "Oh Sinah, you were so good for our team, so good for all of us." As he slipped his hands under her and picked her up, he continued. "Alright now, let's get you home. I'm sure your parents would like to say their good-byes."

Dante refused to look toward them as Bridger carried Sinah passed him. As he began to buckle her up in a seat, he whispered. "I was so sure."

Once Dante climbed into the helicopter, he quickly got into his seat. "I thought so too, Bridger. Well maybe I did. I think I did. Maybe that's what all our Helixes become when we reach a certain point in our development. I mean all double Helixes are supposed to have a physical change. But then that's not necessarily true. I mean the Commander has silver eyes but…"

Bridger cut him off sitting in the seat next to him. "Dante, you're rambling."

Dante looked toward the destroyed corpse of Sinah before he choked on his words. "I… It sto… stops me from crying."

Bridger's expression turned sympathetic as he placed his hand on Dante's shoulder. He gave it a firm squeeze before he called out. "Let's head back Bruno!"

Dante quickly shook his head. "I want to check out the blast zone again. I need to make sure my other gloves were destroyed in the explosion. I don't want to take the chance that our Lab could find them." Dante turned his head as he continued. "I can't let this tragedy happen again."

Bridger weakly smiled as he nodded. "Okay. Bruno, head back to the blast zone!"

One-Hundred

Returning to the Scene

Bridger stared down at the clean-up crew as they hosed the entire area with synthetic gasoline. Dante frantically tapped the green screen from his Combat gloves. Bridger released a loud bored sigh before he spoke. "We've been here a while Dante. The Commander's probably wondering what happened to us."

Dante barely nodded. "Give Alex a call."

Bridger snickered then shrugged. The second he pressed Dante's ear piece rather than his own, Dante tossed Bridger a full frown. Bridger snickered again. "Shouldn't you say 'Hello' or something?"

Dante held his frown as he went back to work. "Alex, has the Commander's life sign reacted yet?"

"No but there's been an order sent down from the top. Soldiers are heading toward the Launch Pad area. If you guys return, you'll be caught."

Dante was hesitant to nod. "We knew the risk when we did this. But we had to try. Even if Sinah wasn't god, we made our choice."

Suddenly a slow beeping spilled through the earpiece. "The Commander's back."

"Remember to get out of there before you get caught. We'll be back shortly."

Dante didn't wait for Alex's acknowledgement before he shook Bridger's hand away from him. Bridger returned to the open helicopter door. He looked down at the crew as they began to use flame throwers to torch the area.

Once Dante finished scanning the area, he lowered his hands. "Unless the crew picked them up, they're not here. Come on let's head back." Dante's tone of voice became slightly upset. "Our punishment is waiting for us."

Bridger looked toward Dante with a sympathetic smile. "It won't be so bad, trust me. Bruno, let's head back!"

Bruno quickly called out in return. "Okay!"

Fallen gave Director Hart a look of confusion as he climbed out of the hummer. Murdoch, who climbed out of the passenger side, looked toward him as well. "The Director never comes to the Launch Pad area."

Any soldier the Director passed instantly saluted him. Fallen frowned as the limping Director approached him and chuckled. "A few of your men have gone AWOL?"

Fallen clinched his jaw but didn't respond. Murdoch glanced toward Fallen then back to the Director. "They-"

Fallen lifted his hand, silencing him. The Director smiled slightly as Murdoch gave a slight nod. "It's good to see that Lucifer still has a handle on some his soldiers. I was beginning to wonder when I heard about your other members."

Fallen's eyebrows lowered slightly. "Is that why you're out here, to question my leadership?"

As the Director opened his mouth to say something, he noticed a lone Med Tech standing by a gurney. His expression shifted to questioning. "All your men have the rapid healing skill. Why do you need-?"

The Director was cut off as a helicopter flew overhead and began to land.

One-Hundred And One

Beginning and the End

The Director gave a slight wave toward the helicopter. Without hesitation, the soldier's raised their weapons and cautiously approached it. Once the engine was turned off and the blades stopped spinning, Bridger swung open the helicopter door. He smiled stepping onto the ground with the obliterated Sinah in his arms. "Well, I wasn't expecting a welcome home party."

The soldier's instantly locked their loaded machine guns on him. As Dante and Bruno stepped on the ground, one soldier yelled out. "Put your hands on the back of your heads and get on the ground, now!"

Bridger sympathetically looked down at Sinah. "Sorry but I need to deliver her first." He looked toward Fallen as he continued. "Then I'll give myself up, no problem."

The soldier's kept their weapons and attention locked on Bridger as he walked toward Fallen. The second Fallen saw Sinah, he expression instantly weakened. Bridger closed his eyes and whispered. "...I'm sorry Commander."

Fallen's hand barely twitched toward the Med Tech. Noticing Sinah, the Med Tech quickly pushed the gurney over to them. As Bridger gently laid Sinah down upon it, he spoke. "She's dead."

The Med Tech barely nodded. As Bridger stepped back from Sinah, the soldier yelled out again. "All three of you get on the ground, now!!"

Bruno instantly began to panic. "Wha..?! I… I…"

Bridger chuckled lifting his hands in surrender. "You're wasting your time with those two."

Dante's eyes instantly darted to him. "But I-"

Bridger chuckled again cutting him off. "I forced them to follow me. I lied and said the Commander gave the command to listen to me. I'm not on his team anymore, so this little rebellion shouldn't really be surprising. Right you two?"

Bruno eyes were full of worried traumatized tears. He wasn't hesitant to nod. "That's right! That's exactly what he said! I didn't know he wasn't on the Commander's team. I swear! I swear!"

Dante on the other hand quickly shook his head. "No, I-"

Bridger looked toward Murdoch and gave a slight nod. Murdoch returned the nod as Bridger spoke. "Don't bother to protect me fellow A Helix. I'm to blame for this."

Dante opened his mouth to protest but Murdoch placed his hand on his shoulder. Dante's eyes darted up to him as Murdoch closed his eyes and shook his head. Dante looked back toward Bridger with a look of shock and anger.

The Director pointed toward Bridger. "If he was the cause of this disruption then he's the one to receive the punishment for it."

The soldier's weren't hesitant to close in on him. Bridger smiled crossing his arms behind his head. "I give up."

From the moment Fallen had laid his eyes upon Sinah, he never once shifted his attention. His expression weakened as he stepped closer to her and removed one of his gloves. He whispered gently placing his cold pale hand on the side of her face. "…Sinah."

The moment his skin touched her flesh, Sinah made a loud gasp as oxygen rushed into to her lifeless body, returning her from death. Fallen instantly doubled over as blood flooded then gushed from his mouth. While Bridger on the other hand, screeched collapsing to all fours. He frantically began to claw at his back feeling his skin burning in agony.

The soldier's nervously took as few steps back from him as large feathered wings pierced through his back then tore through his battle suit. Once they were finished freeing themselves from his flesh, the colour of his wings could clearly be seen. Each feather was a pale bluey white. The tips were touched with gold.

The Director closed his eyes as a cool breeze rushed through the Launch Pad area. It swiftly blew away the once stagnant air. Having never experienced it before, the soldiers looked around not understanding what was happening.

The Director's lips curled into a full smile as he looked toward the unconscious erratically breathing Sinah. "Welcome to our Lab, God."

Acknowledgements

A special shout out to everyone who helped, supported and managed to make this book possible!

Thanks to Mya Barr and the team from iUniverse for everything and having so much patience with me

I know I already dedicated this book to you Carrie, but thanks for your constant encouragement and your ride or die friendship. Rock on!

And to the readers and hopefully my new found fans, thank you so much for taking a chance on this unknown author. Hopefully we'll be able to take many more literary journeys together.

Also to Mike Anthony, though you're not in this world anymore, we all still miss you very much, Rest in Peace.

About the Author

Jillian E. Martyn enjoys cooking, playing video games, and being dragged to many concerts by her cousin. She loves edgy fashion, makeup, artistic people, and her cat, Mini. She currently resides just outside of Toronto, Canada.

Printed in the United States
By Bookmasters